Three of today's
to experience for
to savor overwhelming sensual pleasure…
and to indulge in a desire so strong,
it breaks through the boundaries of time.…

Detective Caitlyn Raine discovers that
sexy Luc Agassou is no pussycat in
**WILD THING by Julie Kenner**

Dr. Bonnie Anders can't keep her hands off
Agent John Cameron in
**TOUCH ME by Susan Kearney**

Anthropologist Eve Baptiste finds out that
some fantasies shouldn't be denied in
**SURRENDER by Julie Elizabeth Leto**

*Essence of Midnight*

**Embrace the fantasy…**

*USA TODAY* bestselling author **Julie Kenner** has always been fascinated with the paranormal, that shadowy world between us and them, between now and forever. Equally enamored with the classic tale of *Beauty and the Beast,* Julie let her imagination wander until Luc and Cate appeared, two soul mates struggling to overcome a secret and a curse. Learn more about Julie and her books at www.juliekenner.com

*USA TODAY* bestselling author **Susan Kearney** likes nothing better than wondering about "What if?" What if a man buried critical information so deep in his mind that not even *he* could remember it? What if a woman could help him—but for her to do so, he must allow her touch? And what if touch reminds him of torture—not pleasure? How will that woman make him think about her? Only her? That scenario is Susan's premise for "Touch Me." She'd love to know what you think. You can contact her at www. SusanKearney.com.

Starting with her love affair with the works of Edgar Allan Poe, *USA TODAY* bestselling author **Julie Elizabeth Leto** has always loved tales of the unknown. She's also a big 'fraidy cat, so she prefers her ghosts to be sexy rather than scary. And since researching Romany culture for the Gypsy king hero of this story so intrigued her, she decided the secondary characters introduced in "Surrender" needed novels of their own. Look for Nicholai to ply his mischievous, sensual ways on a familiar heroine in Julie's upcoming Blaze novel, *Undeniable,* out next month! For more information visit www.julieleto.com.

# JULIE KENNER
# SUSAN KEARNEY
# JULIE ELIZABETH LETO

*Essence of Midnight*

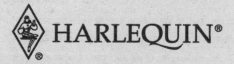

**HARLEQUIN®**

TORONTO • NEW YORK • LONDON
AMSTERDAM • PARIS • SYDNEY • HAMBURG
STOCKHOLM • ATHENS • TOKYO • MILAN • MADRID
PRAGUE • WARSAW • BUDAPEST • AUCKLAND

ISBN 0-373-83614-7

ESSENCE OF MIDNIGHT

# CONTENTS

# WILD THING

## Julie Kenner

For Nena, aka Nana,
because I'm pretty sure she doesn't have one yet.

# CHAPTER ONE

CAITLYN RAINE SAT on the hard concrete bench and watched, mesmerized by the great cat's regal beauty. Muscles rippled under the midnight-black coat as the beast stalked behind the fencing, its copper-colored eyes never leaving her own.

This section of the Audubon Zoo had been her favorite place to escape since she'd moved to New Orleans nineteen months ago. How many times had she come here, walking alone through the famous Garden District to get to this solitary spot? The zoo provided a peace she couldn't find in her job or in herself. The cages and habitats, each specifically designed for a unique species, provided an ordered respite from a world that never quite made sense. A world where Cate just never quite fit in.

But the world would provide no cage for Caitlyn. She'd find no safe haven, and there were no easy answers. She'd spent her whole life stalking demons, the kind on the street and the kind that lived inside her. But still they came. Night after night she hit the streets, hunting down the killers and the rapists and the vandals. And day after day she testified in court. The stalwart detective. Just the facts, ma'am. No need to get emotional. No need to let the jury know you saved their children by getting that monster off the street. Why bother? There would just be another monster to take his place tomorrow.

But no matter how futile, Cate did her job. And she did it well. She had to. How else could she prove that the voice in her head was wrong? That familiar low whisper with her mother's southern drawl. *You're a bad girl, Caitlyn. A cursed girl. You shouldn't never have been born.*

Amazing that the voice could persist even after the woman was gone. The day Cate had graduated from high school, her mother had walked away, taking her anger and her superstitions with her, and leaving seventeen-year-old Cate to fend for herself.

It hurt, yes. But it was also a relief.

The woman herself was gone.

But the voice in her head remained, and so Cate came here to the zoo to escape that proclamation, to silence that persistent voice. And hour after hour she'd lose herself in the sweet pleasure of doing nothing but watching the great cats move about. Their lives were her escape, and she loved them for it. But it was the one called Midnight that she loved the most. Even more aloof than his counterparts, and certainly more violent, the cat had been relegated to private quarters—a smaller habitat off the main panther area. And Cate had kept silent vigil, watching the cat, feeling absurdly, pathetically, as if there was a bond between them.

Today, she'd once again succumbed to the urge to come here, ignoring Adam's offer to buy her a beer and his protest that it wasn't right to spend her birthday alone. She sighed. He was probably right. She probably should have accepted her partner's offer, but she just couldn't handle company or the false camaraderie. Not now. Not when she was alone and turning thirty.

With a tug, she hefted her backpack into her lap, then pulled out a package wrapped in gold paper. It was from Kimberly, the only person in the world Cate might actually call a close friend. They'd met in Los Angeles, and for some reason Kimberly had taken a liking to Cate, managing during the years Cate worked for the LAPD to break through one or two of Cate's thick stone walls.

Cate twisted the package, examining its sides and corners, and imagining that it held something fabulous. Unlike Cate, who'd happily shop at Goodwill for the rest of her life, Kimberly had good taste and knew how to wield it.

With a little sigh, Cate allowed herself to wish that Kimberly was at home by her telephone. But her friend was out of reach, happily tripping through

Europe, and Cate had no idea how to locate her. And despite her law-enforcement connections, using Interpol to track down a girlfriend for a birthday-blues chat seemed a little extreme. Even for a thirtieth birthday.

"Besides," she said, looking once again toward the panther, "I've got you."

The cat stopped stalking and cocked his head, those copper eyes peering at her over the wide, flat nose. Cate shivered, suddenly certain the beast had understood her. She licked her lips. "I hope it's okay if I spend my birthday with you."

A few more seconds passed, and the cat's gaze never wavered. Then he blinked—a gesture Cate took as acquiescence—and resumed pacing the habitat. Cate scowled, shaking her head at her own foolishness as she turned her attention from the cat back to the package in her lap.

She found an untaped section of the thick gold paper and slipped her pinkie nail—the only one she hadn't bitten off—under, edging it along until the tape peeled up. Slowly, she urged the tape away, careful not to let any of the gold color catch on the adhesive. The box was small, but Kimberly had used a lot of tape. It took almost ten minutes, but finally Cate managed to remove the wrapping paper intact. She folded it into a square and tucked it into her purse before turning to the box.

Her unwrapping ritual was grueling and probably a little silly, but Cate loved it. Loved the anticipation that came from peeling back layer after layer of colored paper and tape to get to the goody buried deep inside. With a present, you always knew the digging was worth it. With people, you simply couldn't be that sure.

Now that the paper was off, she lifted the cardboard box lid slowly, revealing an understated wooden box with tarnished hinges. The wood was polished to a high sheen, but other than that, the box was wholly unremarkable. Even so, there was something wonderful about it, as if beneath that simple lid lay the treasures of the universe.

Ever so carefully, she plucked the box free. The wood seemed warm in her hands, and for just a moment she closed her eyes, pretending that this was the crowning gift of a fabulous birthday party and she was seated at the head of an ornately laid table, thirty or forty of her closest friends raising their flutes in a champagne toast to her, her parents sitting tall and proud at the head of the table.

"Utter nonsense," she whispered, her eyes straying toward the cat. The panther blinked, but didn't reply.

Cate scowled, irritated by her own foolishness, both in talking to the cat and in fantasizing about large, unwieldy parties. She didn't like crowds. She didn't need parents or a cadre of friends. She was doing just fine.

She swiped the edge of her thumb under her eye, warding off the tears she simply wouldn't shed. Hell, maybe she should have taken Adam up on his offer. But no. It wasn't a casual drink or polite conversation she wanted. True, Adam might fix her up with one of his friends, but if she wanted to get laid she'd have to arrange it herself. In that regard, at least, New Orleans was the perfect city, and she knew how to work it.

She was a bad girl, after all, and isn't that what bad girls did? Had wild, hot, demanding sex with gorgeous men who never called again? Men who, no matter how much she secretly wanted them to, never bought flowers or candy or told her she was special. Why would they? She was who she was, and no man could save her any more than she could save herself.

A tear slid down her cheek, and she roughly brushed it away. "It's only a birthday," she said, her soft whisper directed toward the panther.

The great cat stared back, then settled himself on the cool stone, his regal head resting on crossed paws.

"Well, time to see what I've got here," Cate said. At midday in the summer heat, the zoo was almost empty, so no one would hear her talking foolishly to a cat. As she lifted the lid on the box, though, all thoughts of idiocy left her head, replaced with an intense sense of wonder.

There, nestled in the velvet-lined interior of the

box, lay the most beautiful glass perfume bottle Cate had ever seen. The product of fine artistry, the bottle evoked an erotic sensuality, warm silver intricately intertwined through cut, cool crystal. "Oh," she whispered, the word little more than a sigh, as she lifted the bottle out.

Obviously an antique, the bottle was more solid than it looked, and despite its almost ephemeral beauty, she didn't worry that she would break it by handling it. This bottle had seen the world, probably decorating the dressing tables of royalty, holding specially commissioned perfumes or scented oils for a king's mistress. The bottle had witnessed both grand passion and grand intrigue.

Kimberly couldn't have picked a better present.

Although the bottle was empty, Cate couldn't resist the urge to tug at the stopper but it was stuck fast. Not that it really mattered. The bottle was bone dry, and probably had been for some time. And it wasn't as if she'd ever take the time to fill it with her favorite fragrance. That was hardly her style. Though she was happy to add the beautiful bottle to her dressing table.

She held it up to take a closer look at the fine crystal. The facets caught the light, breaking it into a rainbow of color.

In front of her, the cat raised itself, then stood rigid, its nose twitching and its eyes near-slits.

"What is it," she whispered. "What's wrong?"

The cat didn't answer. And Cate realized that, in fact, she'd actually expected it would. Absurd.

Instead, it began pacing, more frenetic than before. It circled the habitat, faster and faster, as if searching for a heretofore unnoticed exit.

Still holding the bottle, she stood, then moved to the fence. The cat stopped, turning to face her. Their eyes met, and she lost herself in the deep color of the beast's irises. She stood, mesmerized, as the seconds turned to minutes, the minutes to hours, the hours to eternity. She'd been drawn in, and now the panther was filling her head, overwhelming her senses. She *was* the panther. Stalking. Caged. Anquished.

Wanting. Needing.

*Needing her.*

Gasping, Cate jumped back, the spell broken.

She glanced at her watch; barely a minute had passed. Had she drifted off into her own daydreams? Or had the panther called to her, reaching out to meet her mind?

Nonsense, of course. But Cate couldn't help the overwhelming sense of foreboding. The sense that she was not the hunter, but the hunted.

There were demons in the dark, and they knew her name.

"Do you know?" she whispered to the panther. "Do you know what's happening?"

And then, drifting on a wind that was surely born

of imagination, Cate heard the whispered reply—*I know, Caitlyn. I know that you are mine....*

SHE WAS THE ONE.

From within his feline prison, Luc Agassou watched as the dark-haired woman fled down the path, her backpack slung over one shoulder and a wooden box clutched to her breast. He'd watched her for almost two years now, suspecting but not certain that she was the one. *His mate.* The one woman in all the world who could help him control his curse.

She'd first appeared nineteen months ago, as he was beginning the second year of his self-imposed sentence. He'd noticed her sitting on the bench in a torrential rain, a yellow slicker and rain hat her only protection from the elements. For the first few months after his confinement, he'd examined each female visitor with an intensity born of desperation. Was it her? Or her? Or perhaps that lush blonde over there?

But disappointment after disappointment had hardened his heart, and he'd quit looking, telling himself that if she came, he would certainly notice. And if she didn't...well, then one such as he deserved this dark and solitary confinement.

When this woman had sat on the bench, he'd noticed. That had been his first clue. The fact that he couldn't take his eyes off her had been the second.

He'd almost summoned the change right then, so

desperate was he to take his human form again. But he couldn't risk it. If he took this woman—if he mated with her—and she *wasn't* the one...

He'd trembled at the possibility of succumbing to the change while she was still in his bed. Could he, in the madness that took him as he changed into feline form, prevent himself from mauling that perfect specimen of female flesh? He didn't think so. He was a killer, a beast. That was, after all, why he'd confined himself to this private hell, a majestic black panther who lived only to entertain the masses that wandered the paths of the Audubon Zoo.

He, like all the unknown others of his family, went through life in the body of a man but with the soul of a panther. And at times, the panther fought to get out. When the curse came, it was hard and brutal, attacking both body and mind so that Luc lost all control. He would lose minutes, sometimes hours, and when his senses returned, he'd find himself in feline form, often hungry and on the prowl.

The change could never be predicted, sometimes not coming for weeks, other times coming twice or three times in one day. But once the madness passed and self-awareness returned, he could shift back into human form at will. That was how he'd stayed at the zoo for so long. He'd simply refused to shift back and, instead, had stayed a panther.

Before he'd come here, he'd tried to live a normal life, tried to pass as truly human. It had been easier before his parents had died. Geneticists, his parents had adopted him after his birth mother had committed suicide, leaving him and his identical twin. The infant boys had become wards of the state, and eventually, his brother had been adopted. Luc often mourned their separation, and hoped that his brother had been as fortunate as Luc. The couple that eventually took Luc into their home and their hearts truly loved him. Even more, as scientists, understood him.

*Genetics,* they'd said. Not magic. But Luc knew it didn't matter what they called it. There was only one cure: sex. And even that wasn't a real cure. To stave off the change—and then only temporarily—he had to have sex with his life mate, a woman then unknown to him.

*A curse,* he'd said.

*Science,* his parents had answered. *Pheromones and hormones and all controllable with time, with practice.* When puberty hit, they'd put bars on his room, so that when the change came he would be out of harm's way.

Life had been bearable while his parents had lived. They'd tried to teach him control, to keep some shred of humanity during those first lost moments during the change. And they'd promised him that a permanent "cure" did exist. They just didn't know what or how.

After his parents had died, his world had been turned upside down. He'd searched for his mate each night, instinct telling him that she was in New Orleans, that she would find him. But his efforts were to no avail, and he was careful to spend every night in his cage. Such precautions were insufficient, however. On one tragic day, the change had come, fast and furious, and Luc had been unable to grasp the control his father had sworn was possible.

He'd failed. He was cursed. And he'd confined himself in this feline habitat, hoping against hope that somehow, some way, his mate would wander past his cage.

His days had been filled with disappointment. Until, that is, he'd seen the dark-haired woman.

He fought the urge to take human form immediately. Best to wait, to bide his time until he knew for certain that this woman could quell the fire that burned within him. That her humanity, meshed with his own, could stifle the demons in his soul.

Today, though, his suspicions had finally been borne out. Today, he'd seen into her soul, felt her being, and somehow he had simply known.

She was the one. His mate. His cure.

And he *would* have her.

# CHAPTER TWO

*SHE WAS ON Bourbon Street, and she was all alone. No tourists, no business owners, no cops. Just Cate...and someone following her. Neon lights advertising nude girls and cheap liquor flashed around her, as if lighting a path to her damnation. She stifled a shiver and ran the other direction, into the shadows, into the dark.*

*The pad of footsteps reached her ears, soft and steady, and Cate's breath caught. She reached for her gun, wanting to turn on her stalker once and for all, but he wasn't there. She wore a silky negligee, and though the streets were empty, golden eyes peered from windows that looked down on the alley. The wind whispered with a dozen voices. Give in, Cate. You are his. Give in... Give in...*

*Her heart pounded in her chest as she twisted, trying to see her tormentor in the shadows. No one. And no sound in the night except the whisper of the wind.*

*And then he was there, his hand on her breast, his lips on her neck. "Mine," he whispered, as he pushed the loose strap of her negligee off her shoulder. The garment slid down, the soft material cool against her hot skin.*

*Her nipple peaked and he rubbed it with the pad of his thumb through the material. Then he lowered his head, his mouth closing over her breast, his teeth teasing and taunting her.*

*She wanted to take his head in her hands and lift him up to face her, but she couldn't move, couldn't do anything but lose herself to the heat swirling in her body. She hadn't even seen his face, and yet she welcomed him with her body, with her soul. And with one low, desperate moan, she shifted, spreading her legs as she felt his hand cup her heat.*

*Her sex throbbed, and she swallowed a scream of frustration. She wanted him, wanted him inside her, filling her, possessing her.*

*"Mine, Cate," he whispered again. "Remember that you are mine."*

*And then, without warning, he was gone, and she was knocked to the ground by the force of a leaping panther. The panther lashed out, attacking the man who'd been following her. Not her lover, but someone else. A dark man, with ragged hair and a dirty face. A flash of dark fur and claws, and then the stalker's knife clattered to the ground. It lay there in a pool of the man's blood as Cate screamed, the sound of her own voice drowned out by a single word that filled her brain, scaring her even more than the attack. Mine.*

CATE JERKED BOLT UPRIGHT from where she'd fallen asleep on the couch. Her heart beat so hard she was certain her ribs would crack. She tried to catch her breath, tried to slow her pulse, but the dream still held her in its clutches, and all she could feel was fear.

This was too much. Ever since her birthday two weeks ago, dreams had been haunting her. Each time she closed her eyes, her head filled with dark, erotic thoughts of need and lust and possession. Someone wanted her, was looking for her, *would find her.*

Even in her dreams she couldn't hide.

But that wasn't the worst of it. Those dreams had become familiar friends in contrast to the nightmares that came more sporadically. There'd been three so far, including the one she still trembled from. Each nightmare was awash in violence and blood, and in each one *he* seemed to be coming closer to possessing hcr completely.

Except she didn't know who the hell he was.

And, worse, the horrific foreboding in her mind was seeping out into real life. The sensation that she was being followed. That something was happening to her. That the world as she knew it was about to change, horribly and irrevocably.

Cate shivered, the warm sunlight streaming in from her window no defense against the cold inside her.

*She was in so much trouble.* And she didn't even know why.

The sharp ring of her cell phone brought her back to her senses, and she levered herself off the couch then crossed the small room to grab her phone off the top of the television. She checked the ID, saw that it was Adam calling, and knew immediately what he was going to say.

"It's happened again," she said, her voice flat. Of course it had. Another brutal attack. The third. She knew, of course, because she'd seen it. In her dream. She'd been right there, watching. Just as she'd seen the others over the past ten days. Unable to do anything, to save anyone. Entirely powerless to help.

"About an hour ago. The bastard clawed up some homeless guy this time. Looks like our victim may have been about to pull a gun on a tourist, but no one deserves the slashing he took."

"Where? Let me get dressed and I'll meet you."

"Not necessary. Riz and Beauchamp took the call. I'm heading to the hospital to take a statement. But I can cover it on my own. I know tonight's your big night."

Cate took a deep breath. "Right. Sure. No problem."

Adam laughed. "You're the only person I know who'd rather go to a hospital and interview a vic doped up on morphine than go to a black-and-white ball."

"I have to give a speech," she said.

"Just thank the nice people for your award and shake a lot of hands." To his credit, he didn't even try to tell her she'd be great. Despite trying to drag her out on her birthday, Adam knew she hated crowds. She loved kids, however, and the one community project that had drawn her in was the All Children's Fund, a charitable organization that helped out underprivileged kids. She gave them her time and her money, and had logged the most volunteer hours in the past year. For that, she got an award.

And had to give a speech.

The thought of standing on that podium talking to all the adults in black tie—the kids weren't even going to be there, just the sponsors and volunteers!—was more terrifying than all her dreams put together.

*Her dreams.* For a few moments, she'd actually pushed them from her mind, but now their memory—and that constant looming sense of being watched—returned.

Forcing the dark thoughts aside, she headed into her bedroom, saw the black floor-length dress she'd laid so carefully across the bed. With a little frown, she stripped down and stepped into it, twisting her arm into an awkward angle to do up the zipper in the back.

Finally dressed, she headed toward her dressing table and the single bottle of Chanel No. 5 she'd been hanging onto for years. She dabbed a bit on her pulse points, her eyes drifting toward the birthday bottle from Kimberly. She'd been tempted to pour the perfume into the bottle, but she'd stifled the urge. A bottle like that was a showpiece. If it was ever going to hold perfume again, it would be some zillion-dollar-an-ounce Paris concoction.

Not that she ever intended to put anything in the bottle. It was too special, too different. Too—

*The bottle!*

The dreams had started when she'd received the bottle. She licked her lips, wondering why the hell she was thinking crazy thoughts. After all, the dreams had started when she'd turned thirty, and that was a far better reason for nutty behavior than a perfume bottle, no matter how old or beautiful.

With a wry grin, she picked up the bottle. Color swirled in the glass, drawing her in like some hypnotic dance. She stared, losing herself in the color. Reds meshed with purples, gold danced with green. And there, deep in those transient swirls, she saw the coppery eyes of the panther—watching her, and seeing all the way down into her soul.

Luc TURNED THE SHOWER ON, then paced between the bathroom and the connecting bedroom as he waited for the water to heat. Tense and sore, his muscles screamed in pain. His pulse was rapid, his skin burning hot. He couldn't remember where he'd been for the past three hours, but still he knew. The blood on his hands was testament to his whereabouts. To his sins.

In the bedroom, he grabbed the remote and aimed it at the wall-mounted television. Sure enough, the local news was already covering the attack.

"...*marks the third mauling in the past ten days. This latest victim, whose identity is being withheld pending further police investigation, is currently in stable condition at University Hospital. While the community lives in fear, both police and zoo officials continue to search for the black panther that escaped from the Audubon Zoo...*"

The video cut to a shot of a uniformed officer on the steps of the police station. A young, blond reporter held a microphone to the officer's face.

"*We have not confirmed that the panther is the culprit in these attacks. While our forensic team confirms that many of the scratches are feline in nature, other factors such as location suggest a human culprit.*"

"*Someone taking advantage of the panther's escape?*" the reporter asked.

"*Could be. At any rate, we won't know for certain until the culprit is apprehended or a victim recovers consciousness and can give us a description. In the meantime, we advise all citizens to stay on alert and to contact the police if—*"

Luc clicked off the television. He'd heard enough. The nature of the maulings suggested a large feline had made the attacks. But some of the evidence pointed to a human. It was a conundrum, and one the police weren't prepared to answer. Never would they suspect that the culprit was both man and beast. But Luc knew. And the truth ate at his soul.

He stepped into the shower and let the now-hot water pound away at the guilt...and the blood. With a deep, guttural groan, he pressed his hands against the smooth white tiles and faced down, letting the pulse of water pummel the back of his neck. His body shook as he released the flood of tears. Damn him. He should have moved to South America years ago and lived out his life in the wild. But he'd been selfish, wanting to harness his curse, believing he could find his mate. And so he'd stayed in New Orleans, waiting and watching. And then, two weeks ago, he'd finally found her, only to lose her again. But he knew she existed, and so he'd taken human form to facilitate the search. He'd end his curse; he was sure of that. But at what cost?

Once before he'd tried to wrangle control, relying on his parents' belief coupled with his own will and obstinate personality. But his parents had been wrong. Without his mate, control wasn't possible, not really. And in the end, his hubris had almost killed a child. That was when he'd confined himself to the zoo. Damn him to hell, hadn't he learned anything while he'd been in that self-imposed prison?

He lifted his face to the stream, letting his tears mix with the water. He'd go back to the zoo. Tonight, he'd instruct Martin that when the next change came, Luc was to be restrained and captured. Even the possibility that he'd found his mate couldn't justify remaining free. Days had passed since he'd taken human form, and still he'd been unable to locate the woman.

Decided, he turned off the water and stepped out of the shower stall. He was adjusting a towel around his hips when Martin knocked at the bedroom door, not waiting for a response before he entered.

"Sir," Martin said with an almost imperceptible nod toward the open double doors leading into the master bathroom. Ostensibly the butler, Martin was in fact so much more.

Luc stepped into the bedroom, meeting Martin's gaze. "I'll be leaving tomorrow," he said. "This time, I don't intend to return."

"I saw the news," Martin said, going to the closet and pulling out Luc's tuxedo. "I don't believe you are the culprit."

Luc crossed his arms over his chest and raised an eyebrow. "No?"

"No, sir." The butler smoothed a wrinkle on the tux, then glanced at Luc, his expression meaningful. "I don't."

"Then you're an old fool," Luc said. "Or have you already forgotten that you let me in the back door not thirty minutes ago naked and covered in blood?"

"You have more control than you let yourself believe," Martin said. "You've *always* had more control."

A sliver of anger cut through Luc's gut, and he thought of Clarissa Taylor, the little girl whose life he'd almost taken. "You don't know anything."

"On the contrary, sir. I know everything. That's why you keep me in your employ."

There was more truth in that than Luc wanted to admit. Martin had worked for Luc's parents, and had been a constant figure in the Agassou household. In fact, it had been Martin who had "donated" the black panther on behalf of millionaire recluse Luc Agassou, who, Martin assured the zoo, was taking several years to tour Europe or else he would have been happy to attend the dedication of the new panther habitat.

So, yes, Martin did know most of Luc's secrets. But not all. The man was too loyal, believing the best of Luc when Luc was quite aware that it was the worst that had been manifested over and over again. How else could he explain these maulings?

"I'm going back," he said. "You'll be the city's newest hero when you bring me in."

Martin sniffed. "Nonsense. You're not going any-where except to the All Children's Benefit tonight." He held up the tuxedo shirt and shook it.

"Martin," he began, his tone laced in warning, "these attacks—"

"Will stop once you're with the woman."

Luc cocked his head. What was Martin trying to tell him? "You...?" He trailed off, unable to get his hopes up. He'd searched for a week, but had no clues. Had Martin succeeded where he had failed?

"I took it upon myself to visit the police station three days ago, following the last attack."

"Dammit, Martin."

The butler ignored him. "I spoke with one of the detectives working the case. Caitlyn Raine. A lovely young woman. Apparently she enjoys visiting the zoo...."

But by then Luc wasn't listening. *Caitlyn Raine.* The name cut straight into his soul. She was the one; he was certain. His Caitlyn. *His mate.*

The fact that she was a detective—assigned to find him, apparently—snarled his plans up just a bit, but Luc wasn't worried. This woman belonged to him, and he would have her. He smiled. Perhaps he'd been too hasty in planning a return to the zoo after all.

"You know where she is?"

"Indeed I do, sir." Once again, he shook the tuxedo jacket. "And if you would get dressed, you might even make it to the function on time. I would hate for you to arrive so late that the lady has already left."

Luc would hate that, too. He had no idea when the change would come again. Which meant he needed Caitlyn in his bed.

And the sooner he got her there, the better.

# CHAPTER THREE

SHE'D SURVIVED.

Truly a miracle, but she'd actually struggled through, made a speech to a roomful of people, and hadn't dropped dead to the floor from mortification. Not only that, but at least a dozen people had told her how moved they'd been.

Amazing. In the last five hours she'd lost herself in an erotic, terrifying dream, seen a panther in a perfume bottle and survived a keynote address. On the whole, she really didn't know which was the most shocking.

A waiter passed by with a tray of champagne flutes, and she traded her empty glass for a fresh one. She wasn't exactly drunk, but she'd had a few more flutes than common sense would dictate. Then again, if common sense were running the show, she wouldn't have agreed to make a speech in the first place.

At least the speech had taken her mind off the dreams and the visions. For a few moments she'd experienced something even more terrifying...and she'd survived.

A few more people came up to make small talk, complimenting her on her speech and asking about her involvement with the organization. She answered the questions, managing to put away another flute of champagne in the process.

The room spun a little, and she eased up next to a marble pillar, grateful for its support. She knew she ought to mingle a bit more, but she'd already reached her capacity for small talk. Better to stand here looking interested. If anyone approached, she'd try her best to be witty and friendly. And if they all left her alone for the rest of the night, well, that was fine, too. After all, it wasn't as if there was anyone here she was dying to meet or—

*And then she saw him.*

She swallowed, taking an involuntary step away from the safety of the marble pillar and toward the exotic man in the perfectly tailored tuxedo. The crowd parted to let him pass, but he looked neither left nor right as his long steps carried him across the ballroom toward her. Right toward her.

Cate gasped, then gulped in air as she realized she'd forgotten to breathe. He was close now, and she could see his eyes—copper with flecks of gold. She'd seen those eyes before. In her dreams. Staring down at her as warm hands stroked her body, bringing her to the brink over and over again.

*This was the man.* This perfect male specimen had been filling her nights with erotic fantasies and decadent dreams. Dreams that often faded into the violent nightmares that had made her afraid to fall asleep at night.

She shivered. Despite the nightmares, she was never afraid in his arms. Her blood never ran cold until the panther leapt through the sky. The lover in her dreams kept her safe. And until this moment, she'd had no idea who he was.

But this man *couldn't* be her dream lover; the possibility was absurd. Even so, her body and soul knew exactly who he was, and her body was more than happy to respond accordingly. Her nipples peaked, hard nubs that rubbed against the soft silk bodice of her simple evening dress. Her stomach filled with a liquid heat that seemed to shoot down into her thighs. Her knees were weak, and she wished she was sitting down.

Somehow, her dreams had become reality. Either that, or this man had been invading her dreams, moving into her secret fantasies, her decadent longings. Both ideas were impossible, of course, and yet here he was. This man. And she *knew* him. She really did.

"Caitlyn," he said, his voice somehow familiar. He was right in front of her now, so close she could feel the heat from his body and smell the musk of his cologne. His hypnotic eyes drew her in, and she took a step toward him, barely conscious of her own movements.

"I'm not...this isn't..." She didn't know what she wanted to say, knew she wasn't making sense.

"Isn't it?" His voice was low, husky, with the slightest hint of a Cajun accent. His words surrounded her, flowing over her like warm honey. Her thighs tingled, a moist heat building at their apex. She fought the urge to slip her hand under her dress and stroke herself over her damp panties. She wanted release, needed it, and God help her, she wanted it right then, right there, with that man.

"It's time, Caitlyn." He held out a hand.

Inside her head, she screamed at herself to run away. Far away, and never look back. She didn't know this man, this stranger who had peeked into her soul.

But then she tilted her head back and once again looked into those eyes. And that was when she knew the truth. She *did* know him. She didn't know how or why, she only knew that she did. Somehow, some way, she knew everything about him even if, at the moment, she didn't even know his name.

That didn't matter. All that mattered was the heat that filled her body, the longing for his touch and *only* his touch, and the need to merge with him, to *be* with him.

*To mate with him.*

Oh, dear Lord, where the hell had *that* come from?

She didn't stop to analyze. Instead, she put her hand in his and, as his fingers closed around hers, all rational thought left her head, replaced by the need to touch him.

He leaned down, the coarse remnant of his beard brushing her cheek. "Come with me."

She nodded, her entire body tingling with anticipation, his mere touch sending electricity coursing through her veins.

They moved hand-in-hand through the crush of people, the crowd parting as if in awe as they passed. She heard a few murmurs, saw a few deferential nods, and then, as they left the ballroom, one of the benefit's hosts stepped into their path, his hand outstretched.

"Luc. Mr. Agassou. We're all so glad you're back."

Cate drew in a breath, stopping short, her fingers still trapped in his hand. The host's greeting still rang in her ears. Innocuous words, but with a particular meaning to her—she was leaving the party with a man whose name she had learned from a stranger. Even for Cate, who'd had her share of one-night stands, that was a first.

"I—" she began.

"It's good to see you again, too, Armand." Luc smiled, but irritation reflected on his chiseled features, and that whiskey-smooth voice held an edge.

"I apologize for stealing Detective Raine away. We have business to take care of."

Armand stepped back, his entire manner deferential. Cate started to back away, too. Second, third and even fourth thoughts were coming at her a mile a minute. What was she doing, and who was she doing it with? Had she gone insane? Were her dreams the product of some latent madness?

"I shouldn't be—"

"Come with me, Caitlyn," he said. His fingers stroked her arm as he spoke, and all reason left her head. It was as if she belonged to him, as if he'd tuned in to some primal frequency in her soul, and she was simply on automatic pilot.

For a fleeting moment, she wondered if she had the moral strength to pull away. But the truth was, she didn't want this moment to pass. The pull of the dreams was too strong, and she wanted to feel that intensity of passion in real life, not just in her fantasies. She was bad, after all. Why not be bad all the way?

"Where are we going?" she asked, as he led her onto the elevator. Her voice sounded timid, and she cringed. She was a detective, for crying out loud, not some shrinking flower of a woman. She drew in a deep breath and moved closer, pressing her body against his. "Not far, I hope."

Something dark and dangerous flashed in his eyes. He cupped the back of her neck with his hand,

and she stifled a shiver. "I like your enthusiasm. I'd thought perhaps I would have to entice you. I'm pleased to have been mistaken."

Once again second thoughts filled her head, and she took a step back from him, protests and apologies dancing on her tongue. "I shou—"

He pressed a finger to her lips even as he reached around her to push the emergency stop button on the elevator. "Don't disappoint me, Caitlyn," he whispered, then closed his lips over hers.

All thoughts of objection evaporated. Her knees turned to rubber, and she clung to him, her arms linked around his neck to prevent her from collapsing to the ground in a heap.

His mouth, hot and demanding, worked a magic on her lips like nothing she'd ever experienced. She gasped, and his tongue slipped inside, tasting and teasing. One hand stroked her back while his other hand slipped between their bodies, his fingers expertly easing the silky material of her skirt up to expose her legs.

The pad of his thumb stroked the back of her bare thigh, and she melted a little bit more. She was hot and cold at the same time, a mass of need. Her hands slipped over his shoulders and fisted in the lapels of his tuxedo. She was probably ruining the jacket, but she didn't care. All she cared about, all she wanted, was this man. She wanted to possess, to be possessed, and the depth of her need both thrilled and terrified her.

His thumb eased up, finding her now wet panties. He pushed aside the elastic at her leg, and she gasped as his finger found her core and slipped inside. She gripped him, pulling him in, wanting to take all of him inside her and never have this moment end.

His mouth brushed her neck. "Now," he whispered, "I must have you *now*."

She nodded, unable to respond any other way. And when she heard his last murmur—"Soon, it will be too late"—her mind was too full of heat and lust to ask what he meant. Instead, she did the only thing she could do. She simply succumbed to his touch.

LUC STIFLED A GROAN, fighting back both a wave of lust and the persistent tingling in his bones that always signaled the change. His need for her was like a living thing, and the depth of his want disturbed him. He had known that he would feel a connection with Caitlyn and an urgent need to mate. *Need,* yes. He had expected that. But this wanting, this desperate longing for her, had taken him by surprise.

And he did want her. Wanted to touch her, wanted to taste her, and most of all, wanted to bury himself deep inside her. Not to forestall the change, but because he *wanted* to.

His lack of control fired an anger in him, and he pulled his hand away from her sweet folds, his hands instead gripping her at the wrists as he pressed her up against the side of the elevator. She gave a little gasp of surprise and pleasure, and his body stiffened even further, responding to her desire. The reaction fueled his anger. Was he entirely unable to control his own body? First the change, and now this woman? Everywhere he turned he was forced to succumb to some primal urge. And, damn him, unlike the change, he would willingly succumb to *this* urge.

She was pressed up against him, her breasts soft against his chest. The insistent pressure sent a heat shooting through his body, settling in his cock. He was hard and hot, and the time was now.

"Caitlyn," he said.

"Now," she whispered. She tugged her wrists free, then explored him with her hands. Her fingers snaked inside his shirt, finding bare flesh.

He groaned, reaching out to slip the thin strap of her gown off her shoulder. It fell free, exposing the swell of her breast. He bent, pressing his lips to her soft flesh. He knew he needed to just do it, to slam himself inside her, to hold the change at bay.

Even now, he was dancing with danger. The change was coming upon him, pushing at the back of his head, emerging from his muscles and his skin. Soon, he'd lose his tenuous grip on control. He had to simply take her, without pretense, with none of the courtship that human females so desired. Later, there would be harsh looks and recriminations—and he would make all the appropriate explanations. He would soothe the way for making love to her fully and completely. Now, though, there was no time.

"You're mine, Caitlyn," he said. "Now, and forever."

She gasped, but said nothing, and he covered her mouth with his, forestalling any protests. As he did, he tugged her skirt up to her waist, sliding his hands between her legs. Once again, he slid into her wet heat. His cock hardened when her slick muscles gripped him as he withdrew his finger. With a guttural growl more feline than human, he ripped off her panties, then tugged his zipper down.

He eased between her legs, her slick heat stroking the tip of his cock. She moaned, little mewling sounds that only made him harder. His fingers tightened on her ass, and he lifted her just slightly, planning to impale her on him, to let her take as much of him as she could.

The elevator jerked and shuddered, and he lost his footing. They tumbled to the floor, their clothes and bodies tangled.

He got to his knees, then reached down to help her. As he did, the lights flickered, and the elevator started to move, controlled by someone who'd overridden the emergency stop. Her eyes went wide, her mouth forming into a little O as she adjusted her clothes. She stood up, backing away from him as she shook her head.

"I'm sorry," she said. "I shouldn't have—I wasn't thinking. Please, I'm so sorry, but I have to go."

Her words were like a slap. She couldn't leave him; she was his mate. She was *necessary*. And, damn him, he wanted her.

She turned toward the elevator door, but there was nowhere for her to go. He tugged at her hand. "Caitlyn. You can't go."

He could see the last remnants of the spell break. Her features turned hard, those gentle blue eyes turning to ice. "Watch me."

She punched a button on the elevator, and it jolted, then stopped, and then doors slid open, revealing a deserted lobby.

She stepped off, then turned back to look at him, her stiff demeanor laced with confusion. "I'm sorry," she said. "I don't understand what happened tonight, but I am sorry for letting it go so far."

And with those words still hanging in the air, she turned and ran across the lobby and out into the stifling heat of the New Orleans night.

Luc watched her go, his mind blank, entirely devoid of emotion. Later, he knew, he would think about her departure, and it would anger him, probably even bewilder him. But right then, he felt nothing except a need to run. He was in that place between human and feline. And soon, very soon, Luc knew that he would follow in Caitlyn's footsteps, loping on four legs behind her as he succumbed to the change and wandered loose through the city in search of one more victim in the night.

# CHAPTER FOUR

SHE RACED FROM THE BUILDING, her heels clattering on the uneven stone walkway. He didn't follow, but still his shadow haunted her, his essence seeming to cling to her very soul.

The night hung around her, heavy with the scent of magnolias. Heated and sensual. A night filled with longing and need, and she'd lost herself in it. Lost herself to him.

Cate raced toward Jackson Square, finally stopping and leaning against the iron fence that surrounded the area. Her breath came ragged, and not from exertion. No, her body was hot. Needy. And now it was rebelling because she'd run away from what it had wanted most. Him. Luc Agassou.

She closed her eyes, drew in a breath. Tourists and locals passed, eyeing her curiously, but she dropped her gaze, focusing on the battered pavement. How many times had she come here before, a detective hiding behind her badge and her gun? Now she stood here in her evening gown and heels, feeling stripped naked for all the world to see. She'd exposed herself to that man, made herself vulnerable.

She closed her eyes and drew in a deep breath, her grip tight around the fence post, as the night settled around her.

What the hell was she doing?

Even on her wildest days, she'd never gone at it with a stranger in an elevator. And this wasn't even about the sex. A one-night stand was one thing, but this was... She shook her head, not sure what it was, only knowing that it was *more*. More heated. More sensual. More enticing. More desperate.

More *everything*.

And so help her, she wanted everything she could get.

Her body tingled, and she looked around, staring out into the night, past the corners and shadows, past the clumps of tourists, past the inviting lights of Café Du Monde. She was looking for him, not sure what she would do if she found him, only knowing that she had to look, even as her head told her to get the hell out of there as fast as her legs could carry her.

A sharp crack sounded behind her, and instinctively, her hand went to her hip where she usually wore her gun. It wasn't there, and she turned and saw a couple. The man bent down to pick up the cell phone he'd dropped and then they continued walking toward her, hand-in-hand.

She exhaled, a sense of longing welling in her. She was on edge. Antsy. And she needed to get home. Put on some coffee. Play some Little Feat on the CD player. Revel in the trappings of normalcy.

With purpose, she started walking again, cutting diagonally across the intersection so that she could head back to Canal Street and catch the streetcar back home. The side street was dark, the businesses closed up, the street vendors gone for the night. She walked toward the lights on Decatur, toward the horse-drawn carriages and a vibrant civilization she'd never really been part of.

As she walked away, she caught a shadow out of the corner of her eye and she shivered. A great cat. Watching. And waiting.

She blinked, then looked again, sure she'd been mistaken, and this time it was gone.

A trick of the light, surely.

And yet, somehow, Cate knew that wasn't true. The cat was there. It was waiting for her.

She should be scared, but she wasn't.

And that's what scared her most of all.

BLOOD.

On his hands, his face. Everywhere. The metallic stench of it consuming him, tormenting him.

Naked, Luc collapsed on his back lawn, the twelve-foot stone fence ensuring his privacy. He pressed his face to the grass, his hands outstretched in front of him, a penitent praying to a god he no longer knew.

Forsaken.

Tears clogged his throat, and he pressed his eyes closed, helpless against the onslaught. He remembered nothing more than touching her. She'd calmed him, stilled the raging waters inside him. And then she'd abandoned him, leaving him to the horror that was his life. To the horror he'd been inflicting on the city.

Her taste still hung on him. When their lips had met, nothing else in the universe had mattered. His curse had disappeared. He was only a man wanting a woman.

But he *wasn't* that man, and he knew that he could never really have her in love, only in need. For, truly, what was there to love about him?

He sat back on his haunches, his face toward the sky, his bloodied hands lifted in front of him. It didn't matter. All that mattered was that she was his.

He had to have her.

He would have her.

*Tonight.*

Before anyone else got hurt.

HER EARLIER CHAMPAGNE BUZZ HAD burned off, extinguished by the heat generated between her and Luc Agassou. And though she knew she should simply crawl into bed and lose herself to sweet sleep, Cate couldn't do that. For her, sleep was no longer sweet. And so she opened her freezer, took out a bottle of Smirnoff, and poured herself a shot.

She slammed the drink back, the thick, icy liquid immediately setting her blood to burn. She closed her eyes, felt the warm tingle of alcohol, and knew she was a coward.

She poured another shot, just to prove to herself that she didn't care. She should work. Should review the case file and skim the reports and crime-scene photos. But, dammit, she couldn't do that. Not tonight. Not now.

No, she wanted to sleep tonight. No dreams. No nightmares. Just sleep. And if it took an entire bottle of vodka, then dammit, that's what she was going to do.

Another shot. Then another. Until her entire body felt warm and malleable and her eyelids drooped. She poured one last glass, this time mixing it with water, and went in to settle on her bed. On the way, she plucked the perfume bottle off her dresser, then sat on top of her comforter, squinting at the delicate, curious glasswork.

So beautiful. Swirling patterns of color, the intricate design, the delicate filigree—

She blinked, startled by something she hadn't noticed before. She turned the bottle upside down and blinked a few more times, trying to get her hazy mind to focus. Sure enough, there was some sort of inscription etched into the glass.

Drowsiness had been creeping up on her, but now it was shoved aside, replaced by curiosity about the bottle. She couldn't make out any words, though, and finally she crawled out of bed and stumbled to her desk. She rummaged around until she found a magnifying glass, then examined the bottle again under her desk lamp.

The words seemed to float in front of her. Definitely not English, but not any language she recognized, either. She frowned at the bottle, but not in annoyance. The mystery had pushed past the blur of alcohol and was keeping her awake, yes, but it had also filled her head, edging out thoughts of Luc and the way his hands had felt on her. The way she wanted to pick up the phone and find him, go to him.

Frustrated, she drummed her fingers on the desk. It was already past midnight. She knew she should just go to bed, not get involved in some project. But knowing and doing were two different things, and instead of going to sleep she booted up her computer.

Less than a minute later, she'd copied one of the words into a search engine and pulled up a single hit. She started scrolling through, her brow furrowing as the web page announced that the language was Romani.

*Romani?* That sounded vaguely gypsyish, but she

was hardly an expert. And she certainly couldn't translate the inscription.

She scrolled through a few more pages and finally came across a reference to some professor in Georgia. She scribbled down the woman's name and number, Dr. Evonne Baptiste, an anthropologist with some sort of specialty in Romani. Automatically, she reached for the phone, then realized what time it was. With a sigh, she put the receiver back down. Tomorrow. She'd call the woman tomorrow.

As she headed back to the bed, though, she had to wonder why she was even going to bother. It was just writing on a perfume bottle after all.

But as she snuggled under the covers and pulled the sheet up tight, she knew that she would call. The dreams had started with the bottle, and the nightmares. Somehow, the bottle had opened a door in her soul, and she simply had to know.

*"CATE." A brush against her cheek. "Cate, my darling. My one. Cate."*

*She moaned, lost in the haze of sleep. Another dream, but not a nightmare. Instead, soft and appealing. A touch. A caress. And the burning heat of desire in her belly, between her thighs, in her rockhard nipples.*

*She moaned, arching up, trying to cheat sleep as she pulled him closer.*

*"Yes, Cate. That's right. You're mine. Come to me."*

*His hands stroked her breasts, drifting down to cup her waist. His hand eased around her back as he pulled her up into an embrace. Her lips parted, and he feasted on her, his tongue slipping into her mouth, tasting and teasing. Sensual. Erotic. Enticing.*

*She wanted him. Wanted this to be real. Wanted him there, holding her.*

*Holding her...*

This was no dream!

Cate's eyes flew open, her heart pounding, her breath in erratic gasps. She scrambled backwards, out of his arms, the sheet clutched to her chest as she rolled sideways toward the night table and her gun. She held it out, aimed at his heart. He didn't seem to care.

"You."

A slow, sensual smile eased across that perfect face. "Me." He was already sitting on the edge of the bed, and now he inched toward her.

She waved the gun, just slightly. "I don't think so."

He held up a hand, a silent surrender. "Whatever you say, detective. But I thought you'd be happy to see me."

Insightful little bastard. She kept the gun level. "How'd you get in?"

That damn cocky smile broadened. "The door."

"It was locked."

"Do you really think a lock could keep me away from you?"

"I—" She closed her mouth. Her head wanted to argue with him, to scream, to yell at him to get out of her house and to leave her alone. Her body, though...

Her body was terrified that he would leave.

She tried again. "I—"

He reached out, and she remained perfectly still, her own gaze locked on his haunted eyes. His hand closed over hers, caressed her skin, then gently tugged the gun away. She trembled, just a little, and she felt a single tear roll down her cheek as, finally, she succumbed to this man.

Foolish, perhaps. Dangerous, maybe. But right then this was what she needed. *He* was what she needed.

With the pad of his thumb, he brushed the tear away. "Darling Cate, don't cry. We've found each other now. My life. My mate."

His fingertips stroked her lips, and she leaned forward, opening her mouth to him, her entire body filled with need. She was charged up, vibrating with passion. Lust and want filled her veins and pounded through her soul.

She no longer questioned why; she was beyond caring. She'd been reduced to a primal being, driven only by instinct and need.

She reached out, letting the sheet drop away, revealing the simple, threadbare T-shirt that she'd worn to bed. Her hand snaked around his neck, urging him closer. At the same time, she opened her mouth, and his finger slipped in. She pressed her lips around the digit, then moved back and forth, slowly and methodically, building a sensual rhythm, a promise of things to come.

She kept her eyes closed, but his mouth on her breast came as no surprise, and she arched her back, still sucking on him as he tugged and nipped at her nipple, teasing it through the thin material of her T-shirt.

He slipped his hand from her mouth, and she moaned, wanting the taste of him. His hands cupped her breasts, kneading and stroking, the pads of his thumbs flicking over her nipples.

"Cate," he growled, "I need you." And he clutched the T-shirt and pulled it over her head, tossing it casually aside. Though it was summer and she had no air-conditioning, the air in the sultry, sticky room felt cool against her over-heated skin.

She leaned forward, wanting his lips against her own, but he parried, tugging her down until she was lying on the bed, naked except for a tiny pair of bikini panties. His actions were both rough and gentle, and everything about him, about this wild coupling, turned her on. The panties were soaked, and all she could think was that she wanted more, would beg if she had to.

But she didn't think she'd have to.

This was a dangerous encounter. The kind she was born for. The kind her mother had always warned her about. Rough and demanding. Hot and wild.

Love and caring and family were for other people, not for her, and with this man she intended to push the envelope.

With a boldness born of pure need, she slipped her hand inside her panties, then slid her own fingers over her hot, slick sex. Her fingertip found her clit, and she danced lightly around it, not willing to go there, not yet.

When she came tonight, it would be with Luc inside her. And, she hoped, again and again and again.

His hand cupped her over the satin panties, stilling her hand. "I think that's mine."

The need in his voice came from a place much different than pure lust and sexual desire. But she couldn't think about that. Right then all she could think about was his cock inside her.

His fingers closed over the panties, and then he tugged them. She gasped as the flimsy material ripped, leaving her completely exposed to him.

His fingers took over where she had left off, and she slipped her own hands under his shirt, her nails raking against his skin.

"Off," she said.

He did as she asked, then tossed the shirt into the

corner. She tugged at the waistband of his pants, desperate to free him.

He complied without question, tugging off his jeans and shoes.

They were apart for less than a minute, but during that short bit of time, her mind seemed to clear, and the reality of what she was doing hit her full force.

She knew nothing about this man. Nothing other than his name.

And yet, when he climbed back onto the bed and pulled her roughly into his arms, she knew that there was no place else for her. No one else for her.

He rolled her over, settling her astride his stomach, her thighs on either side of his waist.

"You're beautiful," he said.

She leaned forward, wanting his kiss, to taste his mouth, but he eased her back up, one hand slipping between their bodies to stroke her clit, the other reaching up to caress her breast.

She trembled against the onslaught of sensations coursing through her blood.

Her body was calling to him, building toward climax, and she wanted it. Oh, how she wanted it.

A tiny voice in her head told her to pull away, to roll off, to *run*. She was better than this. *You shouldn't, Cate. Love. You deserve love.*

*Shouldn't?* The word seemed foolish and Pollyanna, especially with his fingers inside her, stroking and tugging and demanding. He'd fired every nerve ending in her body, and still she wanted more. She wanted *it*.

She wanted *him*.

*Shouldn't* was a far cry from *wouldn't*. And she knew for damn sure that she would.

She'd spread herself wide open for this man. Even more, she'd be devastated if he walked away now.

No, she thought. *Shouldn't* was for fools and women without the balls to live the life they were born to. Tonight of all nights, she was grateful she knew who she was. Because with Luc, she wanted to be bad. Very, very bad.

With what she hoped was casual aplomb, she slid off him, rolling onto her back and spreading her legs wide. A demand as much as an invitation. "Take me. Take me now."

Fire flickered in those golden eyes, and with an almost desperate freneticism, he straddled her. He groped her, his hands claiming her, blazing a heated path for his mouth. He reached the apex of her thighs and spread her legs, so wide her muscles ached, and she bent her knees up, giving herself to him.

He laved her, the rough shadow of his beard scraping against her inner thigh. His tongue danced and dipped, tasting and tempting, pulling her closer and closer to the precipice.

She reached down, her fingers twining through

his short dark hair. She bucked against his mouth, wanting him fully, needing him completely.

But he backed away, and she cried out in frustration as he trailed kisses down her inner thigh, then pushed himself up until his face was over her, the hard tip of his cock pressing at the apex of her thighs, so close to everything she wanted and yet a million miles away.

His eyes burned into her, and she slid her hands down until she cupped his rear. She pressed, silently urging him inside her.

"Luc. Please."

"Please what?"

"Inside me." She arched up, lifting her head to brush her lips against his.

He took his time, turning to tease her ear with the tip of his tongue. The spot was sensitive, and she gasped, relaxing back down onto the bed and losing herself to his ministrations. *Go with it, Cate. Let him take you there.*

As his tongue worked one kind of magic, his hand worked another, slipping down her belly, the pressure not so much a caress as a demand.

His finger slipped inside her easily, and her body tightened around him, pulling him in, demanding. Insistent.

Desperate.

"Now, Cate," he said, his voice raspy with need.

Roughly, he spread her thighs, positioned himself over her as he slipped on a condom. She was wide and ready and exposed, and practically tingling with need.

"The time is now," he said, as the tip of his cock pressed insistently against her wet folds. "I must have you now before all is lost."

And then he entered her, hard and demanding. He filled her completely, his desperate thrusts everything she'd wanted since the first time she'd seen him in the ballroom.

Why, then, when her body was filled by this man, did she feel so damned empty?

MINDLESS, HE THRUST, harder and harder, fighting to come. Fighting to stave off the change that, inexplicably, threatened once again.

He could feel it. Crawling under his skin. Threatening to burst through. Threatening to consume him. To consume Cate.

*No.* She *was* the one. She could ward off the change. He was certain of it. He'd simply waited too long and now he was on the cusp as he rammed himself into her, need and fear driving his thrusts.

A haze engulfed him, and the fear grew to terror. The change. Oh, Lord, no. He couldn't be wrong. If he changed...with her in his bed... No, no, he couldn't harm her. Not Cate. Not this woman—

And then the world exploded, and Luc with it.

WHEN HIS SENSES RETURNED he was curled up naked next to her. He sat bolt upright, pulling the sheet back to expose her. Her breasts, belly, thighs.

Unmauled.

Her eyes widened, still heavy with sleep. "Ready for round two?"

He collapsed back against the pillows, felt a crush of tears fill his head and fought them back.

*He hadn't changed.* The sensations had been so similar, yet so different. He'd only come. He'd exploded in passion inside this woman and together they'd held the change at bay.

He'd been right. She really was his. His Cate. His mate.

## CHAPTER FIVE

SHE WOKE IN HIS ARMS, then snuggled closer. His arm tightened around her and he kissed her forehead.

"Hungry?" he asked.

"Ravenous."

He slid out of bed, his hand out to her. She took it, smiling, then followed him into her kitchen. He pointed toward the tiny breakfast table, and she quirked a brow, amused at the thought that the man who'd been in her bed was now in her kitchen. She didn't protest, however. Just sat down and wondered what he thought he'd be able to find that would even remotely resemble food.

Amazingly enough, he managed just fine, somehow turning five eggs, a frozen link of sausage, and a few other odds and ends into a brilliant omelet.

"I'm impressed," she said as he slid the plate in front of her.

"Good." He used his own fork to stab a bite. "That was my intention."

They ate together in comfortable silence until

Cate started to get fidgety. He was watching her, his eyes intense, and she felt the heat rise in her cheeks. "What?"

"You deserve a better meal."

"In that case, I need to go grocery shopping more often."

He ignored the flippant comment. "Tonight," he said.

"Tonight?"

A hint of a smile graced his lips. "May I have the honor of taking you to dinner?"

"I..." She'd wanted to review the case files tonight. Technically, though, she was on her days off. And, so help her, she did want this man.

She drew in a breath, gathering courage. "Yes," she said. Then, more firmly, "Yes."

She'd succumbed to her heart, and it felt good. Even so, when he left, promising to come back for her at eight, she was grateful. She needed some time alone. Some time to think.

She knew nothing of this man. Nothing other than a burning intensity shining deep in his eyes, and a desperate, almost violent need to possess her. To fill her. To consume her.

*To mate.*

She shivered, her body tingling from the memory of his hands on her, his mouth tasting her, his body filling her.

Oh, dear Lord, she was wet again. Wet and needy and frantically wishing that he hadn't left after all.

Frustrated, she headed for the bathroom, then turned the shower full-strength on cold water. Still naked, she stepped under the spray, fighting a scream as the icy blast of frigid water pummeled her.

When she'd finally adjusted to the temperature, she pressed her palms against the tiled shower stall. Her head hung, letting the spray pound the back of her neck.

A thousand recriminations danced through her head, but she shoved them all away, a single question rising to the surface—who was he?

Luc Agassou, yes. She knew that. Prominent, apparently, if Armand's deferential manner was any clue. If she'd been smart, she would have researched *him* on the Internet, not Kimberly's bottle.

But she hadn't, and now Luc remained a mystery. And all she knew for certain was that she craved the man.

CATE GLANCED at the clock above her sofa. Just past two. She'd spent much of her first day off researching Luc Agassou. She'd called in a favor to one of the gals at Division and got her to expedite a search. No criminal record. Not even a traffic ticket.

And her own Internet search confirmed what she'd learned. The man was a pillar of the community, although he'd left New Orleans a few years ago, only to return in the past week. That explained why she'd never heard of him. According to her research, he was the son of internationally known geneticists, and had inherited their fortune when they'd been killed in a car crash almost ten years ago.

She'd felt a stab of sadness for the man who'd lost his family. He'd grown into a well-known philanthropist, donating a huge percentage of his net worth to hand-picked causes. She scrolled through the list—several youth services groups, animal rights funds, literacy programs, the Audubon Zoo, the—

She stopped scrolling, then leaned in closer to the screen, suddenly realizing why his name had seemed so familiar to her. Luc Agassou had sponsored the panther habitat. He'd donated Midnight, the panther that had escaped.

With a start, she sat up straighter, a ridiculous thought occurring to her. *She'd been sitting in front of Midnight's cage the first time she'd heard Luc's voice.*

Slowly, she let go of the mouse and rolled the chair backwards, her eyes never leaving the screen even though her pulse beat wildly, fear-induced adrenaline coursing through her veins.

Luc's voice. She'd heard it. In her head. Right after she'd opened Kimberly's present. She'd been holding the bottle and then, as she'd looked at Midnight, she'd heard it. Heard *him*.

*I know, Caitlyn. I know that you are mine.*

*Mine.* He'd said the same thing in bed.

Trembling, she hugged herself, bending over to stop the threat of tears.

He'd been in her head. He'd been in her bed.

And despite everything she told herself, he'd even started to sneak into her heart.

Dear Lord, who was he?

And even more important, how could she hide?

"THE LADY WILL BE MOVING IN with us." Luc sat at the table, his fingertip idly tracing the rim of his iced-tea glass.

"She is amenable?" Martin looked up from where he'd been fussing nearby.

Luc avoided the butler's curious glance. "She doesn't know yet. I'm taking her out tonight, and I intend to be most persuasive."

Martin didn't even blink, simply moved closer, the crystal pitcher in his hand. "More tea?"

"Dammit, Martin, it's the only way."

"I don't recall arguing, sir."

Luc stabbed at a piece of andouille sausage. "The hell you didn't."

"You seem put out, sir."

"I'm not put out. I'm frustrated. It's entirely different."

"Whatever you say, sir."

"I swear, Martin, if you call me sir once more..."

"I understand...Luc."

Luc pushed back from the table and tossed his napkin on the chair. "I'm out of here."

"May I ask where you're going?"

"I'm going to go get the girl," he said, feeling like a total prick even as he said the words. He headed to the garage. The girl deserved to be romanced and seduced, but he needed her hard and fast and right where he needed her when he needed her. Feral. Wild. Violent coupling to staving off even more violence.

The most vicious of circles, and he was perpetuating it.

His gut ate at him, a tinge of humanity coloring the instincts that drove him. He moved silently through the garage and slid behind the seat of his Porsche, then fired the engine. The garage door was still down, and for a moment, he just sat there.

So easy.

It would be so easy to end the suffering. His own. His victims'...

*No.*

He'd found his cure. He'd found Cate. He could have her. He could have life. And he'd give her as much romance as possible. And even if it wasn't perfect, so what?

Luc had seen enough of this world to know that very little ever was.

He drew in a breath, then another, seeking strength. Then he lifted his hand to the visor and pressed the button to open the garage door. The mechanism kicked in, raising the door and letting the late-afternoon sun filter into the room.

Eerie shadows danced on the walls, but Luc ignored them. Shadows didn't disturb him. He already knew where the monster lived.

With a violence born of frustration, he slammed the car into reverse and peeled out, leaving rubber scorch marks on the polished concrete and the pale asphalt driveway.

He maneuvered the street in a frenzy. The change didn't tingle in his blood right now, but even so, he was desperate to see her.

Her apartment topped a garage in the Garden District, and he parked in front of the stairs leading up to her home. He got out of the Porsche, not bothering to close the door behind him, and climbed the stairs two at a time.

He pounded on the door, anxious for her to answer, desperate to touch her once again.

Nothing.

He pounded again. And still Cate didn't come.

After a moment, he simply broke in as he had the day before.

Her rooms were dark and had an abandoned feel. He shook his head, sure he was simply being foolish. It was after three; she'd probably simply gone to work.

He crossed to the phone and dialed the precinct, his confidence not dwindling until the receptionist told him that Detective Raine was on one of her days off, and could someone else help him?

*No.* There was no one else.

Silent, he hung up the phone, then walked to her bathroom as if sleepwalking. No toothbrush. No hairdryer. No deodorant.

Damn it all to hell.

She'd left him.

"YOU WANT TO TELL ME again why you're camping out in my guest room?"

Cate shook her head, avoiding Adam's stern gaze. "I'm sorry. Bad date. The guy makes me nervous. I...I just thought I should make myself scarce for a while."

He sat on the edge of the bed, tugging his wife, Alice, down beside him. "Shit, Cate."

Alice smacked him on the thigh. "Adam!" She rose and went to hook an arm around Cate, steering her to the bed and shoving Adam aside. "You're welcome to stay for as long as you need. I completely understand." She flashed Adam a meaningful look. "Men can be such asses."

He held up his hands in surrender. "Hey! What the hell did I do?"

"Nothing," Alice said. "Yet." She stood up, pulling Adam along with her. "We'll leave you to unpack or whatever. If you want to join us in the living room, feel free. We'll most likely be watching some television program that drips testosterone."

Adam pointed to himself, an affronted expression drawn on his face. "You see? You see what I put up with? I tell you..."

Alicia rolled her eyes and tugged him from the room with one last sympathetic look in Cate's direction. Alone, Cate curled up on the bed and hugged the pillow, willing herself not to nibble away another nail. The horrible truth ate at her. *That* was what she wanted. What Adam and Alicia had. Love. Camaraderie.

They were soul mates, and Cate was certain that, no matter what, they'd always be together.

Would she ever find her soul mate? She licked her lips, her arms tightening around the pillow as the real question seeped through her soul. *Had she already found him and then run away?*

Restlessness tinged her blood, and she slid off the bed, determined not to think about it. She'd made the decision to stay at Adam's place and it was a good plan. She needed distance, needed to think. And she wasn't about to second guess her own choices.

She glanced at the clock. Not quite six. Time to unpack and then pop into the living room and join her friends. Adam had said something about ordering pizza, and her mouth watered with anticipation. She lived in New Orleans, city of amazing food, and yet a super cheesy pizza always sent her right over the edge.

She hadn't packed much, so it didn't take long to put everything away. Underwear. A few pairs of jeans. A couple of T-shirts. Some slacks and tops for work.

And there, in the little side pocket under a pair of socks, she found the bottle.

With a tiny bit of trepidation she pulled it out. She didn't even remember packing it, and yet for some reason, her subconscious had thought it was important. Why?

She didn't know, but she was determined to find out, and so she rummaged through her purse until she found the name and phone number of that professor in Georgia. Most likely the woman wasn't in her office—or wouldn't have any interest in talking to a superstitious cop in New Orleans—but Cate was just desperate enough to make the call.

With the bottle resting beside her on the bed, she pulled out her cell phone and dialed. One ring, two, five...

She was just about to hang up when a woman answered with a crisp, professional tone, "Evonne Baptiste."

A wave of foolishness crashed over Cate. What

was she doing? What difference did it make what the inscription on some stupid glass bottle said? This was stupid, foolish, completely—

"Hello?"

"I, um, I—I'm sorry to bother you." Cate closed her eyes. She was stammering like a fool.

"No bother. Who's calling, please?"

The woman's voice was so smooth, so pleasant, that Cate's hesitancy evaporated. "I'm Caitlyn Raine. I'm a cop in New Orleans and, well, I have a question." She found herself babbling out the entire story. How she got the bottle, how she'd noticed the marking, how she'd become curious about what the inscription meant. She didn't relay the strange wash of sensations that had invaded her soul since she'd unwrapped the bottle. That little tidbit was simply too personal.

"I copied a word into the Internet," Cate said, winding down. "And it came back as Romani. *Gift.* I also ran across your name and so, well, that's why I'm calling. I'm curious to know what the full inscription says."

Silence hung on the other end of the line, and for a moment, Cate thought the professor had hung up.

"Dr. Baptiste? Are you there?"

"You say the inscription is on a bottle? Glass with integrated silver?" Her voice held a thread of awe, and she went on to describe the bottle in such detail that Cate was compelled to pick it up and feel the delicate weight in her hand.

"How did you know?" Her cop instincts leapt to life. "Oh, good Lord. It's not some sort of stolen artifact, is it?"

"No, no." The professor rushed to reassure. "It's just, well, it's just old gypsy stories."

"Gypsy?"

"Of course."

"Gypsies speak Romani?" Her voice came out tight.

"Is something wrong?"

Cate shook her head even though she knew the other woman couldn't see her. "No, of course not. It's just that my mother believed in gypsy curses." Her mother's superstitions had been almost crippling. And while Cate knew that her mother's beliefs had been one of the reasons her mother had shunned her, knowing the excuse didn't lessen the hurt.

"A lot of people believe in curses."

Cate licked her lips, not willing to press that issue. "Would you mind translating it for me?"

"Read out the letters."

Cate complied, and when she was done, she heard the other woman's sharp intake of breath. "It means 'the strength of the gift.'" The professor paused. "Ms. Raine. Caitlyn. Would you mind giving me your phone number? There's something I'd like to look up. An old legend."

"About my bottle?"

"Maybe. I need to do some research."

"Sure." Cate gave her the number, then laughed, trying to sound amused, but sure she simply sounded nervous. "You're not researching gypsy curses, are you?"

The professor didn't return the laugh. "Not exactly. But Caitlyn, if you have any, well, *gifts,* you might want to be careful around the bottle."

"Gifts?"

"Paranormal gifts. Some say the bottle will enhance them."

"Oh. No. I'm as normal as they come." Except even as she said the words, she knew they weren't true. She'd thought she was normal, yes. But ever since Luc's words had filled her head, she'd known that something extraordinary was going on.

Now she knew what.

She was cursed.

And she needed to stay as far away from the bottle—and Luc Agassou—as she possibly could.

# CHAPTER SIX

"I JUST DON'T WANT IT HERE," Cate said, holding the packaged bottle in her hand. She was on the phone with Bonnie, a childhood friend who'd finally returned her phone call. "Trust me, this thing is more your speed."

Bonnie had always been sensitive, and she'd made use of her gifts in her career. Some sort of shrink, Cate recalled. Now, though, Cate didn't really care about the details of Bonnie's professional life. She just wanted the dreams to stop. And since she hadn't yet heard back from Dr. Baptiste, she was sending the bottle to Bonnie. "Trust me. It's supposed to enhance paranormal powers or some such nonsense. It's right up your alley."

And not at all up Cate's. She might as well pass the thing off. If Dr. Baptiste ever called back, she'd give the professor Bonnie's number. And Cate would hope like hell that passing the thing off meant passing off its effects as well.

"It does sound intriguing," Bonnie said. "You're sure?"

"I'm sure." They chatted for a few more moments until Cate found a good point to ease out of the conversation. In truth, she was more interested in the papers spread out in front of her than in the bottle and its mystical properties. As soon as it hit the mail, it was history. And thank goodness for that.

She hung up, then walked the package to Adam's mail box. Once it was safely secured for its journey, she headed back to the patio and lost herself in her work, barely even noticing as the shadows falling across the pages grew and shrank with the movement of the sun.

"Take a break, Cate." Adam seemed to materialize behind her. He plucked one of the dozen files off the patio table and leafed through it. "Even you have to eat sometime."

Cate frowned, reaching back to lift her heavy hair off the nape of her neck. She was damp and sticky, but she hadn't even noticed until Adam had interrupted. She'd been too absorbed in her work.

"I need to figure this out," she said. "I need to catch him."

"You're supposed to be taking time off."

"No shit," she said.

Adam sighed and took the chair opposite. They'd been working this case since day one, and they'd both kept photocopies of all the relevant reports and key evidence. She'd spent the morning reviewing the

documents once again, hoping they'd missed something before and she'd find the clue they needed.

"Okay," he said. "What have you got?"

She met his eyes. "Our perp is feline." As much
as she hated the thought that the panther she'd spent
so many afternoons with was a mauler, she knew
there was no other explanation.

Adam frowned. "There are some suggestions that
the perp might be human."

She grimaced. "I know. But..." She drew in a
breath. "Adam, I know I'm right."

"Tell me." The playfulness was gone from
Adam's voice, and his expression was totally serious.
All cop. He nodded toward the evidence spread out
on the table. "Tell me what you see in the evidence."

And so she did, trying to convince him without
telling him the biggest clue of all—that, somehow,
she'd *seen* the attacks. She wished she could simply
write it off to her subconscious, her mind process-
ing the details of a case as yet unsolved. But it was
more than that. So much more.

And there was no denying that the culprit was a
great, black cat.

THREE DAYS.

For three days, Luc searched for her, and three
times the earth turned on its axis without any sign of
his Cate. He didn't know her friends, didn't even

know who her partner was. He'd talked to her land-lord, but he'd had no more clue than Luc did. He'd gone to the precinct, but these were her days off, and while they'd offered to have her paged, he'd declined. He knew well enough that she wouldn't return the page.

Something had scared her off. *He'd* scared her off.

But he needed to get her back, and soon. Feline instincts were clamoring just below the surface. He'd gone days without the change, but soon...soon...it would come again. And without Cate, Luc was certain someone else would get hurt.

He'd hit the point of desperation. She was gone, and if he wanted to spare any more victims he needed to lock himself in the basement at his house. A prisoner, but out of harm's way.

With a deep groan of frustration, he stood in the middle of St. Charles Street, his arms to the side. He turned in a slow circle, his head tilted up to the sky. He stood on the cable-car track, but there was no car coming. He wouldn't have cared, anyway. His fate was sealed. This was his one last-ditch effort to find her. If it didn't work...well, he'd worry about that when it happened.

Closing his eyes, he let nothingness fill his consciousness. Somewhere, in the depths of his soul lay the heart of a great beast. And a heart that sang with

Cate's. He called to her now, reached out, his mind finding that silken thread that connected their souls.

*Searching, longing, needing.*

The cable car approached, easing down the track toward him, but Luc neither knew nor cared. All his focus was on this mission. He had to succeed. He had to find her.

His mind found the thread and he held tight, following it through the dark and dank shadows, the hidden places. Further and further as the cable car groaned closer and closer.

A house. A room. A man and a woman. And there, finally, he found her.

He opened his eyes just as the car approached. And as the car glided over the spot where Luc had stood only moments before, he was already racing across the street, heading toward his Caitlyn.

"CATE."

Startled, she looked up from her notes into Luc's copper eyes. She expected anger, a sense of violation, instead she felt almost giddy to see him again.

"How..." She trailed off, the question not worth asking. Somehow, she was his. Of course he'd found her.

"You ran," he said.

She nodded. What had earlier seemed like a survival instinct now seemed kneejerk and foolish. She wanted to be with this man. Wanted to soak up his heat-filled gaze and lose herself in the protection of his arms. She took a deep breath and decided simply to tell him the truth. "I was scared."

"Of me?"

"No," she said honestly. "Of us."

"You feel it, too." Deep relief tinged his voice. "Didn't you know?"

"I couldn't be sure." He took the seat that Adam had sat in earlier, then pulled one of the folders to him, ignoring the bright red Confidential stamp.

"Those are police files."

"So I see."

She didn't object further, even though she should. Instead, she just watched as he flipped through the papers.

"Will you catch him?"

She propped her chin on her fist. "Him? Not it?"

His expression was unreadable. "Human or cat," he said, "it doesn't matter. Both are attacking."

"I know. And, yes, I'll catch it."

"It? Not him?" he said, tossing her question back at her.

"Our perp is a panther. The panther that escaped from the zoo."

His eyes darkened. "I didn't realize the police had confirmed that yet. The news reports suggest that a human culprit is still being sought."

"This is my theory."

"Oh?"

She nodded. "I'm keeping an open mind, of course. But I'm sure I'm right. And in the end, I *will* catch the panther. It's...personal."

His gaze seemed to bore into her. "Personal?"

She felt her cheeks heat. "I'm sure that seems foolish to you, but I used to go to the panther habitat."

"And you feel betrayed."

She squinted at him, surprised he could read her so well. "I...yes. Yes, that's it." She started to gather her papers. "At any rate, I *will* catch him. It's my job. And I owe it to the people he's hurt."

He nodded, somewhat thoughtfully, then held out a hand. "Come with me, Cate. I think it's time we talked."

"I—"

"Cate. Just come."

All thoughts of argument abandoned her. She knew she would go with him. Hell, from the moment she'd left her apartment, she'd known she would go with him if he found her. That was, after all, why she'd run in the first place.

But she wanted this; she truly did. There was something comforting about his presence, and she wondered if that's what happened between soul mates. This soothing, easy compliance. No thought, simply feelings and trust.

The trust frightened her. Except for Adam, and

perhaps Kimberly, she'd never trusted anyone. She'd learned from her mother that loyalty was an illusion and that trusting was the easiest way to get burned.

With Luc, though, trust had bloomed, despite the frantic lust that sparked between them. Or, perhaps, because of it.

Whatever the reason, she *did* trust him.

The trouble, of course, was that now she expected to get burned.

"Wow." Cate turned in a circle, taking in the splendor that was his home. "Wow," she repeated.

Luc couldn't help his grin. Some of the homes in the famous Garden District had started to fall into ruin. But not the Agassou mansion. The house was his only link to the happiness he'd once enjoyed with his family; he could never let it fall into disrepair.

"I'm glad you like it."

"It's stunning." She crossed to the inlaid credenza and picked up a vase that she was sure must be worth more than a year's worth of her salary.

"My father inherited it. His family moved to New Orleans from France, and he can trace his roots back to the fourteen hundreds."

Her eyes widened. "It must be amazing to feel all that history tugging at you. All I know about my father is that he was vile. And my mother ran away when she was sixteen and never told me a thing about her parents."

"I'm sorry."

"It's okay." She shrugged. "It's my life and I'm used to it. But I do envy you."

The irony of her words twisted in his stomach. "Believe me, you wouldn't want to share my heritage."

Her questioning glance was so sincere, so full of interest, that he felt compelled to tell her the truth even if that light might fade in her eyes. Some form of the truth, anyway. "I'm adopted."

She blinked, confusion washing over her face. "But *this* is still your family."

"But they're not my ancestors. My ancestors are—" He cut himself off. He couldn't simply blurt out the truth. "I don't know anything about them."

"You know they exist."

He nodded. "Ever the pragmatist. Yes," he confirmed. "I know they exist. I even know that I have a sibling. A twin brother." He'd often wondered about his brother. Was there someone else out there who shared his curse? An ally he'd never met? Or had his twin escaped the pull of genetics, leaving Luc to bear the burden of their heritage?

Most likely, he'd never know. "He was adopted first. I assume he lives somewhere in the States, though I suppose he may have moved back to our homeland."

"Where's that?"

"South America. My mother and father were from there."

She nodded, apparently satisfied, then moved across the room, her fingers twined with his. "I think you put too much stock on blood ties. Your parents adopted you. They loved you, cherished you and took care of you." A tiny smile touched her lips. "I think that you can claim their ancestors as your own."

*So sweet.* He brushed the side of his hand across her cheek. "You're a good woman, Caitlyn Raine."

Her eyes darkened and she shook her head. "You don't really know me."

"I know enough," he said. "I know you're a cop. Cops help people."

She lifted one shoulder, but didn't meet his eyes.

He stepped closer, compelled to stroke her hair, wanting simply to comfort her.

*We'll find a cure, Luc.* His mother's voice rang in his head, and he saw her there in his mind, holding fast to his father's hand. *We'll find a cure and you, my darling baby boy, I promise you will find someone to love.*

He wanted to cry out, a low moan of pain and longing, a cry to the mother he'd lost and the life he'd always wanted but had never been allowed to have.

Instead he held tight to Cate, to the promise and hope she represented. He knew her, fully and completely, and yet in so many ways, he didn't know her at all.

Even so, she was his. His life, his mate. And, he hoped, the love his mother had promised.

"Luc?" Her voice was soft, muffled by the pressure of her mouth against his chest.

He stepped back, rubbing his temples as he shook his head just slightly, hoping he looked normal but certain that every ounce of pain was reflected on his face. "I'm sorry," he said. "I don't mean to overwhelm you." He took his hand, pressed it to his heart. "But you overwhelm me, Cate. You fill me. You're everything to me, and the knowledge that you are here with me, now, in this house, is—" He broke off, once again skirting dangerous territory. "Well, let's just say that I'm very, very glad that you're here."

He could tell that his words pleased her, but almost immediately she tamped down her reaction, a tiny self-deprecating smile playing on her lips. "I...I don't really understand what's happening between us. But you should know that I'm not the woman you think I am. I'm not remarkable. I'm not even very good."

He moved closer, edging against her, breathing deep of her glorious scent. He bent, lifting her hair to press a kiss behind her ear. "I think you're very, very good."

She didn't answer in words, but the tremor that passed through her body spoke volumes. He wanted her then. Wanted to cherish her, to seduce her. To start on her toes and kiss all the way up to those beautiful lips. This wasn't about need; he had not even a hint that the change was upon him. He simply desired this woman, this mate that destiny had brought to him.

He had told her they would come here to talk, and though they'd spoken of their lives, he had yet to tell her the truth about them—about him. He had planned to, yes, but now his resolve faded. He was the beast she hunted, the beast by whom she felt betrayed. He would have to tell her sometime—he knew that. But not now. Not yet.

First, he wanted to court her, to date her, to win her heart as men had done with women through the ages.

He wanted to be a man with her, not a beast.

He wanted to love her.

And he wanted her to love him. Because only if she loved him would she be able to find it in her heart to forgive him.

His arms encircled her waist and he drew her close to him. He tilted her head back and her eyes, wide and full of desire, looked up at him. Her lips parted, and he didn't wait to discover if she was about to demand that he stop or beg him to continue. He took her mouth with his, his tongue demanding entrance with a force born of purely sexual need. A man's desire flooded his veins—pure human, pure lust—and the only thing feral was the wild demand that fed him, thousands of years of mating instincts driving his need to take this woman, to make her his own, once and for all.

She melted under his touch, her willing acquiescence to his demands arousing his passion even more. He didn't wait—he couldn't—but instead urged her toward the parlor doors, his fingers fumbling for the button of her jeans. He had to have her; he couldn't wait. And she was as desperate as he.

They tumbled to the floor, rolling over an antique Turkish rug until he was straddling her. She wriggled her hips and he jerked her jeans down, taking both the denim and the soft satin of her panties.

She lay before him, exposed and glistening, and her lips formed just one word. "Now."

He didn't hesitate. He was too hard, too ready, and he clambered out of his own clothes, then spread her legs, his cock teasing her slick folds. He played with her, just a little, but he couldn't stand the strain. And he thrust inside her as she begged for him to take her.

His climax was fast and sure, and Luc exploded inside her. He rolled over, taking her with him, his lips seeking hers. And as he kissed her, soft and sweet, a new reality settled around him. His cursed bloodline bound him to Cate, it was true. But also, Luc knew, he was bound to her by the ties of love.

By LATE AFTERNOON, Cate realized that she didn't know herself as well as she thought. She'd always believed she was tough. Certainly not one of those women who bought into the whole Cinderella fantasy.

But she was buying into it now, and the more Luc treated her like a princess, the more she found herself enjoying the role.

They'd spent the afternoon in Luc's castle, because there really was no other way to describe the stunning mansion or the flower-filled gardens. Cate knew nothing about either fine furniture or fantastic horticulture, but she knew enough to recognize the effects of both care and money. And the Agassou estate reflected both. They'd walked slowly through his backyard, her hand tucked inside his, the broad branches of the magnolia trees sheltering them. Fabulous purple flowers spilled out of oversized stone pots lining the walkway, and he'd plucked one, then made a show of tucking it behind her ear before brushing a soft kiss on her cheek.

It had been silly and sentimental and she'd fallen for it utterly.

Because it was New Orleans, the heat was close to unbearable and they now sat at a small metal table tucked into a fragrant corner of a shady arbor. Martin, Luc's charming butler, had brought them tall, cool glasses filled with mint juleps. The whole afternoon had been thoroughly decadent and Cate had enjoyed every minute of it.

She licked her lips. She hated herself for doing it, but she couldn't help second-guessing something that seemed too good to be true.

"Luc?"

He'd been telling her about the history of the house, but she'd tuned him out, simply content to hold his hand and lose herself in her own thoughts. Now he stopped talking, a question in his eyes, but no accusation. Even so, she was certain he knew that her mind had wandered. He squeezed her fingers, the intimate gesture his only response.

"I—I don't understand this."

A grin danced at the corner of his mouth. "It's quite simple. My father brought in two tons of dirt and raised the backyard. That let him—"

She whacked him on the knee, but couldn't stifle the laugh that bubbled out. "That's not what I meant, and you know it."

"I know." This time his voice held no tease, and when he squeezed her fingers, the touch was purely sensual. Her body fired in immediate response and she pressed her legs together, unwilling to let a visceral reaction to this man control every waking moment.

"I don't understand what's happening between us," she elaborated.

He regarded her quietly for a moment, then traced the line of her jaw with his fingertip before curling a strand of her hair around his forefinger. "Must you understand everything?"

"It's my nature."

"And we must all behave in accordance with our nature."

It was a statement, not a question, and so she didn't respond, simply sat, her eyes focused on his face, as she waited for him to continue. Somehow, she knew that he would.

"I won't say that I love you, Cate, because that might scare you away."

She swallowed, not nearly as frightened by his words as she imagined she should be.

"But I will say that we are connected, you and I."

"But that's exactly it." She leaned forward, happy to grasp onto something other than love. Right then, it was a word she feared, a word that hit just a little too close. "*Why* are we connected?"

He grinned, a sudden mischievous look. "Perhaps if I found the connection unpleasant I would seek out a reason. But since I have no complaints, I'm content to accept the inevitable."

"The inevitable?"

"You," he said simply.

She swallowed, the implications hitting her. *Luc* was inevitable. For reasons she didn't understand, this man was tied to her future. And damned if she didn't want him there.

But as much as he filled her soul, violent images still filled her head. Even though she'd sent the bottle to Bonnie, the dreams hadn't stopped. Darkly erotic dreams. There'd been no more nightmares—thank God—and no more maulings to investigate, either. But the cat was still loose, and she knew she couldn't rest until it was found...and the dreams faded into nothingness.

"Cate?"

Those copper eyes were focused intently on her, and she feared that he had managed to read her thoughts. She swallowed, shaking her head. "Sorry. Just thinking."

"The maulings."

"You're very perceptive."

His fingers brushed the bare skin on her arm and once again she fought the urge to tremble. "Perhaps. Or perhaps I only understand you."

He gathered her into his arms, and she clung to him. "Perhaps there won't be any more attacks."

He spoke with an intense conviction, and she wanted to kiss him simply for trying to make her feel better. As it was, his strong assurance was contagious, and she nodded, almost against her will. "I wish I could believe that, but—"

"Believe it."

She met his eyes, found them clear and deter-mined. "Why?"

"Because you have no reason not to. There's been no attack for several days. It's your day off, right?"

She nodded. "It's ridiculous. I've got a huge case-load, and the bureaucrats are making me take two stinking weeks." She hadn't wanted to take them, but the department bean crunchers had finally insisted that Cate, and a few other detectives who'd been squirreling away vacation time, needed to use it. Cate had ignored the memo from brass for three months. But when her captain had finally put his foot down, she'd had no room to argue.

"Then *enjoy* those days."

"I want to," she said. And she did. She really did.

"Good." He leaned over, pressing a soft kiss to her lips that, while not decadent in itself, offered so much. "Because I intend to make sure you enjoy yourself. And I thought we'd start with a late-afternoon siesta..."

CATE DIDN'T ACTUALLY GET to rest during their siesta, but as she stretched naked on the satin sheets after an hour-long bout of lovemaking, she definitely felt sated and relaxed. Across the room, Luc was pulling on slacks in front of the closet, and she was watching him, thoroughly enjoying the view and thinking one very disturbing thought—she could get used to this.

A tiny buried part of her dared to hope that the

voice in her head was wrong. That she could have the whole dream. A husband. Children. A family that loved her.

*No, no, no.* She needed to get that thought out of her head. No matter what this thing was that seemed to be filling the air between them, the bottom line remained the same, and the familiar refrain reverberated through her head. *Not for you. Never for a girl like you.*

"Something wrong?" Luc stood, looking utterly sexy as he buttoned his starched white shirt. Such a short time and already he knew her too well. A blossom of hope dared to bloom, but Cate ignored it, tucking it instead into the darkest corner of her heart.

She shook her head, the lie as natural as breathing. "Just enjoying the view."

"I'm glad you think it's worth watching."

She shrugged. "It's an empirical fact. Can't have you thinking I'm an idiot."

He let his eyes roam over her, and her body tingled in response, the sensation starting at her toes and drifting all the way up to the top of her head until her entire body felt warm and malleable and it was all she could do to keep herself from begging for his touch.

With his eyes lingering on her, he smiled. "I can't believe these words are coming from my lips, but you really should get dressed. I have plans for you this evening."

"It's only five."

As his smile broadened, so did the heat in her belly. "I have plans for a very, very long evening."

"Oh." She licked her lips. Discomfort warring with an intense desire to wrap herself up in this man. A lifetime of putting up walls won out, though, and she licked her lips, at the same time eased the sheet over her bare thigh. "Listen, Luc, today has been, well, it's been great. But I really do need to get going."

"Why?"

The question startled her, though she certainly should have expected it. "Well, I might be off from work, but I have tons of paperwork to catch up and evidence to review for all of my cases."

He nodded, his copper eyes intense as he sat on the bed again. "You've already admitted there's something happening between us. I thought we'd agreed to explore that."

"I..." She trailed off, then shrugged. How could she explain to him that she was fine with the sexual tug between them? If that's all it was, she'd stay in his bed forever. Sex she could deal with. But this was more. The way he touched her, the way he looked at her, the way he talked with her—as if she were special, as if they could have a future...she didn't have the tools to deal with that. All she knew how to do was run.

"I'm not proposing marriage, Cate," he said, once again sitting next to her. He took a strand of hair and curled it around his finger, then flashed a devilish grin. "At least not yet. Just a dinner that you won't run from." He stroked her cheek, his hand caressing her face, then tracing her lips. "And maybe a bit of after-dinner entertainment."

Her buttons. He knew every single one of them. How to manipulate her, how to say exactly the right thing. That reality both frightened and comforted her, and her head screamed that she should run far and fast from this man. That he could get past her defenses, leaving her bare and vulnerable.

She stayed anyway. And she had to wonder if she was being supremely stupid or if, God help her, she was falling in love.

## CHAPTER SEVEN

THEY HAD DINNER AT Commander's Palace and then went dancing at Tipitina's. An elegant dinner followed by the crush of bodies, sweat, and the pulse of music and lust in her veins. They pressed together on the dance floor, moving to a rhythm that the band couldn't hear but that seemed to beat through both of them.

They took a taxi back to his house, and had she been doing her job, she should have cited them both for indecent exposure. In truth, she didn't think the driver saw anything, but it had taken every ounce of self-control in Cate's body not to scream in pleasure as Luc made her come, his fingers buried in her slippery folds.

They'd left her panties on the floorboard of the cab. Just a tiny souvenir.

Inside, they'd made a beeline for the bedroom, barely managing to stay somewhat clothed before the door shut behind them, exercising that tiny amount of propriety in case Luc's butler Martin happened to be about.

All night, Luc's presence had been taunting her.

His scent, the subtle touch of his hand. When he'd finally touched her in the taxi, she'd come right away.

Now, she had no patience to wait.

She reached for his belt, her fingers fumbling as she unfastened the thing, letting it hang open as she moved on to the button. His hands were just as busy, inching her skirt up around her waist, cupping her right *there* as she clenched her thighs together, allowing no chance to lose his touch.

He stroked her, a single finger sliding along her slippery folds. And when her legs simply couldn't hold her upright anymore, she fell backwards onto the bed.

He kicked off his shoes and stripped off his jeans, then climbed onto the bed to straddle her. Her skirt was around her waist, her blouse unbuttoned, and she lay there exposed and needy. He watched her, one hand cupping her breast. "You're beautiful," he said.

"Tell me later." She had to force the words out, past a wall of need. "Right now, I want you inside me."

His face changed with her words, his expression turning possessive. Good. She wanted him to have her, to take her, and dammit, if he didn't do it right then, she thought that she would scream.

When he thrust inside her, she almost did.

He consumed her, filled her, and when he pounded inside her, she was certain she was going to rip apart. She matched him, thrust for thrust, her hips bucking. They were wild, desperate for each other, as if by this frantic lovemaking they could discover the source of their connection. As if, by the melding of flesh, they could become one.

The orgasm ripped through her, and she clung to him, fingernails clenched into his shoulders, her body bucking beneath him. It was primitive and wild, and with this man, it felt completely right.

Exhaustion took her, and she curled up against him, still half-clothed. His fingers played with the buttons on her shirt, finally unfastening them all and laying the material open to expose her breasts. She hadn't worn a bra, and now he stroked her, his fingers dancing lazily around her nipples.

"I'd be careful if I were you," she said dreamily. "I might demand a repeat performance."

"And I might be happy to oblige." He kissed her breast, the heat from his lips shooting straight down between her thighs. She squeezed her legs together, prolonging the pleasure, and sighed. "You're wonderful," he said.

"No, I'm not." The words came out automatically. A simple truth. And she rolled sideways, drawing her thumbnail to her mouth even as she spooned against him. She hadn't meant to bring her past into their bed, but it had come anyway, and now she shrank from the memories.

His hand idly stroked her hip, and she could feel

the light touch of his breath on the back of her neck. For a moment, she didn't think he was going to speak, then he shifted, moving to sit up with his back against the headboard. She stayed where she was, but pulled her knees up to her chest. His fingers found her hair, and he stroked softly.

"I can only report what I see," he said.

"My father raped my mother," she said simply, unable to look at him. Tears welled in her eyes and she squeezed them tight, fighting the pain, trying to hold on to reason. She wasn't stupid. She knew that simply because her mother said something didn't make it so. But that didn't change the hole in her stomach when she thought about her life.

His fingers stilled in her hair. "I'm sorry."

"She tried to end the pregnancy. It didn't work." She licked her lips. "There are days when I wish it had."

She didn't want to cry. And she told herself she didn't want his sympathy. But when he whispered, "Come here," the dam burst. The tears poured out and she rolled over, letting him close his arms around her as she buried her face in his chest. She did want him, dammit. She wanted his sympathy and his support. And for the first time in her life, she not only wanted a man's love, she needed it. She needed *this* man's love.

He held her that way for an eternity, his hands gently stroking her back, his muscles taut and firm under her hands. And when the tears stopped and she was no longer shaking, he said simply, "Tell me."

And she did. She told him about growing up with her mother, about never doing anything right. Of trying anything and everything to get the woman's attention until, finally, she'd forgotten just why she'd been acting out in the first place. "I stayed out late, I drank, I was rowdy as hell. I slept around. Anything and everything to prove my mother right. I was a bad girl."

"You were looking for someone," he said. "Someone to save you from your life."

"No—"

"And when you didn't find him, you became a cop. Now you're helping other people. Doing for them what no one ever did for you."

His words shot through her, the touch of truth cold against her heart. "No." She whispered the protest. "I'm not that noble. All I'm doing—all I've *ever* done—is try to erase my mother's voice in my head."

He pressed a kiss to her hair. "The cause doesn't matter. What you're doing is noble. You *are* helping people, and you are doing good."

She'd been pressed against him, the top of her head to his chest so that if she opened her eyes all she saw was the bed and their bodies. Now she tilted her head up, straining to look into his eyes. "It doesn't matter," she said, "because it never ends. I can't save anyone. Not really. Hell, I can't even save myself."

"Perhaps you aren't meant to save yourself," he said. "And as for others, about that, you're wrong."

"No—"

He pressed a finger to her lips. "You can, Cate. You can save *me*." He stroked her cheek. "And believe me when I say that you already have."

SHE WAS OBSESSED with finding the escaped cat, and Luc could do nothing to dissuade her from her job. Even though she was taking vacation days, she pored over records, checked 911 calls for reports of animals in alleys, and checked in with the hospital, hoping that one of the victims had regained consciousness. She was concerned about the victims' condition, of course. But she also wanted information.

Luc hoped the victims survived, too, though for a different reason. While Cate wanted information, he wanted absolution. He wanted to know that he was not a murderer even though he couldn't erase the fact that he'd surely put those people through hell.

Most of all, though, he wanted Cate to back off the search. If they survived, and if there were no more attacks, then with time he figured she would walk away. The city would assume the animal had been killed by a car or a shotgun, and that would be the end of that.

Right now, though, he knew that her blood burned with the need to capture the savage who was stalking the innocent on the streets of New Orleans. What would she do, he wondered, if she knew that he was the man she sought, the creature she'd come to hate even though she did not know him?

*There was no reason for her to know.* The realization came to him in a flash, and he knew that was the only way. With Cate in his arms and in his bed, he was safe. He'd carry the secret to his grave. She need never, ever know the dark parts of his soul.

Indeed, he tried to escape the dark himself. During the day, when he managed to pull her away from work, they walked the French Quarter, sipping chicory coffee and eating beignets at Café Du Monde before strolling down Royal and peering into the windows of the antique stores that lined the picturesque street. They held hands and laughed and joked.

At night, though, shadows loomed, the shadow of his secret most of all. And even when he was spent, exhausted after losing himself in her arms, still he lay awake, watching this woman who was his savior. This woman that he'd come to love. He couldn't disappoint her. Couldn't ever let her know. The truth, he vowed, would remain hidden.

As he did every night, Luc watched as Cate's chest rose and fell, sleep having finally overtaken her. He'd meant what he'd said a few days ago. She had saved him. This woman who didn't even know her own worth was, literally, his key to salvation.

She deserved his love. And, so help him, she had it.

She murmured in her sleep, shifting against him, and he stroked her hair, saying soft things, wanting to make the world right for her. She stilled, and he simply watched her, amazed that someone so beautiful could doubt herself so much.

They sat like that for a while, him watching, simply absorbing the essence of Cate, until sleep started to overtake him. He was just about to drift off when she tensed, crying out in her sleep and sitting bolt upright, her breath coming in gasps as she clutched his arm. She stared at him, her eyes wild, but she didn't seem to see him.

"Cate. *Cate.*"

She blinked, finally focusing, the alarm on her face fading to relief. "I had a dream."

"A nightmare, more like it."

She nodded, easing herself up to hug her knees and press her body closer to his. It was a subtle motion, but it warmed him. She trusted him, wanted his comfort. And he wanted to give it to her. "Not as bad as *some* of my nightmares, though." She tilted her head a bit, this time aiming a gentle grin toward him. "And not nearly as pleasant as the other dreams I've been having. Though I will say that being with you makes those dreams seem pretty tame."

He had no idea what she was talking about, and his confusion must have shown on his face. "It started a few days before we met," she said by way of explanation. She licked her lips. "It sounds silly, but I've been having these, well, these dreams."

A bone-deep cold settled over him, and for no reason at all, he feared her words. "What kind of dreams?" he asked, forcing himself to form the question.

Color rose on her cheeks. "At first, just erotic dreams. *Very* erotic. As if I was being called by someone and I could feel him touching me."

"I see." His jaw tightened, and he forced himself not to be jealous of a dream. "And was that the kind of dream that woke you just now?"

She shook her head, her eyes meeting his. "No. Those dreams have stopped since I've been with you. I think..." She trailed off, no longer meeting his eyes. "I think I don't need them anymore."

*Good.* But he didn't voice the thought.

"This was a nightmare." She spoke the word matter-of-factly, and he realized that this nightmare was something she lived with.

"Your mother?" he asked.

"No. These are...violent. I don't know. It's hard to describe." She shook her head, as if shaking off a memory. "At any rate, I shouldn't have even called it a nightmare. The *real* nightmares always have Midnight in them."

Immediately, his senses were on alert. "The panther?"

She nodded. "He's there. And he attacks. Violent, hideous attacks."

Nausea rose in his gut. *Him.* She was seeing him in her dreams. They were connected, he and Cate, even more than either of them had ever imagined.

He forced himself to form words. "And these dreams. Do they—" He couldn't finish the thought. It wasn't necessary. She knew what he meant.

"Yes," she said. "They seem to coincide with the maulings." Her face twisted, contorted in anger. "It's as if he's taunting me, showing me that he can attack, that he will attack, and that there's not a damn thing I can do about it." She hugged herself, trembling slightly. "My part in all this though is more than just the job, you see. More even than that I used to go to the zoo to watch him. It's like I've failed."

He frowned. "Failed?"

She nodded, clearly miserable. "I see the attacks in my dreams, and it's like I should be able to do something. But I can't, and now all those people are in the hospital. I couldn't save them. Hell, I couldn't even help them."

His stomach roiled as he remembered that he was the one who put them in the hospital.

Her features hardened. "*That's* why I have to catch him. It's my job, yes. But I have to do it for me. For my peace of mind." She drew a breath. "I have to—I *will*—catch Midnight."

A chill settled over Luc and he trembled, just the smallest shaking of his muscles. She felt it, though, and her face transformed. Gone was the anger, replaced with pure compassion and total beauty. "Are you okay?"

He forced a smile. "Just concerned for you." He pulled her into his arms and pressed her cheek to his chest. He wanted the feel of her against him, but he also didn't want her to see his face. "When did these dreams start?"

"My birthday," she said. "It was the last time I saw Midnight," she added. "I'd spent the day at the zoo. I'd opened my birthday present there. I'd even—" She cut off with a shake of her head, the color high on her cheeks.

"What?"

"You," she said, and his blood ran cold. Did she know? How? How could she know?

"Me?" His own voice was hardly recognizable.

"I think it must be the bottle," she said. "It did something to me. So many things have happened. The maulings. The visions. And..." She broke off with a little shrug, but a smile danced at her mouth. "And this connection to you."

"What do I have to do with the zoo?"

She frowned, perhaps hearing the urgency in his voice. Then she licked her lips. "That's the odd part. I first felt this connection, this thing, between us there. And I heard your voice in my head."

"My voice? What did I say?"

"That I was yours." She lifted herself and pressed a kiss to his lips. "And the voice was right. I am."

He clutched her close to him, terror coursing through his veins. She was right about the connection. What she didn't realize was that it was *all* connected. Him, the maulings, everything.

"Do you still have the bottle?" He asked the question more from curiosity. He had no idea what he'd do with the thing.

"No. I sent it to a friend. I thought perhaps the dreams would stop if it was gone."

"But they haven't."

"No." She frowned. "Well, yes. Since I've been with you, I no longer dream of the cat." She snuggled close to him, her eyes heavy with sleep. "I love you, Luc. I don't really understand what happened between us, so fast and furious. But I want you to know that I love you."

His heart wrenched, and he stroked her hair. "And I love you, my Cate. My love."

She leaned against him, and as the moon rose outside his windows, she slept.

And Luc realized what he had to do.

*SHADOWS TAUNTED HER.*

*She walked barefoot down a darkened alley, the stench of garbage hanging in the dense air. The humidity seemed to envelop her, but even so, she shivered, not from cold, but from fear.*

*He was out there. He was stalking her. And this time, she wouldn't escape.*

*A low growl filled the air, and she spun, looking for the source but finding nothing.*

*And then, when one of the dark shadows moved, taking the form of a leaping panther, teeth bared, eyes golden and lost in the thrill of the kill, she stood frozen to the spot.*

*Unable to move, she did the only thing she could do—*

Cate screamed.

The sound ripped from her throat, jerking her to consciousness, and she sat up, the cold grip of terror still on her as she fumbled beside her for Luc's warmth.

He wasn't there.

She waited, knowing he would have heard her. Knowing he would come running to hold her. To soothe her. To make it better.

But he never came.

And as her pulse slowed, finally returning to normal, Cate hugged the pillow to her chest and told herself she wouldn't cry. This was expected, after all. The people she loved betrayed her. And Cate could rely on no one in this world but herself.

# CHAPTER EIGHT

"If I might say so, sir, you are being most unreasonable."

Luc glared at Martin from behind the bars in the basement confine. He'd left Cate hours before and gone to his study, unable to hold her while knowing the truth—that the passion with which she hunted him was spurred by more than just her job. It was deep and personal.

He had to tell her the truth. He'd been selfish in thinking he could keep it from her, thinking only of his own pain and not his victims'. Cate was right; he *should* be caught. Should be made to pay retribution even though he wanted nothing more than to live out his life in peace with Cate at his side.

And so he would leave the choice to her, even though he already knew what she'd do—she would turn him in. In her eyes, Midnight's attacks were a betrayal. So, too, would be the secret that he'd been keeping from her. And in the end, she'd do what she must. For duty, for the victims. And because, as she'd said, it was personal.

"I've made up my mind, Martin. Now can I please have some water?" He was locked in now, an unfortunate necessity, but he'd felt the change coming on. At first, despite his newfound resolve, he'd thought to go to her, to use her, his feline instincts urging him back to his mate. But he'd fought instinct, fought for his humanity to shine through, and in the end, he'd won the battle.

A dubious victory, considering he felt less than human now, locked in a cage, depending on Martin to bring him food and drink.

"You cannot tell her that you attacked those people."

"I have to, Martin. She deserves the truth. She deserves to find the culprit she's been searching for."

"Dammit, man, you did not injure those people. Your parents taught you control. Don't offend their legacy by not believing."

Self-loathing consumed him. "It's not a question of belief. I've seen the blood on my hands. I attacked. Just as I attacked little Clarissa Taylor."

"The child survived, sir," Martin said.

"I almost killed a five-year-old," Luc shot back.

"Sir, you are—"

Luc never found out what he was because Martin's words were lost, buried beneath the pounding of blood in his ears as the force of the change struck him. The world spun out of control, and he rushed the bars, beating against them with his fists.

And then he was gone, the maelstrom sucking him in, pure animal instinct taking over and, once again, he was floating in the blackness of his own soul awaiting the moment when awareness returned.

CATE HAD WASTED half an hour crying in the bed, tears of anger and betrayal, then finally fallen back to sleep. She'd secretly hoped he'd come back; that she'd been wrong and he'd simply gone for a walk because he couldn't sleep.

She should have known better, of course.

And so she gathered her things and headed for the front door. She'd go back home and bury herself in her job, finding in her work the comfort she could no longer find in Luc's arms.

Now she stopped at the door and scribbled a note, addressing it only to Martin so the gentle old man wouldn't worry. She was just trying to figure out the best place to put it, when the man himself appeared beside her.

Cate jumped, her heart pounding. "I didn't hear you come up."

"It is a butler's job to be invisible." He nodded to the suitcase. "You are taking your leave of us, miss?"

She nodded, but didn't meet his eyes, afraid that if she did, the tears would start up again. "I need to get back to work. If Luc can't find the time to leave a message for me, I certainly can't find the time to wait indefinitely for him."

He bowed just slightly. "He does have a message for you, Miss Cate. Though it will be a hard one for you to hear."

"What is it?"

Martin shook his head. "He wanted to tell you himself, but that's no longer possible. I shall have to speak for him."

Fear coursed through her veins. "Is he hurt?"

Martin shook his head. "Let me bring you to him."

Cate squinted. "Where is he?"

"Not far. But it's not the where that is important. It's the what." He held out his hand to her. "Come, my dear. I'll explain on the way."

A PANTHER.

Martin had told her an unbelievable story, but his explanation couldn't be true. It was impossible, absurd. And yet somehow, deep in her heart, Cate knew that what the butler had revealed was absolutely true—Luc had transformed into the sleek black panther that now paced the basement cage.

And she alone was the key to controlling his curse.

Hesitating just a little, she stepped to the bars, pressing her face against the cool metal. Basements were unusual in New Orleans, and from this vantage point she could see that this was new construction, specially reinforced to survive the boggy terrain. She wanted to ask Luc about it, but the man was nowhere to be seen.

It was just her and a sleek black cat.

She drew a breath. "Luc?"

Nothing.

"Dammit, Luc. Martin told me. He told me everything." She felt like a fool speaking the words, not quite able to get her head around the fact that she really and truly believed it. She did, though. Hell, maybe she'd known the truth all along.

Now, though, she had to see it. Had to see *him*.

"Change, Luc. If you love me even a little, I need you to change."

That did it. The cat rose from the ground, muscles rippling under its thick coat as it walked toward her, teeth bared. She stayed where she was, her hands clutching the bars, her face pressed into the space between. If the cat lunged now, she was surely dead. But she held her breath. And trusted.

And then she blinked, not sure her eyes were functioning. But yes, there it was again. A ripple. The cat's body, changing. Shifting and pulling until—

*Luc.*

Crouched, naked on the cold concrete floor.

"It's true." She whispered the words, then crossed herself.

"You didn't believe?" he asked.

"I did," she said. "But to see it—" She drew a breath. "Oh, Luc. Why didn't you tell me?" she demanded.

He stood and crossed to her. "Tell you what? That I am the man you seek? A marauder? The attacker of innocents? The cat who stalks in your dreams?"

A tear trickled down her cheek and she didn't try to stop it. He was everything she'd sworn to fight against, but she loved him.

And, dear God, she could save him. She could end the curse and be with the man she loved.

But to do that, she had to turn her back on his victims. How could she do that, even for love?

"Oh, Luc." The words were barely a sigh.

"You must turn me in," he said.

She shook her head, not willing to accept that. Not yet. There had to be a way. "No. I love you. And I can save you."

"Yes, but you would resent it. Perhaps not at first, but Cate, I'm the evil you've been stalking. You cannot tie yourself to me, not and live with yourself. It goes against everything you've spent your life doing, all the bad you've overcome. It's not a sacrifice I can ask you to make. Nor one I can accept."

*No.* With a sudden clarity she knew what she had to do. She loved him. Even more, she believed in him. For the first time in her life she'd believed in someone other than herself, *trusted* someone completely. And, so help her, she still trusted him.

And she didn't believe that Luc was capable of those attacks, even when he was in his feline form. "Martin says you can't remember," she said.

"I don't need to remember. I've seen the blood on my hands afterward."

"You didn't attack those people, Luc. There's got to be another explanation."

He just stared at her.

Damn the man, she wanted to throttle him. "Martin says you have control. That you wouldn't attack, even during the change."

"Martin is an old fool."

She held one card, one secret about which Martin had spoken, and she played it now. "He says that Clarissa survived. That you stopped, and that she lived."

Pain slashed his face. "I almost killed that child," he said, his voice barely a whisper.

She wanted to wince, wanted to cry, but she steeled herself. "Tell me."

"It was after my parents' death. I was dining at the home of friends and afterwards we were in the garden. I felt the change, so I made my excuses, determined to reach home and my cage before it happened." He described the scene, his voice passionless, monotone. "Inside the house, though, it hit me. More abruptly than I'd expected. My friends' little girl was in the house, and she was all alone, you see. All alone with the beast."

"Martin says she survived."

He nodded. "She did. Scared but essentially unafflicted."

"You *did* have control."

"I don't know what caused me to stop, to not finish her. And it doesn't matter. I shouldn't have been in a position to harm her anyway." He licked his lips, met her eyes. "The next day I arranged for the donation of a black panther to the zoo, and began to spread the word that Luc Agassou would be traveling abroad."

Her eyes brimmed with tears, still unwilling to believe what he told her. "No." She shook her head. "It wasn't you. You didn't hurt those people."

"Cate. I appreciate the faith, but it's misplaced."

"No, it's—" She stopped, something important tickling at the back of her brain.

*And then she knew.* Dear Lord, she knew, and she was right, and she could save him. This man that she loved, she could not only end his curse, but she could prove that he was innocent.

But to do that, she needed his help.

DAYS PASSED, and Luc paced his cage, knowing that Cate was somewhere above, making futile preparations to prove him innocent. He wanted to believe her. Wanted to buy into her eager and enthusiastic protestations that he wasn't killing. That he *couldn't* be attacking because she'd dreamed of the panther while he'd been locked in the cage.

One dream, however, wasn't enough to convince him. She seemed to think she'd been seeing through the attacker's eyes, but Luc knew that made no sense. Most likely she was seeing raw images, emotions mixed with dreams.

But she'd asked if he loved her, and he'd been unable to lie.

"If you love me, let me try this. Let me try to prove you innocent." She'd smiled that smile he loved so well, and she'd looked at him with dark, professional eyes. "Let me do my job, Luc. And if I'm wrong, I'll leave."

Even though he knew she was wrong, he'd had to take the chance. Because he did love her. And, damn him, he wanted her to stay.

Now they were waiting. Waiting for the fickle workings of his curse to send him prowling the streets again. Waiting—

His soul rippled, and he drew in a breath. *Now.* It was upon him. Soon, Cate would know the truth.

And just as soon, Luc knew, he would be really, and truly, alone.

"I DON'T KNOW HOW MUCH assistance I can be, Miss Cate," Martin said.

"You're doing fine. I'll be doing all the important stuff." She would have preferred he stay behind, but she did need help and, under the circumstances, asking Adam for assistance was simply out of the question.

At the moment, they were in her car, following a dot blipping on a screen. They'd tagged Luc with a transmitter, and now the wonders of technology helped them follow him as he prowled the streets of New Orleans. A great cat, loose in the dead of night. They intended to follow him, and, Cate was certain, the true culprit would appear. Another panther, stalking in the dark.

Luc didn't believe her, of course, but Cate didn't care. She was right. She was certain. And she'd prove Luc's innocence.

"There," Martin said, pointing to the screen.

Cate nodded, then maneuvered the car into a space. "From here we go on foot." She opened the glove box and took out the small pistol she'd prepared earlier. "This is for you," she said. "Just in case."

Martin looked at it, his face paling. But he nodded and clutched the gun.

Cate checked her own weapon, then got out of the car, the tracking device in one hand as they walked through the deserted streets near the offices of the Fifth Circuit Court of Appeals.

"That alley," Martin said, pointing to a service road alongside one of the buildings surrounding the imperious courtyard.

They headed in that direction, Cate's gaze cutting across the open area as they walked. The homeless tended to huddle in the dark corners, finding shelter in the nooks and crannies of the deserted plaza that teemed with life only during working hours. Tonight, though, the place was deserted, and Cate couldn't help but wonder if someone—or something—had scared off the squatters.

As if in answer, a scream ripped the sky, and she raced forward.

*And there he was.* A black panther, his muzzle and feet bloody, as his teeth and claws ripped at the leg of a man, mercifully passed out on the bloodstained concrete.

"No!" Her own scream cut through the sky, pure horror pulling the cry from her. The cat turned, ears cocked, copper eyes focused on her.

The nose flared, and she took a step backwards, the movement foolish, as it only provoked the beast. He lunged, soaring through the sky. She pulled her gun, taking aim, frantic to prevent the claws and teeth from rending her flesh.

She didn't fire, though, because her target was knocked out of the air by a streak of black. As Cate scrambled backwards, she watched, mesmerized, as the *two* great cats warred, claws and teeth bared, fur flying.

"They'll surely kill each other." Martin spoke from behind her, his voice frantic.

He was right. The two panthers twisted, identical except for the collar on Luc. They rolled and grappled, and the rogue cat sank his teeth into Luc's neck. Luc howled, a bone-deep cry of pain and terror.

*"No!"* Cate screamed. Any longer and the rogue would kill Luc. She could only hope that she didn't kill him herself. She lifted her gun, aimed and fired.

LUC CROSSED TO THE BED, his neck bandaged where the panther had latched on twenty-four hours before.

He still couldn't believe it. *She'd been right.* Not only that, Martin had been right. Luc had always had control. He had, in fact, been the only reason that the victims had survived and not been mauled to death by the panther who had attacked them.

His twin. His very own brother.

Just as Cate had felt a connection to Luc, Luc had felt a connection to his brother. He'd always been at the maulings because he'd been called there, following in his brother's path. His feline self had been determined not to allow the carnage intended by his brother, who lacked the control taught to Luc by his parents.

His sibling was gone now. Cate had killed him to

save Luc. The police had been called, of course, as well as zoo officials. The terror was over. The culprit caught.

He slid beneath the sheets, desperate to feel her warmth. "How did you know?" he asked. She'd told him already, of course, but only in bits and pieces. Now, though, he wanted to know the full story.

She curled against him. "I realized that since we were connected, the dreams must fit in somehow. It made sense that I was seeing things through your eyes. That scared me at first, because I thought it meant you were the attacker. But then I realized the truth. If I was seeing with your eyes and I was watching a black panther attack people—"

"Then I couldn't be the one doing the attacking."

"And then I had the dream while you were in the cage, and I knew there had to be another. Someone that *you* were connected to. And you'd said you had a twin..." She trailed off with a shrug. "I'm a cop. I trust my gut."

"You were right." He leaned over, capturing her mouth with his. "You believed in me, Cate. Even when I didn't believe in myself."

"Sometimes it's hard to believe in yourself," she said.

"I love you, Cate."

Her smile lit her face. "I love you, too."

He held her close, just listening to the beat of her

heart. "And, you know, I suppose I should also thank you," he said after minutes had ticked away. "You saved me, after all."

"I'm your mate, remember? That's what I'm supposed to do." She smiled. "Besides, I'd say we saved each other." She stroked his arm, then snuggled closer. "Will you miss it?"

He didn't have to ask what she meant. There was a freedom in being feline, a different perspective on the world. But no, he would not miss it. Now Cate was his world, and that was all that he wanted.

"No," he said simply.

"Good." Her grin turned mischievous. "Because I intend to keep you rather occupied in the bedroom. If you *did* miss it, I'm afraid you'd be out of luck."

He affected a look of shock. "Are you suggesting, my dear, that you would use me for your sexual pleasure?"

"Indeed I am, Mr. Agassou," she said. And then she slid under the sheet and began to show him in excruciating, erotic, magnificent detail, just what exactly that sexual pleasure entailed.

# TOUCH ME

## Susan Kearney

For Brenda Chin,
an editor who knows a good idea when she hears it.
Thanks.

And a special thank you to
Julie Elizabeth Leto and Julie Kenner.
It was fun working with you both.

CLASSIFIED

For Your Information.
Read and Destroy.

The Shey Group is a private paramilitary organization headed by Logan Kincaid whose purpose is to take on high-risk, high-stakes missions in accord with U.S. government policy. All members are former CIA, FBI or military with top-level clearances and specialized skills. Members maintain close ties to the intelligence community and conduct high-level behind-the-scenes operations for the government as well as for private individuals and corporations.

The US government will deny any connection with this group.

Employ at your own risk.

# *PROLOGUE*

DRAGGED NAKED FROM A filthy cell, undercover agent John Cameron dreaded what would come next. Hands tied behind his back, blindfolded, his body ravaged from lack of food, he nevertheless kicked and elbowed his captors. His flesh might be weak, but his spirit remained firm, stoic, resolved.

He couldn't avoid the electrodes taped to his most sensitive places. He couldn't avoid the volts of searing electricity that cramped his muscles and fried his nerves in agonizing attacks. But he could endure and burrow deep inside his mind where his captors couldn't follow.

John retreated behind the thick steel walls he'd built with painstaking care. As long as he still breathed, he would never give them the information they sought. Good men had died to protect thousands of innocent Americans lives. He would do no less.

John didn't welcome death. Nor did he fight the pain. He embraced it. He let it flow through his body as he thought of more pleasant times. His childhood sailing on Lake George. Winters skiing Gore Mountain. The clean scent of falling snow. Rain on the roof of his first Corvette. The crisp scent of frying bacon.

Time and pain tangled in a vortex without edges. In the world he'd created to escape his tormentors, there was nothing but a ribbon of rainbow colors, a string of melodic voices, spinning threads anchoring him to reality.

Although John had retreated to a place all his own, he possessed an uncanny awareness of time. The session suddenly, mercifully, had stopped short. His grateful body sagged, cramped muscles spasmed.

A familiar voice sliced through the darkness. "You're safe, John. We're getting you out of here."

# CHAPTER ONE

*Two months later*

THE MIAMI HEAT SCORCHED, but thanks to John Cameron, the view sizzled. His powerful shoulders and long, tanned limbs churned a frothy wake in the clear blue of the infinity pool, which blended perfectly with the cool azure of the Intracoastal waterway. Swimming with smooth, coordinated strokes, he rotated both arms in perfect synchronization with the forceful dolphin kick of his muscular legs. When he flipped from effortless butterfly to graceful backstroke, a tangle of anticipation and desire sluiced through Dr. Bonnie Anders.

With his glossy jet hair slicked back from a high forehead, Bonnie could see his sensual face, defined by a ruggedly bold nose, carved cheekbones and a square jaw that caused a serious, swooping pull of pleasure inside her. With her swimsuit cover-up

clinging to her body like shrink-wrap under the blazing Florida sun, she couldn't wait to join him.

And not just because John's case fit right into her
psychiatric specialty and piqued her interest. Although she needed to touch John to engage her special gift and help him to overcome his mental block,
she'd never had a patient who made her fingers tingle in anticipation.

Her presence at the end of the lap pool caused him
to stop swimming midstroke. Standing, he revealed
a broad chest with glistening black curls that made
her palms dampen and her pulse flutter buoyantly.
Water trickled down his symmetrical face and spiked
long black eyelashes, a smoke screen for eyes that
were compelling, magnetic and slightly puzzled.
Then as if solving the mystery of her presence there,
his full lips widened into a welcoming smile, flashing straight white teeth.

"Hi there, gorgeous." His voice, a deep baritone
with a slight Midwestern accent, tantalized her like
a sweet caress, yet still vibrated with a hint of vigi-
lance. "Did Logan Kincaid send you?"

"As a matter of fact, he did. I'm Bonnie." After
hearing about Bonnie's success using touch therapy
on a former spy who'd resurfaced with total amne-

sia, Logan Kincaid had hired her to help John recall the information he'd repressed during torture.

She took in the glass-and-concrete mansion behind her, the royal palms holding court over an outdoor bar, a mile-long grill and a stainless steel kitchen. Even better were the wall of citrus trees along the estate's side fences that lent a private intimacy to the spacious yard. A perfect setting for a one-on-one with a gorgeous man.

Bonnie stared boldly at him through her dark shades, enticed by the confident smile that tipped the corners of his mouth and the glint of wary interest in his eyes. She'd never have guessed that one month ago he'd been too weak to walk. The doctors and physical trainers had done wonders, but then again, they'd had great material to work with. And now it was her turn.

She flung her arms wide to take in the grounds, the gazebo, the windsailers on the Intercoastal waterway. "The Shey Group sure knows how to take care of its people."

John's grin widened. "Is that why you're here?"

"To take care of you? Oh, yeah."

She planned to take care of every little part of him—his head, his heart. Whatever was broken, she'd fix it. After all, that's what a psychiatrist did. And after seeing how easy he was on her eyes, doing her job well, touching him, was going to be even more pleasant than she'd anticipated. Already she longed to graze her palms along his tanned skin, wondered if he would feel closed and dark like an underwater cavern or frenetic like a cascade of color rushing by too fast to gauge or simply so still that he seemed to hide at the bottom of a deep green lagoon.

Considered by many to be a maverick, Bonnie wasn't a traditional psychiatrist. However, her unusual success with touch therapy had brought her to the attention of the Shey Group, a covert organization of ex-military specialists who needed her expertise to help John Cameron recover very specific memories that pertained to national security. Through work with a previous patient, Bonnie had learned that the Shey Group took on impossible missions, everything from protecting the nation from terrorism to preventing assassinations. John had discovered some information when he'd gone undercover to infiltrate a terrorist cell but had never had the opportunity to pass it on to his boss. It was critical to national security that John recall this information. With possibly thousands of lives at stake, Bonnie was more than ready to begin.

She peeled off the cover-up, let it pool at her feet, then kicked off her mules. His gunmetal gaze singed her with a toasty glow. She awarded him an extra moment for an appreciative head-to-toe ogle before she dived into the pool, pleased that her breasts, which had less material covering them than a postage stamp, had his eyes smoking.

Let him burn.

To bring back the memories trapped deep in his mind, she needed to keep him aroused and distracted, a tactic that would enhance her methods—until her "secret weapon" arrived. John Cameron's medical file was quite explicit. To get through to him, she had to excite him, provoke him, stimulate him. She had to use her odd but natural powers of touch—and more. Thanks to her friend, Cate, she'd soon have the "more" she needed. In the meantime she'd flirt and distract. She expected to push herself beyond her normal limits, but what she hadn't expected was how much she'd enjoy her role.

After growing up as the only child of a single military mom, Bonnie knew John's type. Hard-core. Patriotic to the bone. A man like her dad, who had never married her mother, but who'd been a good father to her and who'd served his country with pride.

While her parents had roamed the world, Bonnie had lived with her aunt, a civilian who worked for Cent-Com at MacDill Air Force base, and Bonnie considered herself lucky to have lived in the same neighborhood for her entire childhood. However, on that kind of government pay scale, she'd never stayed in digs as fancy as this mansion. Someday, she'd finish paying back her student loans and buy a house in Tampa, but even her Bayshore condo couldn't compare to the luxury here. For this assignment, she'd struck twenty-four-carat gold.

A Miami waterfront estate, a man that could have starred in a James Bond movie and an intense attraction that already placed him center stage in her fantasies. Yeah, she'd fallen into a tough assignment, this time. The sacrifices a woman had to make for her country. She grinned in total satisfaction, dived into the pool, then blew air out of her nose and stroked right past John.

After the short flight from Tampa, then the drive through congested traffic, she was ready to stretch her muscles. A strong freestyle swimmer, she sprinted for the other end, the cool water streaming over her warm flesh, reinvigorating her. When the water frothed and lapped at her feet, then her calves and thighs, she knew he'd joined her, and had easily matched her stroke for stroke.

For ten laps he mirrored her pace, neither pulling ahead nor falling behind. When she turned her head to take a breath, she glimpsed the power of his strokes, his effortless speed and sensed he could maintain this pace for hours. She slowed and stopped in the middle of the pool, pleased when he did the same. Standing, the water came to her midriff. Mischievously, she took water into her mouth, tilted her head back, then let it fountain onto her chest. Just as she'd intended, his gaze followed the water droplets. She dipped under again, this time surfacing and shooting water in his direction.

He cupped his hands together and sprayed her. His gaze was warm, his eyes friendly, but she noted that while he remained by her side, he never came close enough to touch her accidentally.

She released a sigh of contentment. "This is just what I needed."

"What?" He raised one curious brow.

"A few days of R and R with you."

"A few *days*...with me?" His expression bordered on sheepish. Obviously he'd assumed just what she'd intended for him and now was attempting to back-track. "Maybe we should introduce ourselves. I'm—"

"John Cameron. And I'm Bonnie Anders. Doctor Bonnie Anders."

"Son of a bitch." He grinned, taking all the sting out of his words. "You're my new shrink."

She chuckled. "In the flesh."

"Mm. Nice flesh, too." His mouth firmed a tad, as if contemplating a task he dreaded, but would tackle because he must. The pressure on him had to be enormous, but his mind wouldn't cough up memories just because he commanded them to. Sometimes the mind needed to be cajoled, seduced and distracted before the pressure eased enough for it to resume normal functioning. John raised an eyebrow. "I didn't expect therapy to start until tomorrow. So when Kincaid told me he was sending over a woman...and when I saw you, I assumed..."

She grinned. "I'm flattered."

He eyed her face, his expression mischievous, interested, yet with just a touch of reserve gleaming in those gorgeous eyes. "You don't *look* like a shrink."

"I assure you I have all the proper credentials." Or at least she'd had all the proper credentials, until the American Medical Association had suspended her license. She'd known from the moment she'd opened her practice that she'd face some opposition. As long as she achieved the results her patients needed, she figured all the controversy would eventually die down. She'd figured wrong. But she wasn't worrying about that. Logan Kincaid had promised to stop the fuss over her unconventional treatment methods. "We're off the clock until tomorrow, so relax."

He frowned. "Doc—"

"Call me Bonnie."

"Doctor Bonnie, did Kincaid tell you—"

She splashed him full in the face. "Work starts tomorrow, dude. Today we get to play."

He splashed her back. "And what does the lady doctor want to play?"

Although he teased, although he kept up the charming demeanor, he'd just erected a mental wall. She didn't need to touch him to know. His lips had tightened and a muscle in his jaw jerked. Bonnie had always been intuitive and without a doubt the man was in serious need of another distraction. She was grateful for her curves as she swam to the edge and climbed out of the pool, giving him an eyeful of her back and her Brazilian-cut bikini that exposed a good portion of her bottom.

John was wary, but for a moment when she turned and caught his gaze, the banked embers in his eyes riveted her to the deck, telling her clearly that he wanted her as much as she wanted him. No matter his reluctance to touch her, one shared sizzling glance and she knew their eventual coming together was inevitable. It wasn't like that had ever happened before with a patient, but she knew it would with this man. She wished he was far enough along in their sessions for her to reach into her bag, pull out the suntan lotion and ask him to apply it, but just because she ached with a fierce need to touch, didn't mean he was ready. Although he'd also climbed out of the pool, he maintained a careful distance, putting on shades that hid his eyes, wrapping a towel around his corded neck.

Today was a day to establish trust, a day to remind him that he was a charming man with a lot to offer a woman, a day to get back in touch with the salty tang of the sea, the gentle northerly breeze and tidal rhythms. Her sessions with, first, a spy who'd suffered from amnesia, then a crusty diplomat who'd spent a horrible year kidnapped in the jungles of Colombia and, after that, a mountain climber who was the only one to survive an avalanche had taught her that proceeding slowly removed stress and upped the patient/doctor trust quotient, increasing chances of removing blocked memories. However, on the down side, none of her former patients had had an aversion to touch—a gift she depended upon to help break mental blocks. Not since his captivity and his torture would John accept anyone's touch. But on the up side, she'd never had such a sensual attraction to a man—and from his hot glances, the attraction was mutual and one she fully intended to use to her advantage. Perusing the assortment of boats at the dock, she considered the speedboat and two personal watercraft. They all had noisy engines, which would make conversation difficult.

Then she spied the catamaran. "Do you know how to sail?"

"Sure."

She dried off with a few swipes of the towel, applied lipstick to protect her mouth from the sun, donned a straw hat and her sunglasses, then pulled out the suntan lotion. So what if he wasn't ready to touch her. Ignoring her own yen to graze one fingertip down his broad chest, she reminded herself she had other tricks under her hat. "Take me for a ride?"

He chuckled. "You do have a way with words."

Brazen and playful, she winked at him over the

rim of her shades and let her eyes pierce the distance between them. "I'm very direct."

"I noticed. And you always go after what you want?"

"Don't you?" she countered. Turning the lotion upside down, she squirted it into her hand. She began with her forehead, slicking the lotion on her nose, cheeks and chin. She squeezed more into her palm and held out the bottle. "Want some?"

His Adam's apple bobbed. "Not right now, thanks."

"Well, I spent one rotation in dermatology and I never go into the sun without my SPF 30." She smoothed the lotion over her neck, her collarbone, her chest.

He didn't glance away. Not once. He simply watched her hands, a hungry look on his lips, an admiring glow in his eyes, but she didn't miss the wounded slice of pain that glittered for just a moment, preventing him from touching her as he so clearly wanted to.

She took her time, smoothing in the oil over her rib cage and stomach. After sinking into a chair, she crossed one leg over the other and slathered the lotion over her thighs, calves and feet.

"And do you always get what you go after?" he

asked, his tone casual, but she sensed more than nonchalant interest. He might be a wounded warrior, but that wary caution was part of the secret agent persona that had kept him alive through many dangerous missions.

"That depends." She considered telling him she'd attended Johns Hopkins and Harvard, then nixed the idea. She considered telling him about her work with other patients, but she didn't need him comparing his own torture to other terrifying survival stories. She considered telling him that if her natural skill to help him wasn't enough, a special enhancement to her ability was about to be delivered. But trust wasn't about credentials or objects with special powers. Trust was about sharing and getting to know one another. "Are you taking me sailing or not?"

"That depends," he tossed her words back at her, his attitude challenging. "You'll have to wear a life jacket because with all that lotion, you look slippery enough to fall overboard."

"Slippery? That's not an attractive image."

"Doc, if there's one thing you don't have to worry about, it's your looks."

She couldn't miss the blatant approval in his tone and stood, noting that he hadn't offered to put lotion on her back. "We'll both wear life jackets. Because I don't know how to sail at all. And if you fall over, I won't be able to turn around and save you."

She expected him to make some snappy retort, but despite her best intentions, he clearly had other things on his mind. He would be tough to distract. But the more he tried to force the memories, the less likely he'd succeed. She needed him to relax, to let go of the horror and think of pleasant pursuits so he'd drop his mental shields—not an easy thing to do under any circumstances. With so many lives at stake, the task became much more difficult.

"I'll inform security that we're heading out." He padded over to an intercom system and spoke for several minutes, then loaded a cooler from the minibar in the outdoor kitchen to take with them on the boat. When two men went down to the docks and fired up the personal watercraft, John gave them a casual wave.

When she'd arrived at the estate, Bonnie had had to pass through the tight security at the front gate. She understood that John Cameron had vital secrets of national security in his head. To avoid revealing what he did or did not know to his captors, he'd so deeply repressed the information he'd stolen from them that now he couldn't recall where he'd stashed the critical data. His torturers had wanted to know if he'd spilled the beans to law enforcement—but John hadn't had a chance to pass on the information before he'd been caught. So the danger that the terrorists would continue with their plans was very real. To prevent disaster the Shey Group needed to know what John had hidden in his head. Drugs and hypnosis had failed. Now it was her task to help him remember. But only when she saw those men checking their guns as she climbed onto the watercraft did the urgency of her work sink in. Until John Cameron divulged the information he'd suppressed, not only would his life remain in danger, but according to Logan Kincaid, head of the Shey Group, so would the lives of thousands of others.

John Cameron's official file gave her a lot to go on. As a kid he'd grown up in New Jersey and had shown his dedication early, winning the Golden Gloves state championship by age twelve. Then he'd rounded out his skills with judo and karate, and his old army file rated him as an expert marksman. But he wasn't just comfortable with guy stuff. With two sisters and married parents, he came from a stable background of hardworking entrepreneurs.

But Kincaid's unofficial file on John Cameron proved the most interesting. She skipped over the classified missions to the more fascinating stuff. The man loved women. He had women friends and lovers, though no one steady in his life right now, clearing the way for her to approach him any way she wished. Despite all her psychiatric training, Bonnie knew the fastest way to get to him wasn't by talking, but by touching.

And the sooner, the better.

## CHAPTER TWO

BONNIE ANDERS HAD MADE yesterday special. She hadn't poked or prodded him. She hadn't attempted to debrief him. Instead, John and Bonnie had swum, sailed and sunbathed during the glorious day in the Miami sunshine. Their evening consisted of drinking piña coladas and enjoying the sunset, eating oysters on the half shell with fresh lemons and horseradish sauce on the lanai, then watching a comedy on the tube with bowls of gourmet vanilla ice cream smothered in hot fudge sauce. Normal, everyday things that most people took for granted, except John hadn't known rest, relaxation and companionship had been exactly what he'd needed until Dr. Bonnie Anders had carved out this day for him.

Nor had he known how special Bonnie was under all that luscious skin, but after spending hours together chatting, he also appreciated her sharp wit, her playful demeanor and her tantalizing sensuality. With her voluptuous curves, her chestnut hair streaked with shimmering gold and a stunning face, Dr. Bonnie Anders could have posed for *Playboy*. In his mind, she was one hot babe.

Before he'd been tortured John wouldn't have missed the opportunity to spread suntan lotion over her gorgeous skin. But ever since those bastards had shot high voltage through him, the idea of touching or being touched pained him. And being around a woman as sensual as Dr. Bonnie Anders, wanting to caress her and taste her and get naked together so badly, and yet being unable to do something so simple as touch her, deeply concerned him.

He'd figured that today she'd have her hair tied up in a neat twist, wear some stodgy dress and put on her business demeanor, giving him a means to resist her compelling sensual allure. But wearing a spaghetti-strapped top that left her midriff bare, white short shorts and bare feet with candy-apple-red toenail polish, Dr. Bonnie Anders looked like no doctor he'd ever met. Nor did she act like one.

Her every breath expanded her lungs, emphasizing breasts that diverted his normal wariness of all things medical. With her perfectly rounded breasts, her carnally painted mouth and exotic toes, she was his idea of the perfect dream woman. But she was no dream. She was real enough to touch—if he hadn't been damaged.

She'd set their first session in the backyard gazebo that bloomed with a variety of rust, violet and honey-colored flowers. Coffee and Krispy Kreme donuts, his favorites, had been delivered and sat within reach on a glass table. Climbing vines with shiny emerald leaves shaded them from the cloudless sky and bright morning sun, yet allowed the sea breeze to cool them. But the best view in Miami was lounging in the chair right next to him, her toned skin taunting him, within reach yet so untouchable.

She bit into a sugar-glazed donut, her green eyes sparkling with delight. "Yum. Where have you been all my life?"

"Do you always talk to donuts?"

She licked a stray dab of sugar from her lips. "Who said I was talking to the donut?"

He shook his head at her—but with a chuckle. If he couldn't touch her, he sure as hell could feast his eyes on flesh that looked better than a scrumptious gourmet meal. "Surely you don't make those kind of remarks to every patient?"

She locked gazes with him. "Only the ones with silky black hair and smoky eyes. Only the ones my fingers are tingling to touch. Only the ones with bodies hot enough to tempt me."

"Tempt you to what exactly?"

She considered the donuts as if deciding whether or not to indulge in another. "Hey, I'm the one who's supposed to be asking the questions."

"You haven't asked any." He didn't mind waiting as he feasted on her magnificent curves. But despite his interest, his body didn't exhibit as much as a flicker of desire. Normally once his brain engaged, his body quickly followed suit.

The other doctors had told him his damaged nerve endings needed time to heal. But he wasn't so sure. He'd awakened this morning with a perfectly good hard-on and he suspected his problem had nothing to do with his physiology and everything to do with psychology. Perhaps he just needed the right woman to entice him.

Her silky voice held a challenge. "I'm thinking."

"Looks to me like you're thinking about eating."

The creamy filling had oozed onto her finger and she sucked it off unselfconsciously. "I can think and eat at the same time." She popped the lid of her coffee, poured in cream and sugar, then stirred. Finally she sipped and let out a deep sigh of satisfaction. "So what did Kincaid tell you about me?"

"That you were special." He grinned at her. "Logan Kincaid only hires the best. He's always been a master of understatement, but this time he outdid himself."

"Why, thank you."

She leaned back in her lounge chair, sipped her coffee and crossed her lovely legs at the ankles. "Did Kincaid mention that my methods are unconventional?"

"To meet you is to know that." He took a cup of coffee for himself and watched her expressive face, admiring the way she always seemed so on top of her game, as if she had no doubt that she could pry the data out of his stubborn head.

She rolled her eyes at the vine-topped gazebo. "You've already figured me out in less than a day?"

Unable to resist the enticing scent of those sweet donuts, he picked up one and carefully bit into it, appreciating the sugary confection more than usual, no doubt due to the company. "I had you pegged as a rebel from the moment you told me your career choice."

"I see. Would you object to me brushing a feather

over your arm?" She switched subjects on him faster than a channel surfer with a TV remote."

He almost choked on the donut. "You're into feathers?"

She laughed, her amusement genuine. "I'm into all kinds of pleasure. Specifically touch."

He tensed, his muscles rigid as if expecting an attack. "I don't like to be touched, doc."

"Bonnie," she insisted. "Do you know why?"

"The shrink at the hospital tried to explain it. Although he used too many technical words, the bottom line is that it's a result of my...captivity."

She nodded. "That's too simplistic. What you've experienced is complex and gives us quite a challenge. Suppose you loved peach ice cream. You liked the creamy taste in your mouth, the soft texture on your tongue, the cool slickness as you swallow."

"I'm with you so far."

She licked the sugar off her fingers, slowly, seductively as if she weren't lecturing at the same time. "Then someone mixes your favorite peach ice cream with just a dash of peanut butter. Only, you're allergic to peanut butter. Your throat closes up. You break into a sweat. Your pulse skyrockets and the chest pain makes you wonder if you're having a heart attack. EMS takes you to the hospital where they pump your stomach."

"I get the picture."

"Then your mother comes to visit and brings you peach ice cream—but the idea of eating it makes you nauseous now. Your stomach churns. But it's not your body reacting to the peach flavor. It's your mind that is trying to protect you from eating peanut butter. Only the signals are crossed, confused. The stronger the mind, the harder it is to separate the mixed signals."

Finally an explanation that made sense. He admired her ability to avoid the psychobabble other doctors had spouted. "And that's why after they hooked me up to a gazillion volts of electricity I no longer want to touch or be touched. My signals are mixed up?"

"Yep. But have no fear." She held up a white feather. "Doctor Bonnie's here."

"With her trusty feather?" Tense muscles eased a little. Not all the way, but enough for him to ignore the tautness which continually reminded him that failure to recall what he'd repressed might mean the death of thousands of innocent Americans.

"I want this feather to skim over some skin. But we won't touch flesh to flesh."

His aversion to touching was something he was sure he'd eventually overcome on his own. But he needed to remember *now,* before innocent people died.

Because Kincaid had briefed her, she knew that after John and his partner had infiltrated a terrorist cell, they'd uncovered a plot to simultaneously detonate fifty bombs in the U.S., one in every state. Their mission had been to acquire the master list of terrorists with the exact location of where the bombs would be set off. If he'd been able to pass on the information, the entire terrorist cell could have been caught before anyone was killed. Only before he could divulge the information, his partner had been exposed and murdered. John had been captured, and the terrorists had been desperate to know how much of their plan had been revealed. John refused to give up that critical information and had suppressed the information during torture. But after his rescue, no matter how hard he'd tried, he couldn't remember the crucial data. "Look, the goal here is to—"

"You don't have to understand, John. In fact, it might be better if you didn't. Try not to think." She waved the feather. "Just cooperate."

He didn't understand what feathers had to do with retrieving his memory, but none of the regular docs' suggestions had worked, so he'd give the unconventional Dr. Bonnie's methods a try. Kincaid was brilliant, had terrific taste in women and surrounded himself with experts. "If Kincaid believes you can help me recover the missing data, then I'm willing to do whatever it takes." He held out his hand.

"Palm up, please." He steeled himself for the featherlight touch.

But she didn't use the feather. Instead, she uncrossed her legs, sat up and bent over to peer at his palm, revealing deep cleavage encased in a startling neon-yellow bra that peeked out of her clingy red top. "You have a very long life line."

"What?" The woman was incorrigible. He was positive she'd bent forward to distract him, using his natural inclinations against him. He scowled at her because her tactic had worked. He couldn't think too much about feathers with her magnificent breasts right there in his face. "Now you're a palm reader?"

"One of my many talents." She grinned, straightening. "However, I'm also a whiz with a feather."

"And so humble, too." His voice was light. Although he was by no means relaxed and doubted he would be until he recalled where he'd stashed the missing data, he no longer tensed from neck to toes.

Her flirty attitude kept him off balance, just enough to take the edge off his nerves and the horrible pressure of knowing what was at stake. He didn't understand why she needed to overcome his aversion to touch to help him reclaim his memories. Yet, all his work and the death of his partner would be for nothing if he didn't remember.

At the moment, his brain told him that the feather wouldn't hurt him, but as she'd pointed out, his signals were confused. He didn't quite understand how she intended to straighten him out, or how she would help him retrieve his memory and the critical information the Shey Group desperately needed. However, her presence was so delightful, especially compared to the stodgy doctors who'd treated him before, that he'd willingly go along.

"Stop thinking," she ordered.

"How?" he countered.

She glanced at the sun and back to him. "Have you noticed that it's going to be another scorcher?"

"This is typical Miami weather in July."

She placed the feather in his palm. "Hold this a sec."

And then she pulled off her tank top. His lower jaw dropped, leaving his mouth open as he stared at that neon-yellow bra, which he now saw had tiny

holes in the lace. Peekaboo holes that gave him sa-
vory glimpses of coral aureoles. How the bra stayed
up without straps, he had no idea. He stared at her
breasts that were so full they overflowed the lace,
blinked and stared some more. He anticipated that
she would fall right out, especially when she
breathed.

He arched a brow but couldn't stop grinning. "You
are deliberately trying to distract me, aren't you?"

"Is it working?"

"Maybe I need a little more incentive."

"You want incentive? I'll give you incentive." He
held his breath, half expecting her to remove another
article of clothing. When she didn't, he was only
slightly disappointed. Especially when she proposed
something almost as exciting. "Now take the feather
and stroke me."

"Stroke you?"

"Anywhere you like."

He thought she'd intended to touch *him* with the
feather, but her words had just made him a happy
man. "Come here."

He spread his thighs, and she pulled her chair
closer. Close enough for him to appreciate the scent
of her spicy perfume. Close enough to see her pulse

flicker at her elegant throat. Close enough for him to hear her ragged intake of breath.

Twirling the feather between his fingers, he drew out the moment. And then ever so lightly he tickled her neck, her collarbone, the tops of her breasts. Her green eyes flamed, but she didn't move one muscle. When her nipples hardened into buds and one of them actually poked through the lace, his mouth watered and he had the urge to tip his head down and take that sweet bud between his lips.

As if reading his mind, she shook her head, her golden-streaked hair reminding him of a lioness on the prowl. "Don't touch me. You only get to use the feather."

"Why?" That coral nipple surrounded by neon-yellow lace tempted him, taunted him. He was sure that tonight, if he slept at all, he would dream of yellow and chestnut tresses streaked with gold, of tasting her flesh and lips. Of making love. Just the sight of that tiny pucker of flesh had sweat beading his forehead. "Why do I only get to use the feather?"

"Because if I can't touch you, then you can't touch me."

"Did I ever tell you how much I dislike logical women?" He twisted the feather around her nipple, taking immense pleasure as the bud swelled. Shifting his attention to her other breast, he tried to tease out her nipple. This side budded, but the lace interfered, driving him to distraction and preventing success.

"Is that why you've broken into a sweat?" She picked up a napkin and dabbed at the sweat trickling down his brow.

And he didn't flinch! Truth be told, he remained so absorbed in coaxing that nipple out between the peepholes of her lacy bra, her napkin dabbing couldn't bother him. Just a few more strokes of the feather, a few more breaths to shift the lace...and nipple success.

Oh, yeah. She looked absolutely stunning with those two little nubs swelling amid all that yellow. He wished he had a camera, but he took a mental picture he would never forget. He didn't know how they were going to overcome his problem, but the desire bubbling through his veins convinced him that making love to this woman was as inevitable as his eventually finding a new line of work. He'd given his all to the Shey Group and was ready for a change, ready to spend more time with a woman like Bonnie, instead of holed up in some third-world country being shot at. Happier than he'd been in a long time, he swirled the feather over her belly, but he kept returning to her breasts to ensure that she remained just as he wanted her.

"I can see you are a man who likes to be thorough." Her voice was amused, low, husky.

"I'm a man who likes what he sees."

"Would you like to see more?"

"Oh, yeah."

"How do you feel about getting naked?"

John gave her question more consideration than he would have liked. Before his torture sessions, he'd had no compunction about walking around nude. Or taking off his clothes. But now, although he had no physical scars, he tended to wear boxers since nudity reminded him of vulnerabilities he didn't want to remember.

And yet, he'd have liked nothing better than for her to remove that yellow bra. For his gaze to have unimpeded access to her magnificent breasts. Just thinking about those coral tips made his mouth go dry and his pulse skip.

"I don't like the idea of being the *only* one naked," John responded, curious to see how she'd react. He'd never expect Bonnie to blush. She didn't. Nor did her deep green eyes widen. She didn't fidget, cross or uncross her tanned legs or tap her bare feet. She didn't as much as tighten her glossy pink lips, either. With the aura of a sophisticated and experienced woman who appreciated her own sensuality, she arched her back and her breasts strained against the fabric.

"So you wouldn't object to taking off your clothes if I removed mine?"

"Is that an offer?" he countered.

"Maybe." She held out her hand for the feather. "My turn."

Reluctantly, he gave it to her, guessing that she now intended to touch him in return. But he wasn't as tense as he expected. After all, she'd already dabbed him with that napkin and he'd been fine. He hadn't been mentally jolted straight back to the torture chamber like every other time someone had touched him.

She tapped the feather on his nose, startling him. "You're thinking again."

He rubbed his chin. "It's a habit of mine."

"Well, if you must think, tell me where the best place is on this estate to make love." She caressed his cheek.

"That tickles."

"I know." She glanced at her breasts. "I'm still aroused."

Her nipples weren't quite as erect, until he locked his eyes on them. His attention alone seemed to make her swell again, making him quite proud of his effect on her.

"There's a hot tub off the balcony of the master suite. That might be a good place to make love."

"Where else?" She brushed the feather over one shoulder, then the other.

"The walk-in shower?"

The feather brushed his ear. "Do you have a water fetish?"

"I think I'm going to have a shrink fetish."

She chuckled, her lips forming a secret smile. "You know what I'm wearing under these white shorts?"

"I haven't a clue." He swallowed hard as he considered her question. He eyed where her waistband skimmed her flat abdomen and sexy belly button. Unlike the bra that had peeked out onto the satin of her breasts, he didn't glimpse as much as a scrap of material sticking out of those low-riding white shorts.

Light smoldered in her dark green eyes. "This lingerie is a matching set."

A matching set? Oh...my...God.

He imagined her in peekaboo panties and his

blood began to boil as he envisioned what other delectable part of her he could tease with the feather. And when she traced the feather over his pectoral muscles, he had to remind himself to breathe. Because the tiny wisps shot prickles of desire straight to his core.

Blood surged south and he shifted uncomfortably as the seam of his jeans cut off circulation. With just her words and body, she had him fired up as if there were some tangible bond between them. Her vitality captivated him, charmed him. Her brazen sensuality had his heartbeat throbbing and his senses off kilter. His admiration for her methods escalated.

The satisfied curve of her lips told him she knew exactly what she was doing. She glanced at the bulge between his legs and her eyes brightened. "I'll take off my shorts if you remove those jeans."

After that tempting suggestion, she swirled the feather over his nipples, jerking him to his feet.

"Deal." He didn't have to think twice about her suggestion. She had him all geared up. While he hadn't forgotten the stakes, she'd made his memories take a back seat to the temptations she kept placing in front of him. Mostly he thought about touching her. Kissing her. Making love to her. And he most definitely wanted to see those yellow panties. "But I believe it's my turn to use the feather."

## CHAPTER THREE

BONNIE WATCHED HIM remove his jeans with no more inhibitions than a stripper. So far, so good. Very good.

Despite the torture he'd suffered, at six foot four inches tall, John Cameron was lean, fit and the picture of good health. With his tapered muscles and long limbs, he could have been America's poster boy for the Olympic decathlon, until one looked deep into his smoky eyes and saw that he was a man who had been to hell and back.

If she succeeded in helping him remember what he'd lost, not only would she help save thousands of innocent lives, she would alleviate his terrible stress. John was a man of high principles, a man who'd refused to reveal information under extreme duress. For him not to be able to remember vital information that could prevent terrorist attacks had to be its own kind of torture.

John evoked all of Bonnie's sympathy and stirred her compassion, not to mention her fantasies. After all, she'd gone to medical school to help people. And if the exciting man needing her special touch happened to be gorgeous, sexy and willing, and being with him gave her joy, she certainly planned to make the most of this opportunity.

His physical arousal caused her smug delight. And as his face became more animated, his smoky eyes flashing lightning bolts of interest, she would continue to up the stakes. Bonnie hadn't allowed herself a fling in way too long. And this setup couldn't have been more perfect. While military men attracted her with their dedication, sense of purpose and strong codes of honor, they tended to understand only the concrete world of what they could see, hear and prove. Men like John had difficulty with her peculiar gift. And she had no interest in falling for a partner who couldn't believe in her special abilities.

But a fling would not only serve her country and help her mission, it fit into her personal plans perfectly right now. Since she more than liked John Cameron, flirting with him was a no-brainer, especially when it helped to ease the tension blocking his memories. She adored the hard lines and muscled planes of his body. The washboard abs, the powerful shoulders and his sexy chest hair. But most of all she admired his mental strength. Many men would have broken under similar circumstances. Others would have survived, but withdrawn. John Cameron could still flirt and play. Wounded but healing, he was well on the way to recovery on his own. But time was of the essence. The Shey Group couldn't afford the luxury of waiting for his memories to trickle back on their own.

The terrorists could carry out their attack at any time. If she could help John retrieve the forgotten information she would be doing him, the Shey Group and her country a huge service. That she could enjoy the process jazzed her.

She liked the way John made her feel when she was with him—free to say whatever she wanted. Free to act out any insane idea. Free to be herself. Free to use her power of touch that so many people found abnormal. Women often considered her a freak. Men usually avoided her, fearing she could read their minds, or they remained skeptical that she could open blocked pathways. While she hoped her ability by itself would be enough to help John, she suspected that his mental block might be stronger than any she'd previously encountered. She'd take advantage of additional help, pleased that the object that would enhance her powers would arrive soon. Meanwhile, she'd make do with her natural talents.

Their swim in the pool yesterday had helped to ease the normal mental and physical distance between strangers. Their chats had established a measure of trust. And their dynamic attraction to one another served as yet another catalyst to fuel spontaneous combustion.

His feather play over her breasts had her hot as a smoking Fourth of July firecracker. And her nipples seemed to have gotten stuck in the aroused position due to the netting that tugged on them every time she breathed. The lovely feeling only served to make her more eager to touch him.

Damn, he looked hot in baggy boxers. And his erection tenting the navy cotton indicated quite clearly that very soon he'd be ready for her touch. Conventional therapy hadn't worked on John, so Kincaid had given her permission to do whatever it took to cure her patient, and if her methods went outside the bounds of accepted medical practice, so be it. She was authorized to do whatever it took.

But was John ready to cope with a simple touching of flesh? With the strong tide of need surging through her, she couldn't be sure she was thinking analytically. Because as much as she wanted to forget all her training, as much as she'd like to be first and foremost a woman, she wouldn't forget what she'd come here to do. Too much was at stake. John was doing as she'd asked, trusting her, and she was determined to help him—but before she could work on retrieving his memories, he had to accept her touch.

If she enjoyed herself, that was a side benefit. If her heartbeat tripped madly over the thought of touching him, she had to take extra care. Because she didn't want just to touch him, she craved that first touch like a skydiver lusted for freefall.

Touch was her natural element, like an artist relied on his eyes to mix a palette and paint a seascape, like a musician relied on hearing to pick up a cadence. She wouldn't feel complete until she held John's hand, until she merged with the flow of his essence, beheld the vividness of his color, savored the flavor of his soul and discovered his well-hidden secret.

"Come on, doctor darling," John dared her, gesturing to her shorts. "You've teased me for long enough. Take them off."

"Okay." She unfastened the top snap. Watched his nostrils flare. Undid another snap. Took pleasure in his ardent stare. Taking her time, she ever so slowly unsnapped, until the fly parted just enough to reveal the tiniest sliver of yellow.

Hooking her thumbs into her belt loops at the sides, she cocked her hip and tugged down the white shorts an inch. She kept her tone light, suggestive. "Maybe I ate too many donuts. They seem to be stuck."

"Uh-uh." He shook a finger at her in mock irritation. "That excuse won't work. Your tummy is as flat as that table."

She cocked her hip to the other side, tugged the shorts down another inch. "They really don't want to come off."

John picked up the feather and twirled it over her nipples, recreating a direct line of heat between her breasts and her legs. "You're going slowly on purpose to tease me."

"Am not," she lied, thinking that if she didn't touch him soon she was going to melt into a puddle.

When she finally stepped out of the shorts, wearing the tiniest thong bottom she could find in the International Mall, she held her breath in anticipation of his reaction.

She'd intended to sunbathe in the lingerie in the privacy of her condo balcony. However, after she'd glimpsed John's erection standing at attention, she was glad she'd brought it with her.

His eyebrows rose. "Wow."

"You like it?"

His voice deepened to a huskier baritone. "You're the sexiest woman I've ever seen. Turn around and let me see the other side."

"There is no back." She saw confusion in his eyes and turned. "It's a thong."

"Nice. Real nice. But are you sure you aren't trying to give me a heart attack?"

"There's nothing wrong with your heart. Only your head." Facing and approaching him, she gestured to his hand and the feather, narrowing the distance between them until she could feel the heat radiating off of him. "I thought you were going to put that to good use."

"Oh, I intend to, sweetheart." They stood mere inches apart, so close that if he leaned forward onto the balls of his feet, his chest would brush against hers. She ached for him to close the last centimeter. He didn't. Instead he flashed her one of those charming grins. "Same rules? Anywhere I want?"

Excited by the exhilaration and anticipation on his face, she nodded, her mouth dry. "Same rules. But it's my turn next."

She expected him to tease her through the netting as he'd done before, but hoped he'd make a breakthrough and touch her, skin to skin, despite the boundary she'd set earlier. Wondering what he was thinking, wondering if giving up control to him had been the right thing to do, she waited. Torture victims felt a loss of control and by turning over to him the place and method of their first touch, she hoped to make him feel secure.

He stayed close enough for his breath to fan her cheek. Taking care not to so much as whisk against her belly with a knuckle, he slid the feather into the front of her panties.

Inch by inch, he pushed the feather downward until the tip nestled between her curls. "How does that feel?"

"Wicked."

"Look at me," he demanded.

"Why?" She tipped her head back, enjoying the pulse of heat between her thighs.

"I want to watch your face. I want to watch your eyes dilate. And your cheeks flush."

She ached so badly for a real touch from his flesh that she wanted to stomp her foot in exasperation. But he was playing her game, abiding by her rules, so she had no right to complain. Except that he felt too good. She held his gaze, expecting him to pull the feather out slowly again.

But he wriggled the feather from side to side and it was all she could do not to squirm as she longed for more. Longed for him to touch the flesh that he'd teased into a fury of need. Her mouth parted and she yearned for his lips to angle down on hers, for him to forget the rules, for him to lose control and take what she offered.

By the time he finally extracted the feather, her hands were shaking. Her belly quivered and her knees had turned to putty. It took every atom of restraint for her to take the feather from him calmly. "My turn."

He jerked the feather out of her reach with a mischievous glint in his eyes. "I'm not done yet. Unless you're calling it quits."

"I don't quit."

Frazzled, rattled by the desire simmering through her veins like hot brandy, she breathed in through her nose and out of her mouth. She reminded herself that the longer the foreplay, the better for him. He needed time to rewire, for his brain to reconnect with his body, so that he reached out to touch without thinking, like a forgotten reflex. That's what the psychiatrist in her said. The womanly part of her wanted to tackle him onto the lounge chair, kiss him senseless and jump his bones.

He tickled the feather between her knees. "Darling, I could use a little working room."

She parted her legs, wishing he'd toss the damn feather away. But she had to leave that critical decision to him. Only he would know when she'd pushed him into breaking through. Until then she had to give him rules to make him feel safe enough to play this sexual game with her. Only he would know when he was ready to touch.

On the surface, he seemed eager. He exhibited no reluctance, no struggle. But she knew better, and from the mixture of desire and despair in his gaze, so did he. Clearly, he ached to touch her, yet he didn't try and that told her the shields he'd erected were close to impenetrable. She'd expected the barrier he'd raised to have broken down by now—it hadn't. She'd failed.

And damn. Every cell in her body called out to her

to reach up and tug down his head so she could kiss him. Every part of her soul yearned to touch him so she could know him. But for his sake, she waited. Waited and hoped that while he again stroked her nipples, her belly and her mons with the feather he'd find her so irresistible he'd reach for her. Touch her.

He teased the insides of her thighs and then for a moment she thought he was going to take her into his arms, but he simply reached around her. Featherlight caresses over her back and bare bottom created delicious circles of swirling need. But even through her desire, disappointment surged through her that she hadn't incited him to a state where he would let down his guard and do what they both wanted.

And when she couldn't stand another second, she plucked the feather from his fingers. "My turn."

"But I was having so much fun." He sounded so charmingly innocent.

"You can still have fun." She slid the feather up the leg of his boxers, hoping he was ready.

He didn't retreat. He didn't move. He didn't utter a sound.

"You okay?"

"I'm not sure." His voice was tight, his eyes narrowed, his struggle clear.

Damn. Had she let her own hunger push him too fast?

He gestured downward. "If you keep on doing that I might not be able to hold back."

If he was worried about ejaculation that meant what she was doing felt good to him. Okay, she might not have driven him to the brink, but she was closer. She laughed, wanting to share her pleasure with him over how far he'd recovered in such a short time. "Who said you had to hold back?"

She stroked the feather, grateful for the wide boxers that gave her access to him. While she couldn't see exactly where the feather was arousing him, she didn't care. He was feeling pleasure, not pain. Not shock. And the more pleasure she could give him, the easier he'd recognize touch as something to be welcomed and relished.

At the same time as her mind was in psychiatrist mode, she was marveling at the attraction between them. They hadn't as much as shaken hands, never mind kissed, but she couldn't ever remember wanting a man like she wanted him. And he wanted her, but that he'd held back proved to her that without giving him enough time to heal, she might not succeed. What she needed was to incite him to the point he had to touch her because he couldn't stop himself, because it came naturally, like a starving man who couldn't resist a hot meal.

However, if she pushed too hard, too fast, he might never recover his memories—but time was of the essence. With the urgency of the situation in her mind, she only held back a little. After withdrawing the feather from his shorts, she skimmed the cords of his neck, his wide chest and rugged back before gliding the feather up his other leg and once again under his shorts. From his groan of pleasure, she must be hitting a sensitive spot.

He sucked in a hiss of air. Sweat broke out on his brow and his body quivered. "I can't take much more."

That he was telling her, instead of reaching for what he wanted dismayed her. Bonnie wasn't accustomed to failure. "You want me to stop?"

"I...want...you."

The words were too tight. Forced. Despite his arousal, he still hadn't reached for her. While her efforts might have softened his resistance a little, she hadn't done enough.

"I'm not ready," she lied, knowing that she'd never been more ready in her life. But she didn't want him disappointed in himself. She didn't want him to know that she'd expected him to go further than he had. "Why don't we cool off with a swim?"

"HOW COME YOU HAVEN'T asked me about my mission like all the other shrinks?" John asked after they'd swum in the pool and were lying out on the lanai to dry. The sexual tension between them simmered, but unlike people who knew exactly where they were going and enjoyed the journey to get there, he had no such luxury of time. Every minute that he wasted might be critical.

While she didn't pressure him to perform, he'd glimpsed disappointment in her gaze when he hadn't moved on to the next level. While she'd tried to get him to relax and follow his natural inclinations, which were bubbling up at a frenzied pace, every time he considered touching her, he held back. If touching her elicited painful shocks, he didn't want to see her desire turn to disgust, or worse, pity.

Bonnie was different from his other doctors in more ways than he could count. But most importantly, he cared what she thought. He didn't want her to see him as weak. He didn't want her to see him cringe from the pain caused by touch. He didn't want her to think of him as anything but a healthy, desirable male who found her irresistibly attractive.

While he'd pretended to buy her lie that *she* wasn't ready, he knew why she'd pulled back for him. Her generosity made her all the more precious in his mind. He was lucky to have her, and although he still feared touching or being touched, too many lives were at stake for him to play it safe.

Bonnie was lying on her stomach, letting the sun caress her lovely bottom. The round, lean flesh tempted him, almost enough to stroke. She turned her head and gazed at him with a lazy gluttony that reminded him of a cat eyeing a dish of sweet cream. "I do my best work while I'm touching."

He rubbed lotion over his chest, recalling the pleasant graze of the feather there and the way her eyes had darkened in pleasure when his nipples had tightened. "You sure that's just not an excuse to have your way with me?" he teased, expecting her to laugh, but she went shrink serious.

She also turned onto her back and her breasts distracted him. "I don't suppose you've ever heard of extrasensory tactile awareness?"

He frowned. "Extrasensory tactile awareness? Sounds like a disease."

She did laugh, this time. "While I was in med

school, some of the doctors acted as if I was contagious. But I try to think of what I have as a gift."

"Tell me about your gift." His curiosity burned. Despite her careful tone, he hadn't missed how the skeptical comments from doctors at medical school had hurt her. She was such an unusual mix of science and sensuality that right from the get-go she'd intrigued him, enticed him, enchanted him. And he found himself wishing he could protect her from people who dismissed her abilities and caused her anguish.

"Ever since I can remember, when I touch people, I sense where they hurt." At her outrageous claim, he schooled his features not to reveal his skepticism. The last thing he wanted to do was hurt her. "Over the years my skill has evolved. Recently I've had some success combining touch therapy with the elimination of mental blocks. Since my ability cannot be measured, or seen or smelled, others have doubts, but when I touch, I visualize the blocks."

He kept his tone even, repressing his disbelief. "You can read minds?"

She put on her sunglasses, seemingly not the least bothered by his question. "Mostly these emotions come to me in streaming colors. When I touch people as they speak, I can help ease them through a block that I sometimes feel or see as a wall, or rushing water or thick mud. It's difficult to put into words."

"If you touch me...when you touch me," he corrected himself, "what would I feel?" He wanted to hear some shred of proof to validate her claim. Because he wanted to believe her.

"Some patients have told me that my touch makes them stronger. Others say they don't feel so alone. And occasionally a patient catches a reflection of what I'm feeling. But mostly, patients don't notice anything at all."

So there was no proof that she could offer. "What kind of success rate do you have?"

"That depends on how you define success. Some patients need to recover the memories so they can deal with the pain and move on with their lives. Others don't want to remember at all."

"What do you do for them?"

"I never force a patient."

Somehow, he'd already known that. While he suspected she would be a ferociously passionate lover, she had a gentleness about her that suggested she always put the patient first.

"Suppose forcing is what I want?" John asked,

knowing that whatever he'd blocked might be critical to saving many innocent lives, willing to give anything a try—at least once.

Bonnie sat up and swung her legs over the side of the lounge chair. She peered at him over her shades, her voice serious.

"You'll break through soon. We needn't rush."

"Time might be of the essence."

"We don't know that."

But he couldn't take that chance. If she could touch him and help him remember, he had to let her—even if he cried out from the pain, even if she never again looked at him in the same way. He couldn't put his own selfish pride ahead of what could happen if the information remained locked in his head. He might soon end his affiliation with the Shey Group, but he would complete his last mission and do it to the best of his ability. While he doubted her method would work, he was desperate to retrieve the missing memories. Trembling, he stuck out his arm, offered her his hand. "Do it. Touch me."

## CHAPTER FOUR

BONNIE'S HEART WENT OUT to him as she shook her head. "Forcing a mind...might cause a setback."

John had to be skeptical about her gift, but he'd still been willing to give her a chance. His attitude was unusual. Most people laughed outright or considered her one step away from a mental institution. Others placed her in the same category as fortune-tellers and magicians. Most of her life, she'd known she was different. Only a few close friends had accepted her. Cate was one of them. Could John be another? At his open-mindedness, her respect for him rose several degrees.

John kept his arm out and wiggled his fingers. "I'll risk it."

"I won't."

She gently refused him, careful to keep her concern from her eyes. The man's bravery was not in doubt. Neither was his willingness to sacrifice for his country. And if those traits alone weren't enough to win her compassion, she found his urgent resolve to overcome his block admirable, but reckless.

She'd gone into medicine to help people, studied psychiatry because the complexities of the mind fascinated her. Positive that her gift shouldn't be wasted, she'd often found herself caught between the scientific method that required proof and her gift which had to be taken on faith. But no matter how unorthodox her methods, she'd taken the Hippocratic oath. Her first duty to her patient was to do no harm.

John dropped his arm to his side, but determination carried through his tone. "You don't understand. The group that I infiltrated were fanatics. They hate our country. They hate our way of life. They don't care how many innocent people they kill to make a point, and I have a feeling that time is running out."

"I understand better than you think. Both my parents served in the military." She didn't like his premonition, suspecting it came from a deep recess in his mind that might be factual.

He stuck his arm out again with a bravery that

amazed her. "Then you understand that my welfare cannot be put before others. You need to try your power of touch on me before people die."

He'd been open-minded and perhaps she needed to do the same. Perhaps he was right. While she was accustomed to putting the needs of her patient above everything else, his case was extraordinary, the information in his mind vital to national security. "Are you sure, John?"

"Worst thing that could happen is I'll feel the same kind of shock I did during the torture."

His courage made her heartbeat stutter. He might withstand the agony, but the pain might also reinforce his mental block.

But just maybe, her special ability would allow him to break through to the critical memory. Certainly his willingness to experiment could speed the process along.

"All right." She took a deep breath, released the air from her lungs. "Let's do it."

She touched his hand with the tip of her finger.

As if turning on a switch, her touch linked into his emotions. And she found herself on a rocky black shore lit by blazing flames at her back. At her feet, a sea of molten tar bubbled and seethed, rising up like a hellish tidal wave with flaming tentacles of angry red. Incredible heat ignited her flesh.

Burning.

Agony.

She screamed. He jerked his hand back, breaking their connection.

"Are you okay?" he asked, his eyes full of concern.

She stared at her feet, trying to rid her mind of the notion that her toes were seared, to grasp that the stench of burned flesh, the torment of burning alive had all been in her mind. Never had she encountered anything like John's turmoil. And even through the vestiges of her receding pain, she realized that he had suffered, too—yet despite his own agony, his concern had been for her. "What happened?" she managed to ask.

"I felt a shock."

That had to be the understatement of the century. She hid her fear of failure, hid her surprise, hid the fact that she hadn't a clue how to deal with the kind of mental anguish he carried around in his head. "Yeah, me, too."

And they'd talked enough. She didn't like the tense set of his mouth or the hard look in his gaze that told her his mind had snapped his mental barriers firmly back into place or that he, too, was worried about his mission. She needed time to think, and he needed a diversion, then lunch and maybe a boat ride where talking would be difficult.

When John suddenly stood, his gaze focused, his muscles tensed, his wrists cocked, he looked like a soldier expecting attack. She turned to follow his gaze and saw a man approaching. However, John must have recognized him because he relaxed.

One of the Shey Group's security men approached, moving with the silent grace of a jungle cat, but with legs like tree trunks. John's eyes narrowed on the package the other man carried. "What's up, Web?"

"A package just arrived for Dr. Anders. Did I hear a scream?"

"Just part of the therapy," Bonnie responded automatically, still stunned by what had just happened and excited that the item had finally arrived. She hadn't made any headway alone, had never encountered a block so strong it caused her pain, but perhaps the talisman might tip fate in their favor.

Web held out the box to her, the ridges on his hands a testament to his prowess in hand-to-hand combat. "Ma'am, we opened the package to make sure it was safe." Web's gaze settled on Bonnie and her attire or lack of it seemed to affect his vocal cords. "And Kincaid said it might...be important...."

"Thanks." Bonnie forced a smile, realizing that not only was Web distracted by her lack of clothing, but John was bristling. And as the aftereffects of touching John faded, her fingers itched to explore the object Cate had sent her.

John glared at Web, apparently not the least bit intimidated by the other man's mass, or the fact that he was heavily armed. "Go find your own woman to stare at."

Web shrugged. "I can't find one as good to look at as—"

John jerked his thumb back toward the front gate. "Go."

Web gave Bonnie one more long, slow look, almost as if he enjoyed John's irritation, then swaggered back the way he'd come.

"You weren't very nice to him," she admonished John as she pulled back the already open cardboard box. However, she was pleased that John had implied that she was his. More forward progress. He wouldn't have had a twinge of jealousy if she hadn't aroused his emotions as well as his sexuality. And on the non-doctor level, she was pleased because she liked John. She liked him a lot, admired him more than she'd thought possible. But that he'd let her touch him, had kept an open mind about her gift, then hadn't blamed her for the failure left her stunned.

"Web will get over it." John peered over her shoulder. "Why did Kincaid send you—"

"I asked him to forward the package. It's from a childhood friend of mine from New Orleans." She plucked out a note and read aloud, "Hi, Bonnie. Here is the perfume bottle. Be careful, but I really do think it's right up your alley. Love, Cate." She placed the note to one side. "When I told Kincaid the perfume bottle might help you, he arranged to forward it here."

John chuckled, shaking off his own pain as if it were nothing. "First feathers. Now a perfume bottle is going to help me?"

After their painful touch, she couldn't blame him for his skepticism. "This is no ordinary perfume bottle."

"Right."

"Cate said that it has a gypsy inscription and it's somehow tied to magic, though I'm not exactly sure how. She claimed the perfume bottle had a strange effect on her, freaked her out, so she contacted an expert who says the bottle enhances paranormal powers." She spoke enthusiastically, trying to gauge his reaction. "Cate was sure that I'd adore it."

"She knows you well, all right."

Carefully, Bonnie removed the bottle from a heavy wooden casket that was probably as old as the glass. Crystal facets sparkled in the sunlight and the silver formed an intricate lace pattern around the glass, making the perfume bottle look old, rare, expensive. "It's gorgeous."

"If it freaked her out, why do you want it?"

"Don't you?" She tried to unplug the stopper, but it wouldn't budge. "I'm hoping this bottle will enhance my gift."

"Extrasensory tactile perception. Right."

She gave up trying to convince him with a shrug. According to Cate, she didn't need to open the bottle to use the power. "I'm hoping it'll work for us."

John leaned over, peered at the bottle, then shook his head, unimpressed. "I don't believe in fairy tales. I'm not sure I believe in extrasensory touch awareness, either."

"That's okay." But it wasn't. She wanted him to believe. She wanted him to trust her. She set the perfume bottle in the middle of the patio table, admiring the crystal facets, the rainbow reflections and the exotic stopper. "In the Middle Ages, most scientists didn't believe in germs. That didn't mean they weren't there."

His full lips mocked her, although he kept his voice steady. "So I don't have to believe in your power of touch for it to work?"

"Not at all." However, he did have to *welcome* her touch. Or both of them would suffer horrible pain. At the memory of that searing tar, she barely repressed a shudder. The bottle had better work its magic or she might not be able to help John or the people depending on him.

She glanced at him, caught the tangle of pain, confusion and doubt in his eyes. "Don't worry so much. I know what I'm doing."

JOHN'S FRUSTRATION LEVEL ROSE every time he thought about his shrink. He'd looked forward to discovering the texture of her flesh, the taste of her mouth, the heat of those pouty lips. But one touch of her finger to his palm had caused agony. Clearly, she didn't want to discuss what had happened but neither of them had been prepared. When she'd touched him, he'd braced for the usual shock that set his nerves on fire. What he hadn't been prepared for was that she'd seemed to feel his pain, and he couldn't account for that. Her shout had rocked him to his core. That she hadn't given up on him right then and there attested to her determination and courage.

While the thought of touching her after he'd caused her such pain made his guts churn, he still wanted her. Earlier, during their boat ride, he'd virtually forgotten their first painful touch and he'd almost leaned over and kissed her.

Keeping his hands to himself had been difficult, too, especially after she insisted on again dousing herself in lotion that made her tanned skin glisten like a sparkling gift he couldn't unwrap. And then, as if she hadn't shouted out in pain when they'd touched, she'd taken every opportunity to tease him, until his dick might as well have been a yo-yo that she controlled on a string.

He'd never been so sexually frustrated in his life. After they'd returned to the dock, he'd excused himself to head to the shower and take matters into his own hands. His blood pounded through his veins, his skin so tight that he had to have release. He ran up the stairs three at a time, stripped off his clothes and dropped them on the floor on a direct route to the shower and blessed privacy.

The walk-in glass block shower of the master bedroom had six showerheads, its own garden filled with split-leafed green plants and enough room for four people. He turned on the stereo system, choosing the smoky jazz of Norah Jones, and then adjusted the spray's temperature to soothing warmth.

Closing his eyes, he let the water sluice the tangy salt spray from his skin. However, nothing could eliminate the images of Bonnie from his mind. Her powerful scent of coffee, perfume and suntan lotion seemed to linger with him. So did her impish smile. And the careful distance she put between them whenever she spoke about her "gift." But it was his memory of her nipples peeking through the yellow netting of that itty-bitty scrap of lingerie that had all his blood heading south, again. He'd soon be suffering from blue balls if he didn't take care of—

"Mind if I join you?"

His eyes popped open and then widened at the sight of Bonnie in the shower area with him, naked as Eve in the Garden of Eden—and twice as tempting. All that bare skin made his mouth go dry. He couldn't speak, just stared in amazement, fascination and awe. She possessed flawless golden skin, and wonderful proportions; with her ample breasts, slender waist and rounded hips, she could have

modeled lingerie or swimsuits. Under normal circumstances he would have considered himself one
lucky man.

But these weren't normal circumstances. He
couldn't touch her without causing them pain. And
he was beginning to care about her in ways he hadn't
expected, which made his sexual yearnings even
worse. But he could only look, and as easy as she was
on the eyes, looking didn't solve his problem, but ex-
aggerated it.

She appeared so innocent as she stood there before him. But he knew better and scowled, while she
ignored his expression.

"I would have knocked, but this shower doesn't
have a door."

"You should leave."

"No. We have the perfume bottle now." Carefully
she set it down in a corner of the shower. "Let it do
its thing." She moved under the spray opposite him,
lifted her hair off her neck and tilted back her head,
exposing her graceful neck. Water cascaded down
her perfect breasts and, perfume bottle or not, he was
sure those coral tips would give him erotic dreams
for weeks. He'd been aroused before, but at the sight
of her, he swelled another centimeter.

# An Important Message from the Editors

Dear Reader,

Because you've chosen to read one of our fine romance novels, we'd like to say "thank you!" And, as a **special** way to thank you, we've selected <u>two more</u> of the books you love so well **plus** an exciting Mystery Gift to send you — absolutely <u>FREE</u>!

Please enjoy them with our compliments...

*Pam Powers*

Lift here

Peel off seal and place inside...

# How to validate your Editor's "Thank You" FREE GIFT

1. Peel off gift seal from front cover. Place it in space provided at right. This automatically entitles you to receive 2 FREE BOOKS and a fabulous mystery gift.

2. Send back this card and you'll get 2 brand-new *Romance* novels. These books have a cover price of $5.99 or more each in the U.S. and $6.99 or more each in Canada, but they are yours to keep absolutely free.

3. There's no catch. You're under no obligation to buy anything. We charge nothing—ZERO—for your first shipment. And you don't have to make any minimum number of purchases— not even one!

4. The fact is, thousands of readers enjoy receiving their books by mail from The Reader Service. They enjoy the convenience of home delivery...they like getting the best new novels at discount prices BEFORE they're available in stores... and they love their Heart to Heart subscriber newsletter featuring author news, horoscopes, recipes, book reviews and much more!

5. We hope that after receiving your free books you'll want to remain a subscriber. But the choice is yours— to continue or cancel, any time at all! So why not take us up on our invitation, with no risk of any kind. You'll be glad you did!

GET A *Free* MYSTERY GIFT...

SURPRISE MYSTERY GIFT COULD BE YOURS **FREE** AS A SPECIAL "THANK YOU" FROM THE EDITORS

## The Editor's "Thank You" Free Gifts Include:

- *Two BRAND-NEW Romance novels!*
- *An exciting mystery gift!*

# Yes! I have placed my

Editor's "Thank You" seal in the space provided above. Please send me 2 free books and a fabulous mystery gift. I understand I am under no obligation to purchase any books, as explained on the back and on the opposite page.

**PLACE FREE GIFT SEAL HERE**

393 MDL DVFG                    193 MDL DVFF

| | |
|---|---|
| FIRST NAME | LAST NAME |

ADDRESS

| | |
|---|---|
| APT.# | CITY |

| |
|---|
| STATE/PROV. | ZIP/POSTAL CODE |

(PR-R-04)

# *Thank You!*

## The Reader Service — Here's How It Works:

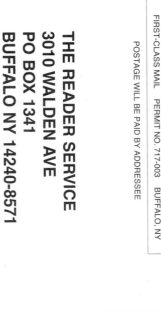

If offer card is missing write to: The Reader Service, 3010 Walden Ave., P.O. Box 1867, Buffalo, NY 14240-1867

**BUSINESS REPLY MAIL**
FIRST-CLASS MAIL    PERMIT NO. 717-003    BUFFALO, NY

POSTAGE WILL BE PAID BY ADDRESSEE

THE READER SERVICE
3010 WALDEN AVE
PO BOX 1341
BUFFALO NY 14240-8571

NO POSTAGE
NECESSARY
IF MAILED
IN THE
UNITED STATES

Finally, he found his voice. "This house must have at least eight other bathrooms."

"But those bathrooms are empty, and it's so hard to get the water temperature just right." She grinned at his sex. "Besides, I like the view in here."

She was impossible. He didn't know whether to be annoyed or amused. He couldn't decide how one woman could be both so naughty and nice at the same time. A tangle of conflicting feelings ran through him, and he didn't stand a prayer of sorting them out. Not with her lathering her hair and the soapy suds caressing her golden skin. Not with her tan lines emphasizing the minuscule triangle of pale skin and tawny golden curls between her legs.

"Don't mind me," she murmured. "Just go on doing what you were doing."

He ground his teeth in frustration. No way was he going to jack off in front of her. And apparently she had no intention of leaving. Of course, nothing was stopping him from making an exit—except she was soaping her breasts with a loofah pad and his pulse had skyrocketed. He found himself holding his breath in anticipation of what crazy stunt she'd pull next. She'd been teasing him all day, and now she stood in front of him all wet and soapy, that loofah pad caressing what he wanted to caress, stroking what he wanted to stroke.

She didn't look at him as she carefully washed. His blood surging, he watched the show, knowing that staying only made his condition worse, but unable to resist. No man could have. Maybe the perfume bottle would work. He was only human, with human needs. And that need was quickly upping the steamy heat in the shower several more degrees.

She soaped her tummy, her mons, her legs, and then when she turned around to rinse, he plucked the loofah from her hand. "Let me get your back."

"Thanks."

He slid his fingers into the strap of the pad and rubbed more soap on it. He might not be touching her skin, but he could feel her shoulder shiver right through the sponge. He took his time, skimming the delicious curves of her shoulder blades and the elegant arc of her neck as she raised her hair for him. He washed her back, his jaw tight in anticipation of running the loofah over her round, firm bottom, so tempting that he had to force himself to slow down.

And all the while he could have kicked himself for not taking the sponge sooner, for losing the opportunity to wash her beautiful breasts. He lingered over the curve of her derriere, enjoyed her soft moan as he teased the soap suds over the insides of the back of her thighs.

He barely controlled the overpowering need to turn her around, slant his mouth over hers and seize the treasure he hungered for. He ached to find out if she felt as good as she looked, if the passion sparking between them would fizzle or escalate or melt them down into a puddle.

Yet, she'd given so much of herself and her time that he didn't want to risk hurting her. He tried to console himself with the thought that showering with her would be enough. However, certain parts of his anatomy disagreed and ached for so much more.

Gently, carefully, John slipped the loofah between the gap of her thighs. He couldn't quite reach the desired spot, and yet, when her legs trembled and she braced her hands against the shower wall, he suspected that she was almost as aroused as he was.

"You'd better stop," she told him, her voice raw.

"Why?"

"Because I might attack you, that's why." She spun around and took the loofah from him, the coral tips of her breasts puckered and perky. "My turn."

Excitement leapt through him. His need was obvious and perhaps she'd use the loofah to...hot... damn. The woman had read his mind. She rolled the loofah around his sex and pumped it up and down, heating him up hotter than a firecracker on a short fuse. His breath came in quick gulping gasps. His fingers clenched and his legs strained.

As if she realized how close he was to finishing, she suddenly stopped.

His eyes flew open and found hers. With her hair wet, her cheekbones appeared more angular, her eyes more needy. She held his gaze, grazing the soap over his shoulders and chest. And all he could think about was when and if she'd dip lower again. He so needed her to... "Ah."

She slid the loofah over his balls, so lightly that he could barely stand still. He drew in a ragged breath and breathed out slowly, but nothing could calm his pounding heart or the building storm. "You're driving me insane."

"That's the idea."

She swirled the loofah in circles, careful not to miss one part of him. When she slid the loofah up the sensitive skin behind his balls and then over his flanks, he squeezed his eyes shut tight and clenched his fingers again. He would not grab her. He would not kiss her. He would not lose control and thrust into her like some madman.

But then she leaned toward him, her head tipped back, her mouth too tempting. No man could resist what she was offering.

He tried to stop himself.

But with her moving the loofah back and forth over such a sensitive area, with the water sluicing over him, with her breasts just inches from his chest and her hips tauntingly close to his jutting arousal, he could barely hang on.

"Tell me what you want," she demanded.

"You."

"Uh-uh," she denied him. "If you can't touch me, what's the next best thing?"

"I don't settle for second best."

She closed the loofah around the base of him, then inch by inch, moved it slowly upward. "Then I'd say you have a big problem."

When, by accident or design, the loofah stopped just under his sensitive ridge, his body tautened. He grabbed her shoulders and tilted his mouth over hers.

And he kissed her.

# CHAPTER FIVE

OH...MY...OH...MY...heaven. Bonnie had been touched before. She'd kissed before. But...not...ever...like... this.

Unlike the pain of their first touch, his kiss sucked her into a vortex of rushing color. A powerful twister that spun her senses, that made thinking impossible, that made her clutch his shoulder just to stay on her feet. The sheer power and depth and brilliant hues of his kiss were unlike anything she'd ever experienced and she suspected the bottle was doing its magic. Cate had been right. The perfume bottle increased Bonnie's paranormal power of touch—because she only felt pleasure, no pain as she had when they'd touched without the bottle's magical properties. Comparing his touch to other men's was like the difference between a breezy day and a windstorm. With the strength of a class five hurricane, he blew her away with his torrential need to have her. Right there in the shower, up against the wall, with the water cascading over them.

She'd been hoping this breakthrough would happen with the arrival of the perfume bottle, but she hadn't known the effect would carry her away. She'd arrived prepared with a condom that she'd hidden under the soap, but there was no time to use it. He was simmering, sizzling, on the edge of shattering.

Influenced by the perfume bottle and their own pulsing needs, inundated by the electric deluge of pure pleasure, she kissed him back with an intensifying zeal. Dropping the loofah, her hungry lips, ready tongue and eager hands played out the erratic and primitive rhythm of her excitement. He responded with a tumultuous need that pierced her core and fractured her illusion that this was only passion, only lust.

She had no name for this chaotic jumble of thoughts and heightened sensations. His. Hers. A melding of sensation and emotion. His extraordinary spirit rippled through her.

And when he fired into her hand, the spasms of his orgasm sent her on a roller-coaster ride that took her right over the edge, triggering her own release.

If not for his powerful arms that closed around her and carried her to the bed, she would have collapsed.

Light-headed, she closed her eyes and waited for the tremors in her belly to cease, waited for the spinning in her head to stop. She'd touched hundreds of people, and never had anyone pulled her into them until she'd lost her sense of self. Not friends. Not family. Not other lovers.

The bottle was pure magic.

When her breathing approached normal, she opened her eyes to find him covering her with a sheet, not the least bit concerned that she was soaking wet. If touching him had made her lose control—and she was more experienced than most with the tactile sensation—what had it done to him?

She studied him. He exuded masculinity, along with a rugged and vital serenity. In fact, he appeared much better adjusted than she felt at the moment. Good. The last thing she'd wanted to do was upset him.

An air of command emanated from him as he slid beside her under the covers. He didn't touch her, as if realizing she needed time to regroup. "You okay?"

"What just happened?" she asked him.

"I had a sensational orgasm." He peered at her, his

square jaw visibly tensed. "But you look as though you just came down off LSD."

She bit her bottom lip. "You felt nothing strange?"

"You did?" he guessed, his brows narrowing a fraction, but she read no disbelief in his eyes, just puzzlement. "Is that why you practically fainted on me?"

"I've never established such a strong connection. Your pleasure triggered my own."

He raised an eyebrow in obvious confusion. "Is that good or bad?"

"It was overwhelming. Wonderful. Out of control. Wild."

He grinned that charming grin at her, as if he accepted her explanation. "Does that mean you might want to do it again?"

"Yeah, but now that you finally touched me, we have work to do." And if the bottle's magic extended to her sense of touch, they might make fast progress, especially if he believed in her. Trust always tore down the blocks faster.

"What do you mean, 'finally'?" Resentment filtered into his tone. "You told me not to touch you."

She pulled a blanket over the sheet. "I didn't want you to force yourself to touch me out of a sense of duty."

"So that's why you wore the tiny bikini and drove me wild with the suntan lotion and soap?"

"Sexuality is a strong basic need, right up there on the top of the list with water, food and sleep. I tapped into that part of you to overcome your aversion to being touched."

"So all these games were just part of curing me?" His voice remained level but she read a mixture of anger, hurt and betrayal in his eyes.

"I haven't ever gone this far with anyone else," she attempted to reassure him. "Sure I flirted and did my best to turn you on, but if I wasn't attracted to you, I would have used other methods."

"Really?"

"Yes."

"Why doesn't that make me feel better?"

"Because you always like to be in control," she teased. "And you now realize that I manipulated you."

"I do."

"And you don't want to believe that an object like the perfume bottle has the power to banish pain when we touch."

"You've got me there."

"And you resent my actions—even if they were for your own good and your own pleasure."

"Damn." His mouth turned into a sheepish grin. "Remind me not to ask a shrink an open-ended question about feelings."

"It might make you happy to know, I'm in way over my head here."

"You?"

She debated how much to share and how to put her confusion into words. "Something unusual happened when we touched."

He turned onto his side, rested his head on his palm. "It must be the magic bottle."

She ignored his jibe. "Normally, when I touch people, I sense colors and feelings. It's like being inside a maze. When I reach a dead end, I simply try to open another doorway."

"And with me?" He asked the question with no intonation except curiosity. He was making her abnormal gift seem normal and she couldn't have been more grateful. Instead of defending herself, she could focus on what had happened, confide in him and get his take on things—something all too rare for her.

"I was sucked into a violent storm. I lost my perception of self in your twisting colors and vivid senses and got caught up in your swirling emotions." She paused in an attempt to explain the unexplainable. "I need time to assess what happened with you and the bottle and evaluate the best way to proceed."

"I don't know whether to be insulted that you make me sound like a puzzle—"

"You are a puzzle."

"—or pleased that you're curious enough about me—"

"Fascinated, intrigued and beguiled might better describe my feelings about you."

"—to try again."

"Oh, yeah." She smiled at him. "I most certainly want to do that with you again."

"I'm not an experiment."

She chuckled. "Oh, yes, you are. You're the best experiment in my life right now."

"I'm not a lab rat. You can't just ring a bell and expect me to salivate."

"I'm sorry. I didn't mean to sound so clinical. But give me a little slack, please. I'm just trying to figure out how I felt *your* orgasm. The perfume bottle must be as magical as Cate claimed."

"You felt my orgasm? That's impossible." But he scratched his head as if he wasn't quite sure.

"So now I'm either a liar or crazy. Either way, I like you, John."

"I like you, too."

"And now that we've broken through the touch issue, we can go to work on your memories. Isn't that what you want?"

"Yes. But that's not all I want." His voice deepened into dead seriousness. "I want you to be straight with me."

"Okay." She could give him honesty, especially when he was so open-minded about her work.

"Are you in any danger when you touch me?"

In danger of losing her heart, perhaps. She kept that idea to herself. She didn't want to go there when there was already so much on their plates. "What do you mean?"

"Could the torture have altered my mind into something ugly and you'll be sucked into it?"

"No. Absolutely not. My gift doesn't work that way. The first time we touched, I felt your pain, but now I just shared your pleasure. Yet I can't read thoughts. I'm not telepathic. What we shared were the most intimate feelings on a level I hadn't known possible. The sharing was wonderful, clean and exciting, but I wasn't expecting that kind of sensory overload. Next time, I'll control our pace."

"What if you can't?"

"Next time I'll know what to expect, and even if I can't, so what? Nothing bad happened. I feel great."

His eyes darkened with concern. "You're sure?"

He'd asked her to be straight with him, so she was. "No, I'm not sure of anything concerning that bottle. But all I have to do to break the connection is to stop touching you." She took a deep breath and held out her hand. "Nothing is going to convince you. So let me show you."

He hesitated, this time, for her sake.

And the cell phone rang.

"DON'T ANSWER IT," Bonnie requested.

John reached over to the nightstand and checked the caller ID. "It's Kincaid."

"He said he wouldn't interrupt," Bonnie muttered.

"It must be important." John pressed down the talk button. "Hello."

The phone would digitalize his words, and the satellite uplink would encrypt them, then decode it on Logan Kincaid's end. They had no fear of anyone listening in to their conversation and so could speak freely.

Kincaid's voice, always calm, held a bite. "How's it going?"

"Dr. Anders is working miracles. My aversion to touch seems to be gone."

"Have you remembered anything?"

"Not yet. Why?"

"Let me speak to Dr. Anders, please."

John handed Bonnie the phone. "The boss wants to talk to you."

"Interruptions and stress delay the process," she chastised Kincaid without giving the leader of the Shey Group a chance to speak.

John restrained a grin. Bonnie sounded as protective of him as a mother defending her children. Perhaps she didn't realize that Logan Kincaid had a direct line to the White House. He was tight with the CIA and had the ultimate respect from the men who worked for him. He'd repeatedly risked his life for his country, and when it came to the lives of his men, money had no meaning. So he wouldn't have called unless the situation was critical.

She paused to listen while Kincaid said something that John couldn't hear. Bonnie's face paled. "I understand." And she hung up while he waited for her to explain.

He didn't like his boss tiptoeing around him as if Kincaid feared John couldn't handle the situation.

He didn't like that it was up to Bonnie to fill him in, and felt only slightly better when she did so with no hesitation.

"Kincaid has a date for the attack. Confirmed by two independent sources. He didn't want to tell you in case it would make things worse, but I believe you can handle—"

John's stomach tugged into a knot. "How long?"

"July fourth. They want to time the attack with the holiday."

"Today's the second. That gives us two days. Is that enough time to free my memory?"

"I don't know." She threaded a hand through her damp hair. "The perfume bottle may help us and we'll do our best. That's all we can do. But whatever happens, I want you to know one thing."

"What?"

She stared at him, her eyes green chips of flint. "If we fail, you can't blame yourself for what will happen."

He shook his head. "If I have the power to stop the loss of life and fail, then those lives will be on my conscience."

"No, John. If you don't remember the necessary information, then you have to blame the men who set the bombs and the ones who tortured you. Not yourself."

"We're wasting time, Doc."

"You let me worry about the time. And this is important. The less stress you feel, the easier it will be to recall the pertinent facts."

"Okay. Got it." This discussion would be moot if he could recall the intel in time. "Can we please get started?"

She made him eat a light dinner of a grilled chicken salad with fruit for dessert before she'd entertain the idea of work. But finally the meal was finished and she led him to the roof, carrying her tote bag. He hadn't been up here before and realized the architect had taken advantage of the flat roof by creating a deck with a tropical garden and a soothing rock waterfall that tumbled into a whirlpool.

Bonnie opened her tote bag and removed the perfume bottle, which she carefully set on a nearby table. Then she tested the temperature of the whirlpool with her fingers and smiled. "It's perfect."

"I thought we were here to work."

She patted the back of the lounger. "Pretend this is the couch in my office."

He removed his shirt. "You have an office?"

"And a secretary." She gestured to his shorts. "Those, too."

"What about your clothes?"

"This time, I'll be the one doing all the touching."

He frowned at her, but removed his clothes. She made no effort to hide her appreciation of his body. "You're enjoying this, aren't you?"

"What's not to enjoy? A rooftop garden...a full moon...and a handsome man stripping at my command."

John shook his head at the enthusiasm in her voice. She had to know how serious this was. She knew lives were at stake. Yet, she took the time to appreciate life in this moment, and he couldn't help admiring her for doing so. He also liked how, earlier, she'd so easily admitted that he was not her typical patient, that their situation was different, that she had feelings for him. Nor had she denied manipulating him, and her honesty made it easier for him to relax and made him realize that she was one special lady. A lady he was coming to care about for her intelligence and her candor as much as her sensuality.

She sat on the edge of the whirlpool, dipping only her feet into the water. "Remember how I told you that when I touch, I see a maze?"

"Yes."

"Well, what I also do is listen to you speak. And

when you reach a part that you can't remember, I try to open a new path. So, tell me about the mission and expect roadblocks, then give me time to open them—that's my job. All you have to do is stop and point them out, then wait for me to clear the way."

"So you're doing all the work?"

She nodded. "Your job is just to lead me in the right direction."

She took hold of his hand. After their earlier conversation, he shouldn't have expected her touch to feel like anything different, but he did. He figured there would be sparks, or a kind of special connection. Something. But her hand felt like a normal hand, with firm tapered fingers interlocking his—nothing otherworldly. He was looking for proof of what she'd told him because he wanted to believe her.

"Where should I start?" he asked.

"Tell me about the mission."

"I was undercover for two years. Through an introduction from a college professor, I inserted myself into a terrorist cell. I proved myself to the group by feeding them information and supplying them with sources for equipment."

"You worked alone?" Her fingers laced with his, maintaining a constant connection.

"I had backup. We tapped their phones, bugged their cars and watched their homes. I worked my way up the ladder inside the cell until I was a trusted member. Then I brought in a partner. His name was Ali Kareem, an Egyptian immigrant, totally dedicated to stopping terrorism after his brother died during the collapse of the World Trade Center."

"Tell me about Ali."

"I can't...remember." She'd told him this would happen, and he tried to wait patiently for the memory to come. Meanwhile, she loosened the clasp of her fingers on his and began to trail them up and down his arm.

## CHAPTER SIX

TOUCHING JOHN THREW HER into an overload of speed and chaos, like the world's busiest highway intersection during rush hour. With some lanes speeding, others merging and others at a standstill, Bonnie had to feel her way carefully. Mindful not to let his vibrant aura suck her into a traffic accident or bump her into the fast lane, she tried to set her own pace and avoid all fender benders, unsure if even the bottle's magic could protect her if she had a collision.

John's active mind made finding the block he'd erected more difficult than usual. She sensed a complexity to him that was rare, a courage that was unique and a warmth that attracted her with an undeniable pull. Off the roadway, vivid hues of rolling mists hovered over serene aqua pools. The hot colors—crimson, scarlet and vermeil streamed by—but the magenta lightning called to her as he spoke about his friend Ali.

Tracing the purples back to their source was relatively easy, except for opal sparks that kept licking at her, but with the bottle's protection, she felt no burning sensation, just flickers of heat. Knowing the flames were all in her mind, she ignored the fire and advanced, determined to find the critical information.

At the same time, she stroked her hand up and down John's arm. The texture and heat of his flesh mixed with the hot tub's water, insulating her a little from his overwhelming psyche and allowing her to go in slowly. "Easy," she instructed. "Just relax."

"I'm trying."

"Take deep breaths. Fill your lungs. Let the air out fully."

As he breathed, his roadway lightened from browns to sand. But the reds remained sharp and the lightning flashed with fury. "I'm almost there."

She reached the base of the lightning, and between the series of flashing strikes, she spied a threatening silver-black wall of massive proportions. "Okay. I'm where I need to be." She let her hand brush the hair from his neck and she basked in the sexual potency of him that made him so confident. It was like dipping her fingers into a sea of lapping need, cresting male confidence and a sparkling wave of sensual awareness.

"Think about Ali for me again."

"He had black hair. Dark eyes. A ready smile. I can almost see his face."

Her hands seemed to be drifting along his surface happiness, and slowly peeling back layers of satisfaction, joy and determination. When a warning cloud of tension told her that they'd neared another block, she soothed her fingers into his neck muscles.

Jagged lightning bolts encompassed a solid door, the electric jolts pulsing and preventing passage. She timed her advance maneuver between flashes, reaching through the snapping high voltage and carefully thrusting open the door to the passageway.

"Ah, I see Ali now," John sounded relieved as the memory returned. "He's smiling, playing cards. Ali loved to gamble."

Bonnie stepped through the portal, but John was rushing ahead of her. As his story poured out, she drifted in the streaming colors, hoping the journey was almost over, but suspecting they had more blocks to overcome and doors to open since he'd buried what they needed so deep within the intricacies of his mind.

The process couldn't be rushed. As much as she wanted to stop these terrorists, she'd learned to accept that the mind would give up its secrets at its own pace. And so far, their unusual connection with the bottle seemed to be helping the flow.

Never had she been able to progress so quickly. By now, she would normally be exhausted spiritually and emotionally from her efforts—especially when working with barriers as stiff as his, with a mind so complex, with emotions so strong. But the bottle lent her stamina.

She continued to touch John's arm, his shoulder, his back. The connection linked her so strongly to him that as he spoke, she could translate his colors into blue excitement, emerald dread and gray worry. Never had her vision been this clear, her gift so strong, making her that much more certain the perfume bottle had special powers. She couldn't help wondering if her attraction to this man made their bond even stronger. Nothing else could account for her optimism.

*Don't go there.*

She needed to focus. To stay with John.

Fighting her own almost overwhelming need to be close to him, to dig into the safe areas, she determinedly moved forward, allowing him to show her the way. Where she would have lingered, he tugged her forward.

"Ali and I got a lead on where the cell intended to buy the explosives. Apparently someone lifted a shipment of C-4 from the military and sold it on the black market."

"From *our* military?" She had difficulty keeping the outrage from her tone at the thought of U.S. soldiers making a profit from the sale of an item that would kill the civilians they were supposed to protect.

"It happens." He sounded accepting, casual, but she saw the flare of orange temper, a corresponding vexation to match her own.

She'd gripped his shoulder too tightly, and now she loosened her hold. "Go on."

"The guy selling the C-4, his name was Eric Dawson. Eric was hard to read. He was from the backwoods of Tennessee, and mostly he ran moonshine, so I don't know how he ended up with the C-4. But Ali took it upon himself to make friends with the guy."

John shut down on her.

The traffic stopped in one huge jam. The mists clouded over the aqua pools. No lightning lit up a wall. In fact, she couldn't see a wall. The streaming colors had been sucked into a gravity well that reminded her of a black hole where all light disappeared.

Recognizing the block, John tensed under her fingers. "I've just hit another roadblock, Doc."

"I'm on it," she told him with more confidence than she felt. Never had she seen anything like this. She felt as if she were locked into a steel cage, with no windows or doors, no color. It was as if his mind had isolated her presence and locked her out.

Not only couldn't she open the door—she couldn't see the door.

Reaching for him with her other hand, she doubled how much of her flesh touched him. Strengthening the connection flooded light on the dark walls around her, but didn't show her a way out. The wall was smooth, seamless, infinite. She saw no cracks. No way under or over or around.

"Doc? Doc, talk to me."

She'd popped out of his mind, with no idea how much time had elapsed, fuzzy about where she was. She was now sitting on the edge of the pool, John's back pressed between her legs, her hands kneading his shoulders. When had they changed positions? She'd been concentrating so hard on finding a passageway through the blackness that she'd lost track of her physical body. But it was the dark cage in his head that concerned her. "How long were we..."

"You haven't spoken a word in at least ten minutes."

She'd been totally stuck. Even with the bottle, she'd come to an impasse. Perhaps a distraction would show her something new and give her time to adjust to what had happened while she'd been inside his head. "Tell me about Logan Kincaid."

As she stroked him, she linked with his mind again, but she still couldn't see a way through the cage. John's voice came to her clearly and although the timbre of his tone vibrated with enthusiasm, inside the cage she couldn't see any sparks. "Logan Kincaid's background is classified. He's worked for NASA and helped the CIA with the Star Wars missile defense programs. He's a genius when it comes to writing code. Rumor has it he worked for the CIA as a kite."

"Kite?"

"Someone who works so deep undercover that if they are caught, the government cuts the string and denies all responsibility."

"So your boss knows his stuff."

With John so full of admiration for the man, his enthusiasm thinned the cage. She kept him talking about Kincaid. And soon she could see definition to the barrier. Again, she sought out tiny cracks.

Still working at the cage, she simultaneously ran her hands down the front of his chest, the effort costing her precious energy. She leaned forward and rested her cheek against his. "Isn't it great to work with people you like?"

"We aren't talking about Kincaid anymore, are we?" He reached up and squeezed her hand.

She'd deliberately taken his mind off of Ali with her carefully chosen questions. Now she sped right back, hoping that the cage wouldn't again thicken and keep her out, that she might follow a crack and slip through. "I was talking about Ali. He was a good partner?"

"Yeah. He liked to laugh and he didn't sweat the small stuff."

The cage thickened but not as badly as before. She could still see through tiny chips and fractures but she was tiring. She pulled on her own inner strength to keep going. Perhaps misdirection would work again. "Tell me about your family."

"My dad is completely old-fashioned. He wouldn't approve of where your hands are right now."

"Is that so?" She let her hands dip over his flat stomach. She wanted to go lower but couldn't quite reach him.

"Maybe you should just climb in here with me."

She didn't need him to ask twice. She needed more skin-to-skin action to beat back the cage. But she hated to break contact, so she used one hand, then the other, to remove her clothes before joining him in the tub.

With a sigh of satisfaction, she floated over his lap and intertwined her feet with his. Her bottom snuggled against his hips and he wrapped his arms around her.

Nice. She wished she could stop pressing him, turn around and kiss him. But pleasure must be delayed. They needed to work until they could go no further. But that didn't mean she couldn't enjoy the moment.

Tilting her head back against his chest, she released a soft moan as he fondled her breasts, taking great satisfaction in the tingling that shot all the way to the pit of her stomach. But she didn't lose concentration. "Was Ali old-fashioned?"

"Oh, yeah. He believed women should wear burkas, those black hooded dresses where only their eyes showed."

"That doesn't seem like a laid-back attitude to me." The cage was there, but stretched so thin that she could see swirling reds and yellows just beyond.

"That's because you're a woman." John cupped her breasts from underneath and flicked her nipples with his thumbs, shooting delicious licks of heat between her legs and making her ache for more of his touch.

She massaged her hands over his thighs. And the cage disappeared, allowing her to view a nexus of roads in milky quartz, black pearl, dove-gray and terra-cotta brown. The vivid reds were gone. As were the lightning bolts.

In fact, all around her seemed still and peaceful. Too still. So she looked deeper and found black goopy tar holes ready to cement her in place and prevent her progress. He hadn't deliberately erected those roadblocks to stop her—they had been in place a long time, probably since he'd been captured. Carefully navigating around the pits, she maneuvered forward, unsure where he needed her.

She had to keep him talking. "So Ali was laid-back about everything except women?"

"He didn't like me messing with his clothing, either."

"His clothing?"

"Yeah, I knocked a pair of his slacks onto the floor and when I reached down to pick them up, he overreacted."

"Keep going." He was telling her details he

couldn't remember before and making extraordinary progress.

"His annoyance made me suspicious. So I checked the pockets and found a key to a safe deposit box."

"So?"

"We never take personal items with us when we go under. And if he'd needed the safety deposit box for the mission, I should have known about it."

His hands on her breasts were caressing, stroking, plucking and she wanted to slap him away so she could think without the distraction, but she needed him relaxed and she needed as much touching as possible between them to keep the link open and strong. And since she already knew the best way to relax the man was to sexually arouse him, she let him continue to tease her. But working and playing at the same time was more difficult than she'd expected. John seemed to know exactly where to touch her to excite her, which elevated his own arousal, so the side benefits to him outweighed her distraction. She could see flickers of red lighting a path for her, showing her the way through the maze.

"So you confronted Ali?"

He shook his head, then licked a hot stroke on her earlobe. "I tailed him to the bank, and later, Kincaid secretly had the box opened."

She grasped his thighs tight, his constant attention twisting her insides into warm knots. While her mind remained curious over what had happened, she still had difficulty focusing. "What was inside the box?"

John nipped her ear, her neck, a sensitive spot on her shoulder, and all the while he kept his hands moving, caressing, taunting. "We found a passport with a fake ID, a hundred grand and a numbered Swiss bank account."

"What did that mean?" she asked. He went taut under her, his thighs bunching and his breathing ragged.

Inside, large tar pits boiled, expanding in circumference to trap her, but she skipped between them, heading for burnished red flickers at the end of a long gray tunnel.

"We figured Ali must have betrayed us. We didn't know if he'd blown my cover yet. Kincaid intended to call off the operation, but I asked to make one quick strike into the offices of their leader, Mustaffa, copy his files and get out."

"Kincaid agreed?" He dipped his hands between her legs and she opened to him, marveling at how his lightest of touches made her squirm inside for more. As if his physical touch wasn't enough to arouse her, she had to deal with the hot flares of red light inside him, showing her how much touching her meant to him, how much he trusted her.

"Kincaid said to wait."

"And did you?"

He parted her flesh with one finger and sank into her heat. At the same time, a ring of red fire surrounded her, holding her in place. She wanted to move and had to wait. Had to wait for him to show her the way through. But with his finger deep inside stroking her, she had to bite back the words to urge him on with his ministrations. Had to use all her determination not to gyrate her hips and demand more.

The red flames around her shot higher. He arched under her, his sex jutting between her legs. "I don't know what I did. But I've never been good at waiting."

"Okay." He'd obviously reached another block but they'd come a long way in just the one session. If the time factor hadn't been critical, she might have stopped. Instead, she tried to do more. "Relax and let me do my thing."

"You go right ahead. Don't pay any attention to me."

He kept one hand between her legs while the other roved freely, devoting a good amount of attention to her breasts. She didn't think her nipples could tighten or her breasts could swell any more, but they did. Concentrating on his block was almost impossible when she burned for completion. But inside his head, sexual excitement was weakening the mental blocks.

He kept up the pressure inside her, while his thumb sneaked gently onto the place where all her nerve endings centered. She was so sensitive, but he was, oh, so gentle. His thumb moved deliciously slowly, while the finger deep inside her continued to caress. And his free hand kept her breasts so excited that she could barely think. Especially with his mouth and lips blazing their own trail of fire over her neck and ears.

Inside his mind the red flames spread, scorching the dark walls. His passion obliterated the tar pits and the traffic jams until she could again see a path before her. But a heavy-duty barrier of massive granite block-aded this path. And there was only one way to go on.

"John, you feel so good. Slow down."

He kissed a sensitive spot behind her ear, increased the tempo of his hand between her legs. "I don't think so."

"You must. We have work to do."

"We are working," he insisted, but he withdrew his hand, turned her around, then lifted her until she sat on the lip of the pool. Then he lowered himself between her legs, with his face positioned between her thighs.

He found her with his tongue, and the sensual shock made her cry out in wonder. While his tongue played delicately and teased the tips of her intimate folds, she clutched his shoulders to steady herself and let out a soft whimper of desire. He felt so good.

So totally good.

Too good.

Her body ached for him. Her thoughts spun. With every ounce of strength in her, she jerked back.

## CHAPTER SEVEN

"WE MUST...STOP." She grabbed his hands from where he held her knees apart. "We need to...reevaluate."

John looked up at her face. It was alive with passion. Desire clouded her eyes. Need had her lips pouty and pursed while her breath came in pants. Water trickled over her breasts, which rose and fell as she took in huge gulps of air. Obviously she was having as much difficulty stopping as he was and no matter how much he wanted her and cared about her, he also admired how she put the mission first.

"We're going too fast."

Instinctively he understood that she wasn't talking about sex. She was talking about touching him and whatever she did to help him remember. And as much as he wanted to deny her strange ability, he couldn't, not if he wanted to be fair. Because her method was working. He was remembering details he hadn't recalled until now.

"I'll slow down, darling." He reached for her again.

"No. You can't be the one in control."

He didn't like the sound of where she was going. If she needed to touch him to help him, he didn't see the difference in who touched whom. "Why not?"

"For one thing I'm having trouble concentrating when you distract me."

"And?"

"Your passion is like a wildfire. It's burning out of control and I can't see past the flames."

He didn't understand what she was talking about, but he believed that she knew what she was doing. He didn't feel her gift when she touched him, though the passion it elicited was potent. But sometime during the last few minutes she'd convinced him that she had a special ability. He'd be a fool to deny that he was remembering things that he hadn't previously been able to recall. And as much as he wanted to enjoy her delicious body, now that his emotions had cooled, he realized she knew better than he how to proceed.

"What do you want from me?"

"You have to let me take the lead."

"Okay," he agreed.

"It's not that simple. You agree now, but once we start touching, you take over."

He acknowledged the truth of her statement. "But you want my hands on you to keep the connection, right?"

"Your passion is feeding off my excitement. It's not enough. We need to go deeper."

"I don't understand."

"You need to let me touch you where and how and when I want."

He sighed. He might start out agreeing to her demands, but when the pleasure accelerated, he was a man accustomed to taking what he wanted. "What do you suggest?"

"You need to trust me."

"I do."

"Prove it and let me tie you up."

He swallowed hard, the hair on the back of his neck standing up. "Tie me?"

"In the hammock. Hands over your head. Feet spread wide."

The idea of making himself that vulnerable clawed at him. Every cell in him rebelled. It was too much like returning to captivity. Yet, she wouldn't torture him—except with pleasure.

She wanted to tie him up.

When he remained silent, his mouth dry, his heart hammering, his chest and head pounding with pressure, she tugged him from the soothing warm water into the cool night air. Goose bumps rose on his flesh. His mind might rebel at her suggestion, his heart might have even skipped a few beats, but his erection remained.

He trusted her.

It was himself he didn't trust.

Didn't trust that he would relax enough to let her work her "magic" on him.

He wouldn't be able to pull away from her touch to escape his memories. But he wanted to recall them, didn't he?

Despite the cool night air, sweat beaded on his scalp.

She wanted to tie him up.

And he wouldn't be a mass of raw energy if he wasn't seriously considering her proposition. Realistically, even if the Shey Group recovered the information, disseminating the intel to the FBI, the military and local law enforcement would take time. If she could entice the data out of him tonight, it would be safer for all involved.

Since there was only one decision he could live with, he didn't really have a choice. "Okay."

She didn't break contact with him. Instead she accompanied him to a comfy-looking double hammock with a four-point tie that allowed it to rock, but not flip. From her tote bag, she withdrew restraints made of sturdy strapping. She fastened them around his wrists and ankles, then gestured for him to lie in the hammock.

Blood roaring in his ears, he did as she requested. First she positioned the bottle close by. And when she fastened the straps to the hammock, her breasts swaying close to his face, his mouth watered and he fought against lifting his head in an attempt to take one nipple into his mouth. Still, he kept his hands overhead so she could restrain him. She moved away, the soft underside of her breasts grazing his cheeks.

After she manacled his hands with the soft straps, she delicately licked the center of his palms, and the erotically sensual move had him questioning his sanity in allowing her to tie him down. When she sucked on each finger individually, he kept dreaming where else her inquisitive mouth might go.

She kissed his eyebrows, and her moist lips and tongue traced his eyelashes, forcing his eyes shut. His heart raced in anticipation. Already he ached to gather her into his arms and pull her closer. Instead, he had to wonder what she would do next.

He didn't have to wonder for long. She ran her fingertips along his neck up onto his scalp, massaging his temples and the sensitive skin around his ears. Meanwhile she licked, nibbled and nipped the side of his neck with her teeth.

Right about now he would have welcomed the distraction of answering her questions about the mission. But she seemed intent on arousing him. Slowly. With wet strands of her hair trailing along his shoulder, her clever hands in his hair and those wickedly nipping teeth, he found himself tensed, holding his breath.

She withdrew her touch and he opened his eyes to see her backlit by the stars and highlighted by the underwater illumination from the whirlpool. With her damp skin so close, her scent wafted to him on the night breeze. "Enjoying yourself?"

"Oh, yeah." She strode to the far end of the hammock and he got an eyeful of her round buttocks as she leaned over to strap his ankles.

"You're deliberately teasing me with that pose," he accused her, his voice hoarse.

"Maybe I am," she admitted without any apology in her tone.

She bent further and waggled her butt, and he

picked up his head to catch the enticing sight of pink lips between two sleek half globes. Automatically, he tried to sit up, but the restraints kept him a voyeur. He dropped his head back in frustration while she tightened the second ankle strap, pulling his thighs open as wide as possible.

She returned and carefully climbed into the hammock next to him, setting them swaying. She snuggled against his side, turned his head with her hand for a kiss. With tiny nips and licks around the corners of his mouth, she kissed him, teasing just above the Cupid's bow and at the slope of the lower lip and chin. When he opened his mouth, she sucked just the tip of his tongue between her lips and flicked it with her own. At the same time she twisted his nipples between her fingers until he found himself testing the strength of his straps. They didn't budge. Engorged, stretched to the point where he was harder than he'd ever been, he let out a groan of frustration, a moan of pure pleasure.

He strained against the restraints, aching for more of her. "Do you have any idea how much I want to be inside you right now?"

"Probably almost as much as I want you there." She let out a breathy sigh. "However, our satisfaction must be delayed...."

"So you keep telling me."

She tapped her finger to the tip of his nose. "You are in no position to argue. But I did notice that the more of my flesh that touches yours, the more you remember."

She sat up and at the same time lifted her leg over him. The hammock swung and for a moment he hoped that she would take him inside her. But she'd positioned her open legs over his stomach, leaving his sex to dance against her warm bottom.

When she leaned down and nestled her head under his chin, pressing her breasts against his chest, he felt her heart beating against him. She kept most of her weight on her knees, yet they touched chest to chest, belly to belly. "Comfy?"

"I'd be much more comfy if you'd move down my body another four inches."

She reached up and threaded her fingers through his hair. "When you decided to speed up your mission and go into Mustaffa's office, what did you hope to obtain?"

He sounded resigned, hopeful that they would get the information out of his head. "Names, addresses, places of targets. Suppliers of weapons. Bank accounts. A money trail. Anything that could give us intel on the cell. We especially wanted to know how they communicated with one another, how they funded operations and who was in charge."

Taking his earlobes between her thumb and index fingers, she rubbed him there and he found the motion both erotic and calming at the same time. When they'd spoken in the whirlpool about the mission, he had drawn a blank about whether he'd entered Mustaffa's office, but now he saw the room clearly. He didn't understand exactly how she'd just freed his memories, but clearly she was very good at her specialty.

"I waited for Mustaffa to depart. The man never kept a schedule, waking and sleeping at all hours of the day and night. I had no idea how long he would be gone, since I didn't know where he was going."

"Sounds nerve-wracking."

She changed her position, lying by his side. This time she let her palm wander over the inside of his thigh.

Her teasing hand helped him relax about the mission, but it built excitement within him about where she'd touch next. "No one ever questioned Mustaffa's movements. Kincaid requested satellite surveillance, but Mustaffa lost himself in a crowd and disappeared."

She tugged on his pubic hair and he tried to arch into her hand. "You went in anyway?"

"Yeah." Those long slow tugs of hers made his stomach knot. "It was risky because Mustaffa could return at any time, but we thought it would be worth it. His office was a bedroom in the back of his house and his subcommanders had left for the mosque."

"And Ali?" Her hand closed around the base of his shaft and began to move up and down.

"He was with me."

He couldn't remember more, until she increased her tempo and tightened her grip, creating a marvelous friction. She asked, "But you didn't trust him?"

"I figured the best way to keep an eye on him was to keep him by my side." She maintained her hold on him and talking became more difficult, but the memories were right there within reach. "Ali couldn't warn anyone while he was with me, and I didn't give him advance notice that we were going in."

"Makes sense. So you entered Mustaffa's office," she prodded, slowing her hand but maintaining her grip.

He used the opportunity to catch his breath, but he felt as if he were about to burst. Sweat trickled down his neck, and he was sure he'd never been so aroused in his life. Yet all he could do was lie there while she teased him.

"It was dark." He could see it all so clearly now. "We used tiny penlights. Ali guarded the door. I headed for the computer and hacked my way in."

She sped up her hand. "And?"

"I hit the jackpot. Ah..." His back arched, his hips thrust upward, but she kept to her new slower pace, driving him wild. "There were names, dates, places, money transactions. I didn't read it, just downloaded it to a disk. I would have preferred to send it out over the Internet, but there was no connection."

She stopped her hand to flick his sensitive ridge, her finger tapping the tender groove on the underside. He bit back a growl, unwilling to admit that he could barely concentrate on her questions. He wanted her so badly he trembled with the need for her, the need for release.

But she didn't stop her caressing, not for a second. Nor did she stop asking her questions. "What was Ali doing while you copied the disk?"

"He opened a window...in case we needed to retreat out the back of the building."

"Go on." She increased the tempo of her hand, then slid down to cup his sac. She palmed his fullness, her fingers seeking the flesh behind his balls, stroking him to distraction. He gasped and she had to repeat her last request before he could answer.

"It took forever for the files to download. Maybe sixty seconds. I'd just popped the disk into my pocket when Mustaffa returned. I dived out the window, hoping Ali would follow. He didn't."

Her hand stopped all movement. "He stayed behind to betray you?"

"No. He died covering my retreat."

"I'm sorry. I thought you said he had fake ID, money in a Swiss bank account." She ran her palm up his hip, over his chest, playing lightly with his chest hair. Then she leaned over him to take a nipple into her mouth. As she swirled her tongue around it, her hand dived back down to pump him.

Talk about distractions. He could barely think with the sensations pouring through him. He felt so tight, so hard, so full. He ached to thrust into her heat, but she denied him. And again he forced out an answer. "Kincaid traced the money. Ali's family had been wealthy when they left Egypt. That money was his."

Straightening, she asked, "And the fake passport?" She played with the very tip until he went light-headed.

"Ali had always feared that America would kick

him out, or worse, suspect him of being a terrorist due to his background. The fake passport was simply extra security." He breathed in long, steady breaths, but her hand on him was relentless. "I'd suspected the man of being a traitor and he died saving my ass."

She scooted down his side, her breath fanning his flesh, her moist lips just an inch from where he needed her. "Ali died so you could recover the information and protect innocent people."

"Yeah."

When she took him deep into her mouth, the warmth was almost his undoing. But she pressed firmly at the base, preventing him from going over the edge. However, he was yanking on the restraints now, his muscles so tense that he had to come soon.

And she stopped.

He groaned.

"So what happened to the disk?"

Despite every distraction, he couldn't remember. Disappointment almost drowned him. "I wish I knew."

"Relax. I can't let you come yet."

"Why not? Maybe if I climax, you can get through."

"Remember what happened last time? Your orgasms are too powerful for me to keep control," she explained.

Then her mouth went back to licking him and nipping him, and if he'd been free he would have had her on her back, or against a wall, or on the deck. He would have plunged into her and...*ah*... She sucked on him and his fingers clenched so hard his knuckles cracked.

"Dammit, Bonnie. Untie me, right now."

"What happened to the disk?"

"I don't know."

She straddled him again, her head facing his feet, her mouth busily creating more havoc. With her bottom in the air, just inches from his face, the scent of her made him frantic. He lifted his head, trying to reach her with his tongue, but she remained just out of reach.

"Did you drop the disk?"

"No."

"Did you bury it?"

"No." He shook his head back and forth. She held him on the edge of pleasure and release, the torment drowning him in sensations. She would surely kill him.

"Did you give the disk up to the terrorists?"

"No. I was running through the woods. I couldn't let them catch me with the information."

She arched her back and tipped up her bottom, her pink lips tempting him, teasing him, taunting him. "So where did you hide the disk?"

"In the hollow of a tree." The triumph that filled him burst into pure joy. She'd done it! He'd remembered where he'd placed the disk.

"You're sure?"

"Yes. You did it!"

"We did it together," she corrected him, turning and planting a blissful kiss on his lips.

"Untie me so I can call Kincaid." His head was swimming with joy and the desire to have her, but she'd stopped and climbed down from the hammock. "What are you doing?"

"Calling Kincaid just as you wanted."

She took a cell phone from her tote bag, dialed and held it to his ear and mouth. When Kincaid answered, John gave him the exact location of the tree, centered between a telephone pole, a fence post and a rocky crag. The Shey Group would retrieve the data and disseminate intel to the proper authorities within the hour.

Bonnie snapped the phone shut with a pleased grin on her face. "My work is done."

He didn't like the sound of that. As if she would

leave him hanging out to dry, with unfinished business between them. However, if she didn't want to make love to him now that she considered her job done, he might have to accept that. "So untie me."

"Uh-uh. Now it's time to play."

## CHAPTER EIGHT

"I AM NOT A BOY TOY," John growled, but he couldn't keep her from hearing the pleasure in his tone.

Bonnie had told him the truth. She wanted him. And now they were free to enjoy one another.

She sauntered over to him and tweaked both his nipples. "Actually, I think that if I were in your position, I would be more accommodating."

He groaned. "You like having me at your mercy."

"What's not to like?" she teased. "I have this hard-bodied guy ready to please me—"

"I'd please you a lot more if you'd untie me."

"—and all the time in the world to enjoy him." She made a ring with her thumb and forefinger and rubbed it over his sex. She loved the feel of his silky-smooth hardness, but most of all she loved the throaty desire in his tone, the passion on his face and the challenging glint in his eyes that told her to push him to his limits.

She held up a condom from her tote. "What do you think it would feel like to have me take you inside me and then rock the hammock from side to side?"

"There's one way to find out."

She tore open the packet, then rolled the condom over him. "Perhaps I'll untie your hands, but only if you promise to let me be on top."

"Darling, you've got yourself a deal."

She leaned over him, rubbing her breasts along his cheeks as she slowly untied his hands. This time she allowed him to capture a nipple with his mouth and the delicious sensation made her hands fumble with his restraints. There was no hurry, except he'd ignited a fire in her that would soon be raging wildly. And only he could put it out.

She wished she could have seen his face when she climbed back into the hammock, facing his feet. She had to be satisfied with his gasp of surprise. But then she straddled him, took him inside her and grabbed his calves.

He sat up, his hands immediately roving over her bottom and between her legs. And when she raised her hips, he slid his fingers into her moist heat, seeking her clit, urging her to ride him hard, to stoke the fires inside him that earlier she'd so carefully prevented from flaring out of control. This time there was no need to hold back, no need to temper the heat.

No need to pretend this was business, because he was so much more. John pleased her on levels she'd never known existed. He pleased her sensually, emotionally, physically. She couldn't seem to stop herself from touching him. The connection between them made the sex more intense, the emotions more powerful. The heat inside her was building when he grabbed her hips and held her still.

He slipped one hand between her thighs and the other reached around her and caressed her breast, plucking at her nipple. His fingers worked in tandem while he pressed kisses along her back. She couldn't hold still and tried to move, but he pinched her nipple, holding her exactly where he wanted her.

"John, please. While I was touching you, I could feel your need...as well as mine. Ah...oh, my...I still can feel what you feel.... It's like a...double whammy."

"Good." He sounded way too satisfied. He released her breast and stretched back onto the hammock. Then he guided her hips off of his erection, pulled her back toward his mouth. And then his mouth found her heat. She buried her head in his sex, but she didn't dare use her mouth on him. With the sensations rocking her, she feared she might bite.

With his hands clasped on her hips, he kept her right where he wanted her. And when his splendid tongue drove her right over the brink, she shook, her muscles clenching. But he didn't stop. He just kept going. She had no time to recover from the explosion before the next one came, this one more intense. She didn't know if she cried out. She didn't recognize the whimpering sounds coming from the back of her throat. And still he didn't stop. The bursts kept coming, until she thought her body couldn't possibly take more. But when another spasm rippled through her, she began to buck.

John's hands remained firm, and his mouth stayed on her intimately, his tongue flicking over her until she lost track of how many times she exploded. Her thighs trembled, her body shook and her heart quivered. She couldn't take one more climax. And yet she did.

And when he finally let her take him back inside of her, she was so limp, she could barely move. He guided her until her back lay against his chest, and then he began to move his hips from beneath her. And all the while he kept one hand on her nipple, the other between her thighs. The hammock swayed, his hips pumped into her and when they both exploded together, she knew the Fourth of July fireworks had come early this year.

She had no idea how long it took her to recover. But with him pressed to her back, she was in no rush to move. In fact, she considered sleeping right in the hammock all night and using John for her pillow.

He cupped one hand over each of her breasts, lightly stroking her. Warm and snuggled against him, she looked up at the stars and the crescent moon and wished she could wrap this moment up and keep it forever.

"What are you thinking?" he asked.

"I was thinking about how life has wonderful surprises waiting for us if we're only open to them."

"Like multiple orgasms?" He sounded so pleased with himself that she chuckled.

"Like finding a man who enjoys giving them as much as I enjoyed receiving them. Like finding a man who trusts me, who believes in my gift."

"What else do you want from me?" he asked.

"What do you mean?" Her heart tripped over the way his tone had turned serious and his aura had changed from red to a steady blue flame.

"I was hoping for more than a two-day fling."

"Are you asking me for another day?"

"No. I'm hoping that being together might go from a fling to something steady. I'm not willing to give you up and simply recall this weekend as the best of my life. It wasn't just great sex—it was much more. All my life I've roamed the world, searching for something I couldn't name. When I'm with you, I no longer have the need to search. I'm content. What about you?"

"I don't know. I'm not sure."

"I can live with that." He kissed her temple.

"You can?" Spending more time with him opened up entirely new possibilities. John's trust in her, his open-mindedness about her gift, allowed her to be herself with him. She'd never had that kind of freedom with a man she adored.

"My work for the Shey Group is on a mission-by-mission basis. Right now I'm owed several months of R and R. I've thought about retiring, but now that I'm healed I'm not sure what I want to do with my career. However, I am sure that I'd like us to be together as much as possible."

"Kincaid came through as promised. The suspension of my medical license is suspended. So I guess my work and home are in Tampa."

"I like Florida." He teased her nipples. "The heat has lots of advantages."

She teetered on the brink of pulling back, of walking away. Yet his steady inner blue flame, as rich in color as the hues in the perfume bottle's crystal, dared her to accept his offer. How could she turn down a man so honorable? So sincere and charming...and so good in the sack? She'd have to be crazy to say no to him. In fact, if she said no, she knew she'd regret it.

If she let John into her life, she'd be much better off than she was right now. Her world would become more complex, richer, broader. "Promise me that whatever happens between us that we won't end up hating one another," she whispered.

"I promise."

And he meant it. She could hear his sincerity in his tone and feel it inside him, too. "Okay."

"Okay?"

"Let's spend some time together and see where it takes us," she agreed, her heart light with happiness.

"That's the answer I was hoping to hear." He crossed his arms over her chest and together they rocked in the hammock, gazing up at the stars.

"We'll have fun, John. Count on it."

# SURRENDER

## Julie Elizabeth Leto

To Donna Cromeans, aspiring author, bookseller and friend, for orchestrating the wonderful trip to Jackson, Mississippi, (excluding the trip to the emergency room) and for introducing me to Penny Boswell, who gave me the seed that grew into the idea that is this story.

And to Julie Kenner and Susan Kearney— always a pleasure to work with.

# CHAPTER ONE

"WHAT IS YOUR SECRET?"

Evonne Baptiste ran her fingertip from a swath of crimson velvet to the rigid center of her prize. She finally had what she wanted. After all this time, all this expense. She expected a cold sensation from the thick shaft as she smoothed her finger up the jutting curve, but instead, a tingle of warmth teased her skin. Before she could react, a splinter of fire jabbed her. With a gasp, she withdrew her hand.

*Just what are you?*

Cradled beneath the bright light of her Tiffany lamp, the two-hundred-year-old perfume bottle flickered and shined as if reflecting a dangerous flame rather than the glimmer of a sixty-watt bulb. Fashioned from cut crystal and entwined with an intricate lace of fine silver, the bottle evoked a million impressions at once—most of them innately sensual. The facets of the glass seized the color around it—

from the lamp shade, the velvet, the light—then threw back a reflection that Eve couldn't tear her gaze from. The bottle mesmerized her and, reportedly, had had the same effect on anyone who spent more than an instant admiring its exquisite artistry.

Well, not the same. Yes, the decorative phial intrigued everyone who saw it, but the full breadth of its purported magical properties remained the secret of a privileged few.

The perfume bottle had a small date etched on the bottom. Only Eve, an expert on all things associated with Romani legend and lore, would have recognized the significance of the year. 1905. The year *he* disappeared. No way could that be a coincidence, not when she'd seen the diaries, too—the diaries that corroborated the legend passed orally from gypsy clan to gypsy clan for the past century.

The bottle was historically tied to Viktor Savitch, a notorious Romani clan leader from the early twentieth century. As an anthropologist with an expertise in Romani cultures, particularly those in Great Britain, Eve had run across the tales of this gypsy king many times. Little by little, the man and the myth had seeped under her skin, into her fantasies. His story brimmed with dramatic highlights, but so much was missing. The details, the reasons—the truth. He was a desperate, driven leader, a man devoted to keeping his wandering clan intact. She also knew he'd been a notorious charmer, with whispers regarding his prowess in bed.

She'd been fascinated by his story from the first breath about him. She couldn't explain the instantaneous connection she'd felt to this man she'd never meet and, though she tried to attribute her response to simple scholarly curiosity, she knew better. Viktor Savitch appealed to Eve not as a subject of study, but as a man.

Eve wouldn't define her interest in Viktor as an obsession—yet. But with the purchase of the bottle, she drifted closer. Even before she'd cleaned out her savings account in order to own a reputed piece of his illustrious history, she'd done all she could to know everything about him. She'd traveled to England, walked the same forest trails, explored his unique culture—something that separated them more than death or a century of time ever could. She'd never know him, but with the bottle, she now had a chance to put together all the pieces of the puzzling story.

If she figured out how to work its magic.

Any number of her colleagues could have easily translated the words on the base, a Romani phrase that loosely meant, "The strength of the gift." But few would have suspected there was more to this bottle than aesthetic beauty. If the rumors were true—and she had every reason to believe they were—the bottle was a powerful conduit for paranormal activity, an amplifier for any supernatural gifts the owner already possessed. Eve couldn't imagine her particular talent growing any stronger, but she hoped.

Eve had the power to communicate with those who had passed on, but had not crossed over. With their spirits trapped on Earth for a thousand different reasons, the ghosts often reached out to living people who were sensitive to their voices. Like Eve. But where were her friends?

For nearly forty-eight hours straight, she'd tried to unlock the secret. She'd utilized all her knowledge, and still remained in the dark. But her fascination never wavered, not since the bottle had arrived via special courier, trussed in dark red velvet edged with ruby-colored beads and cradled in a sturdy wooden box. The box had sealed Eve's suspicion that she'd bought more than a fancy knickknack for her vanity table. Underneath the tattered satin lining, she'd found another etched symbol—faded and nearly imperceptible—but her trained eye recognized the unmistakable seal of the Dulas, a Gypsy clan whispered to have dabbled in black magic.

She put the bottle on her dresser, then lifted the box from the floor, running her fingers over its smooth grooves. "Just what happened to my gypsy king?"

With a deep breath and deliberate swallow, Eve closed her eyes and concentrated. She cleared her mind and lowered the tentative walls she'd learned to erect long ago to keep the voices at bay. The voices of the dead.

Though she'd been communicating with ghosts for as long as she could remember, she rarely invited contact, except with the ghosts that haunted her garden. And even then, most of the time, they slipped into her mind without warning. The souls of the dead could be very persistent. What else had they to do, trapped on Earth between planes of existence?

Besides, on a night like tonight with the wind howling through the mournful willows surrounding her house and flashes of deceptively silent heat lightning slicing the night sky, Eve could use some company. Even the kind that wasn't alive, wasn't solid and apparently wasn't to be relied on.

With a sigh, Eve tossed the box onto her unmade bed, the sheets tangled from her unsuccessful attempt to go to sleep early. With no summer courses to teach at the university, Eve had planned to fill her break between semesters exploring her pet project—

Viktor. She'd told herself she would write a book, combine the many legends and stories and myths into a dramatic tale of adventure, seduction and loss. A high-profile success on the publishing front could aid her professional standing. That rationalization had tipped the scales in her decision to buy the bottle, no matter the cost.

But mostly, she'd cleaned out her savings so she could finally have a piece of Viktor Savitch to call her own. She didn't exactly know how the bottle tied into Viktor's life, but she'd heard a variety of legends. Yet, so far, the exquisite perfume decanter remained as much a mystery as the man who'd reportedly once owned it.

Her gaze slid back to the bottle just as a knock sounded on her kitchen door.

Three hard raps in quick succession.

Eve smiled. With a quick tug on the sash of her robe, she dashed to the door. From the counter, she snagged the unfinished glass of wine she'd poured earlier to help her sleep. As she sipped, she tore aside the curtain that covered the window panes in her door.

She saw no one. But her visitors had finally arrived.

For as long as she'd lived in this centuries-old cottage on the fringes of modern Marietta, Georgia, the souls that wandered the grounds had never entered the house. Well, almost never. Mainly, they haunted the garden and yard, keeping close to the three weathered grave markers in a far corner beside the fence— the markers that had convinced Eve to buy the property on the spot, despite a perpetually leaky roof. One of the entities—a young woman, from what Eve could gather, likely named Alexis if impressions were correct—sometimes sneaked into the parlor while Eve watched television, especially when she screened a film of a sexy or lurid nature. Alexis couldn't resist *9 1/2 Weeks* or *Chocolat*. Then again, neither could Eve, so she didn't mind the intrusion.

But tonight, she needed more from her ethereal friends than company and she only hoped they could help. They too had been gypsies, immigrants to the United States. From where exactly, she didn't know. But there was a slight chance they may have known her gypsy king.

The minute Eve stepped off the screened porch and onto the back step, the wind whipped beneath her silk robe and tossed the material aside. She clamped the edges tighter, nearly spilling her wine, then sat on the bottom step and tucked the silk beneath her. She sipped more wine, knowing from experience that she received messages from the dead more easily if she relaxed.

In July, the air outside Atlanta brimmed with stifling heat. Lightning burst and streaked behind slim
gray clouds, illuminating the sky at uneven intervals
and with eerie silence. Still, as the breeze flurried
across her skin, trickles of a chill tapped her. They
were here. Quiet Alexis. Her cousin, the mischievous
Nicholai. But Eve didn't sense Jeta, the old woman.
The wise soul. The one who likely had the answer
she needed.

Eve took another long draft of wine. The explosion of rich flavor warmed her mouth and throat,
then eased down into her belly, settling the quivers
that always snaked through her whenever she
sought contact with the dead. She formed the question, then watched with closed eyes as the letters
and words formed in her mind. With one sweep of
thought, she translated the phrase into Romani and
pictured the query again. She had no idea if the
dead were bound by the barriers of language, but
she wasn't taking chances. She needed an answer.
She needed it now.

*Do you know the gypsy king?*

The wind kicked up and Eve sought to warm herself with another mouthful of wine. Whispers of words
teased her ears. After a moment, she understood.

*Which? Which? Which?*

She cleared her mind of the first question. When she pictured his name, the letters were blocked and bold.

*VIKTOR SAVITCH.*

The wind blasted the walls of her cottage, the weathered wood groaning, the wind chimes clanging like a discordant alarm. The cold threads of air slicing through the wind injected her with iciness and all at once, Eve was inundated with an eruption of emotions.

This was how she most often communicated with the dead—not with full sentences, but whispered words and impressions. But these burst at her, exploding in her brain, attacking with an intensity she'd never experienced.

*Cursed!*

Fear.

*Black magic.*

Anticipation.

Excitement?

*Legendary.*

And then...arousal.

Eve shot to her feet. A burst of warmth raked across her breasts, caressing her nipples, erect from the cold. Another tendril of heat slithered up her bare leg, teasing her thighs before dipping into a sudden pool of moisture in her panties. Eve stepped back, forgetting about the porch behind her. Her balance lost, the wineglass slipped from her hand, drenching her in crimson. But before she toppled to the ground, a final blast of air scooped behind her, buoyed her, and settled her down on the porch swing.

Eve gasped, then scrambled toward the door. They'd touched her! She shook her head wildly, fumbling with the doorknob as reality slammed down.

They'd touched her! Not like usual. Not with tiny pinpricks of iciness. But with warmth. With potency! With intimacy.

Eve wrenched the door open, threw herself into the kitchen and slammed the door behind her. Her heart pounded against her chest and her eyes had trouble adjusting to the bright indoor light. Sapped of breath, her body flush against the wood and curtains, she panted, desperate to fill her tight lungs.

What had happened? And why was she suddenly afraid?

Never in all the years that Eve communicated with the lost spirits of the dead had she ever experienced real fear. Once or twice, she'd been spooked a little, maybe. Distressed, sometimes, when exposed to an angry or malevolent entity, but never terrified. They couldn't touch her. They couldn't hurt her.

Only that wasn't true anymore, was it? Outside, she'd been touched. Intimately. And her body had reacted in kind, stirring with need that even for the briefest instant shocked her with its intensity. Yet she didn't feel violated in the least. Instead, she felt intrigued.

She swallowed and remembered the bottle settled inertly on her bedroom dresser.

The rumors were true.

The bottle must have strengthened her gift to communicate with the dead. Her possession of the magical object had broken the boundary between the two planes of existence—allowing stronger impressions and, more shocking, physical interaction.

Suddenly exhausted and light-headed, Eve dragged herself to her bedroom, blew out the candle she'd left burning and fell onto the bed face-first. Maybe this was all a huge mistake. Maybe this time, she'd taken on more than she could handle.

Or maybe, she was in for the ride of her life.

# CHAPTER TWO

I CAN TOUCH HER!

Viktor Savitch peered through a pane in his prison
of glass and watched Evonne Baptiste drop onto her
bed, her dark blond hair falling like a curtain over her
face. Exhaustion and shock had played a sinister
game with her delicate features, but as she drifted
into the serenity of sleep, he imagined her a creature
of light and magic.

And he'd touched her! The experience had apparently sapped her energy, but he hadn't felt this
alive in one hundred years. A great trick, since he was
still very, very dead.

Despite that fact, he could almost feel his hands
thrust onto his hips as he threw his head back and
laughed. He didn't have a body for such an action,
but the impression remained the same. Blood surged
through invisible veins. His nonexistent chest rum-
bled with mirth. His vision, cloudy before, now stood

blocked only by the curve of the glass. For the first time in ages, the essence of life swelled around him.

An essence he would harness. Soon. To live again, he'd do whatever he had to do, knowing that some tasks, like seducing Evonne Baptiste, would be more pleasant than others.

When he'd first died, the phantom presence of his physical self had been strong and vital, just as he had been. But over time, he'd faded. Slowly. Painfully. His punishment for a life of arrogance exacted a precise toll. But now, had the powers of the ethereal world decided that he'd done his penance? Had they gifted him with the means to escape?

To hell with them, Viktor cursed. He'd get out, and he'd do it on his own.

Nearly.

Evonne stirred, a soft murmur spilling from her wine-tinged lips. Once again, Viktor reacted, as if a heart slammed beneath the imaginary ribs of his chest. Even the crick in his thigh from where he'd been stabbed so long ago throbbed again.

He'd deal with the pain if he had to. After all this time, he'd found a means to communicate with the world outside his prison. And he couldn't have ordered a more perfect medium. This one, this Evonne Baptiste, not only possessed the ability to speak with those who had died, but she was haunted by an unsatisfied hunger for those intimate needs Viktor had once commanded above all other men, dead or alive.

Passion. Lust. Desire.

Could he find the means to satisfy her? Of course. He could feel his power increasing, even as she slept. For her part in his rejuvenation, she deserved the greatest gift he could bestow. A woman so beautiful, so responsive, so open to the possibilities of the magical world deserved more than just his gratitude. He would grant her whatever she wished, whatever he had the power to give.

Not for a century had he felt so strong and aroused. Had he ever experienced such an intense craving in life, when seduction had simply been his means to attain power? He'd twisted so many Romani traditions to keep his family together. And he'd paid the price—with his life, with a long, torturous and painful death. With denied entry into the Otherworld.

He hadn't been dead long enough to forget his final living moments. His murder at the hands of the witch was as clear in his mind as the supple curve of Evonne's backside as she lay prone on the bed. But he wouldn't think about his death now. The possibilities for revenge had long lost their sweet flavor, especially when the chance of life was just a concentrated touch away.

Outside, he'd manipulated the breeze, calling on *Bavol,* spirit of the air and wind, something he'd accomplished only once as a young man when studying with his shaman grandfather. After the great *Chovihano*'s death, Viktor had been sent away, forced to live in the *gaujo* world of the English aristocracy, where he'd forgotten his shaman magic and instead learned other means to attain power. At twenty, he'd returned to his tribe, keen to use non-Romani methods to rule as *sherrengro,* as chieftain. As gypsy king.

After a decade of rule, his skills to call upon the elements, to foresee attempts on his life, had been so unused in his adulthood that he hadn't been able to block the blow that killed him. But tonight, he'd tapped into that long-dormant power. Could he do so again? Could he convince the woman on the bed that she was the key to his release?

He sensed a breeze in the room, soft and gentle, flurrying from the fan that swirled above her bed. Another whisper of air blew out in intervals from the grate above the dresser. He concentrated. A ripple fluttered her silk robe aside, exposing her long, naked leg, the curve of her buttock.

Yes, he could use the air, but he needed more.

She stirred, but still slept. He'd been in her house for only two days, but he already knew by heart the soft little noises she made when she dreamed. With every owner of the perfume bottle so far, nearly all female, he'd watched and listened and learned. Just in case one of them released his essence, he'd sought to remain ready, prepared to do whatever possible to retain his corporeal form.

But until this evening, he'd gotten no further than watching and wanting from inside the bottle. Not that observing the conquests of other men—and in one case, other women—excited him, but at least he'd been entertained. Those who possessed the perfume bottle nearly always stored it in their bedrooms, giving Viktor much to observe over the past century.

Now, it was time for him to *have*.

As far as Viktor knew, he had no face, no body. When he smiled, the action was more a shift in his aura than anything else, but he enjoyed the emotion all the same. Nothing fired him quite so powerfully as a hearty dose of desire.

Across the room, on Evonne's bedside table, water trickled over the sides of the small fountain she had turned on before her first attempt at sleep. She'd extinguished the candle at the center of the water, but with a thought from Viktor, the wick flared to life. A flickering flame, centered amid glossy, wet stones, threw erotic shadows on the walls, covered in a verdant green fabric that looked like silk. Viktor chuckled, amazed at how the *gaujo* always sought to steal the peaceful perfection of the outdoors and trap it inside their homes. Had Eve ever slept under the stars, with only a fire to warm her and the sound of a bustling stream to lure her to her dreams?

He doubted so, but he was glad for her attempts tonight. He could use the water, the fire, the wind. Tradition barred him from calling on the spirits for seduction, but Viktor had shunned those customs years ago when his people had betrayed him by giving him to the *gaujo*. He would use whatever power he had at his disposal to free himself of his prison.

Including Eve's power—the ability to speak to the dead.

*Evonne?*

His voice echoed. Tinny. Contained. He concentrated, hoping to contact her while she remained bound by dreams.

*Evonne.*

She stirred, rustling the sheets as she turned so that half her face caught the glimmer from the candle.

With a single shot of thought, he doused the electric lamp beside the bottle. Yes, she looked delicious in candlelight.

*Eve, my love. You're so beautiful. How can I resist you?*

She whimpered.

*How will you resist me? I'll pleasure you beyond all pleasure, if you want me. Show me you want me. Show me.*

Viktor directed a stream of the breeze and coiled it up her bare thigh. She curled her legs closer to her body, loosening the knot of her robe.

He repeated his plea. *Show me.*

With drowsy clumsiness, her hands pulled the robe aside. Her knees partially hid her, but her breasts, which he'd seen before as she'd dressed and undressed over the past forty-eight hours, sapped his breath. Aroused, her nipples were tight, hard and long. Had he a mouth, moisture would have filled it. Oh, to taste the sensitive flesh against his tongue!

Moisture. Yes.

He concentrated again, muttering the charm he'd learned by rote as some children learned nursery rhymes. He focused on the trickling fountain beside her bed, watching with anticipation as the water, a gentle stream skittering down the stones, now gushing with large, fat drops.

*Yes.*

He combined the spells. The wind he commanded grabbed a suspended orb of water and dropped it on her breast, then twirled around the wetness in a tight eddy of air. Like fingertips squeezing.

She gasped, but didn't wake.

Why would she? To wake would mean to stop this luscious dream. He told her so, soothing her with words only she could hear as he stimulated her with his magic.

He repeated the charm twice, then three more times until her skin glistened with streaks of wetness and her silk robe clung to her skin. She turned onto her back and with her knees still drawn against her, he could see shadows of her *yoni*—the tight dark curls, the plump pink lips.

The atmosphere inside the perfume bottle tensed and for a moment, the object that contained him shook. He shook. To the very core of what remained of him, imprisoned in the glass.

*Sweet Eve. You are too tight. Too tense. Enjoy the sensations against your hot skin. You are beautiful beyond reason. Beyond this world.*

With a soft sigh of surrender, she relaxed her legs. Her knees hung over the bed and widened, her toes tickling the carpet below. When Viktor caught full sight of the treasure between her thighs, the water flew from the fountain so furiously, he nearly doused the candle.

He looked away and broke contact, determined to rein in his irrepressible lust. This wasn't about his satisfaction, his need. This was about her. Seducing her. Enticing her. Proving he could give her what no other man could—if only she would release him from his prison. He didn't know how she could accomplish this feat, but with all that remained of his soul, he knew that if anyone had the power, she did.

Again, he focused on the fountain, this time warming a droplet with the candle before placing the moisture in a gentle puddle on her belly. She shifted and a drizzle of wetness worked downward through the curls into her sweet center.

She cooed.

*Yes.*

He warmed another droplet, then another, and another, splashing them in soft intervals on her nipples, her lips, her stomach, her thighs. Still captured by sleep, she writhed against her sheets. Except for her sash, a strip of silk across her stomach, the robe had nearly fallen away entirely. Then her hands began to wander.

*Feel me on your body, sweet Eve.*

He splashed another steaming drop on her nipple,

then twirled the wind around her, imagining his own breath on her skin. Her hand drifted to her breast, her fingers reaching out as if to capture his ghostly caress.

*Touch where I touch. Eve, the pleasure is yours to take.*

He repeated the command several times, and for a moment, he felt a weakening of his connection to her. But when she tweaked her own nipple with one hand, then allowed her other hand to drift between her parted legs, his essence surged.

He sent no more commands into her mind, but instead communicated nothing but the intense eroticism that her actions played on his phantom body. He wove fantastic tales, worthy of his Romani blood, of how her fingers, now dipping deep inside her, mimicked the hard thrust of him, pressing inside her, giving her everything she wanted, making her every wicked sensual fantasy come true. Oh, how he adored her. How he wanted no one other than her. Forever. How he begged to hear his name upon her lips as she came.

She panted, tossed her head from side to side as pleasure battled with sleep, which still held her captive. She drew her knees up again, and when she touched that secret spot deep within her body, a rush of a cry spilled from her mouth.

"Viktor, please," she pleaded and the reverberation of her desperate voice sent the bottle toppling over.

And with a flash of light, Viktor's essence expanded and then like a night mist, completely faded away.

## CHAPTER THREE

IT WASN'T A DREAM.

At least, not completely. Even before Eve opened her eyes to the pale blue light of the impending dawn, she accepted that the sensual thrum beating through her body was real. She stirred. Her muscles cramped and the damp sheets sent a quick flash of cold over her skin.

She reached for the comforter, but couldn't stretch that far. She struggled with her robe, but the tangle of silk was wet and uncooperative. Drawing her hands to her face, she rubbed the sleep away, blinked long enough to find one corner of the comforter still clinging stubbornly to the edge of her bed. Despite the intense ache constricting her body, she grabbed, grunted, then twirled the soft downy fabric around her and decided to go back to sleep.

Then she felt a man's hot stare.

She sat up, her eyes slits, and patted the bed beside her as if she might find a sleeping lover on the mattress. But as it had been for the past year, the bed was empty except for her. She touched her forehead, half expecting to find her skin hot from a temperature. She hugged the comforter tightly. As consciousness completely beat heavy sleep out of her system, she realized what had happened.

She'd had a real live wet dream.

In her sleep, a ghost had made love to her, prodding her with silken words, pleasuring her with warm drops of water, then inspiring her to indulge in some major self-gratification. Not that she hadn't masturbated before, but never at a man's suggestion—and certainly not when the man wasn't alive.

"Viktor?" she asked cautiously. She called his name again, concentrating as much as her muddled mind could. "Viktor?"

No response.

She shook her head, her craving for coffee battling with her need to stay huddled beneath the comforter. When the phone rang, she nearly jumped out of her skin. She forced her hand out of the tangle of bedclothes and grabbed the handset, shaking as she answered it.

"Eve? What's wrong?"

Eve let out a strangled sigh, both happy and

shocked to hear her sister's voice at—she squinted at the clock—five fifteen in the morning.

"Nothing. I don't think." A long yawning moment elapsed before Eve put all the pieces together. "Wait a minute. How did you know something was wrong?"

For a split second, Eve indulged in a surge of hope. She'd been damned annoyed all these years that she was the only Baptiste sister to have inherited strange abilities from their grandmother, a reputed clairvoyant who had died before either girl could meet her. From an early age, Eve had had the ability to communicate with the dead. Her younger sister, Lacey, however, seemed content with speaking only to the living, particularly those who caused other people to be dead. She was a top-notch FBI agent currently assigned to FBI headquarters in Washington, D.C.

"You called," Lacey explained, slowly, as if she was fighting a big yawn herself. "You left a message on my machine."

Eve closed her eyes. Did she call? When? And what had she said? She growled. Why was her brain so addled?

"I did?"

"Does 'Lacey, call me. I have a problem' ring any bells?"

"Vaguely," she admitted, not entirely truthful. She really didn't remember. "I'd probably think more clearly if you'd called after the sun rose."

"Replay that message in your mind again, sis. Like I was going to wait for dawn when you might need me. I've been out on assignment for a week. I just got back five minutes ago and the way your voice sounded worried me."

"Oh," Eve said, once again disappointed that nothing remotely psychic had inspired her sister's call.

Just once, Eve would have liked to discuss her strange ability with a kindred spirit who understood firsthand what it was like to communicate with ghosts. And preferably, she'd like said confidante to be alive, too. The dead understood, but they weren't much help with sorting out the difficulties that often arose for the living when they were trapped between two worlds. Eve had devised her own defense mechanisms to block out the voices—some simple, some complicated, but they usually worked.

Until last night.

"Eve, what's going on?" her sister asked, this time sounding much more like the FBI agent than the little sister who, at eight years old, chained garlic around their bedroom window in case Eve decided to expand her communication talent to vamps and ghouls. "You sound funny. And don't deny it because I'm trained to ferret out liars, remember?"

"Something strange happened last night."

"Something strange is always happening at your house. You should move."

"It wasn't them," Eve insisted, but for the first time since she'd purchased her cottage outside Marietta, Georgia, she wasn't so sure it had been the smartest move. The ghosts of the dead gypsies buried in her backyard where an old plantation used to stand had never acted malevolently toward her. Not that what she'd experienced last night had been the least bit evil, either. In fact, it had been nothing short of deliciously erotic.

Still, a tiny part of her felt intruded upon. And the presence, the voice that had whispered into her mind and made the bawdy suggestions she'd been all too quick to follow up on, had been definitely male. Viktor Savitch? Could he have manifested inside her home? He'd disappeared and likely died nearly a century ago and on another continent. How could he be here, with her?

The only male ghost hanging around her house was the prankster, Nicholai. He couldn't have seduced her. He wouldn't have.

*He didn't.*

With a squeal, Eve dropped the phone. She spun around, knowing she'd heard a voice here, in this room. At least, in this house. Very loud and very male.

And not just in her head, either.

The tiny echo of her sister shouting on the other end of the phone brought Eve back to the problem at hand. She grabbed the discarded handset, wincing. "Sorry, I dropped the phone."

"Eve, what's going on? You're not a jumpy person and I can't remember the last time you called me to ask for help. Do you need me? Because I can get on the next flight to Atlanta."

"Hold on, sis."

Eve took a deep breath, centering her aura. She closed her eyes, watching as a square formed in her mind. The shape altered, became three-dimensional. Then it multiplied. And as the mental tiles grew in number, they started the ritual wall-building. She could block out the voices this way, a method she'd devised as a child while watching her father restore an old wall in their house. She continued to breathe purposefully, stacking the tiles in her mind and after a moment, her heart calmed to a steady beat.

"No, Lacey, you don't need to come. I'm fine." In her newfound serenity, Eve remembered why she'd called her little sister a few days ago. "I just wanted to let you know that I'm not going to meet you and Seth out at Virginia Beach next month. You'll have to make it a romantic weekend for two."

Lacey chuckled. "As if it wasn't going to be one with you there anyway. Seth has his ways, you know. He had it all planned. Fun for you, romance for me."

"Lucky us," Eve said, pushing back those third-wheel feelings again.

"No arguments here. But I thought you were looking forward to some relaxation. This is your first summer off in years. I wanted us to hang out. I want you to get to know Seth."

"I know." Confident she had the spirits at bay, Eve untied the tight knot of her robe and discarded the damp material on the floor. As pink sunlight teased the floor through the slats in her blinds, she hooked the phone between her shoulder and ear and pulled the sheets from her bed. Today just became laundry day. "I've got a special project going. Something fascinating. I can't relax until it's done."

Lacey should buy that. Eve was notorious for filling her time off with researching or writing the scholarly works that had established her as an expert in Romani culture. Her sister would never suspect that her new "project" was something much more personal.

"Bring the project with you," Lacey suggested.

Eve folded her lips inward. If last night was any indication, the bottle had indeed enhanced her ability to communicate with the dead. She needed to stay here, find out as much as she could from Jeta, Nicholai and Alexis about the elusive gypsy king, if they knew him at all. She had to put this obsession to rest or he'd invade her dreams forever.

*Viktor.*

A memory flashed in her mind. His name, spilling from her lips. Desperate. Wanting. Orgasmic. She sucked in a breath. Her gaze darted to her vanity table.

The perfume bottle had toppled over, the top lying beside it. She'd tried a hundred times over the past two days to open the bottle, but if she'd tugged any harder, she'd felt sure she would have broken the glass. The phone still clutched to her ear, she crossed the room and lifted the decorative stopper.

The edges were smooth, uncracked.

Now the bottle was open? On its own? How?

"What the—?"

"Eve?"

Her mind clicked back to her sister. "Sorry, Lacey, I'm distracted this morning. Look, I just can't go, okay? I need to stay here and work from home. My research is here." She forced a smile into her voice, which proved more effective when she swung around, turning her back on the perfume bottle that, until last night, had represented nothing more than a wild attempt to gain insight into a man who no longer existed.

Or did he?

"You and Seth don't need me hanging around, do you?" Eve asked. "We'll schedule another vacation, maybe when I have someone interesting to bring along."

"I thought you swore off men. A year's celibacy to clear your heart, figure out what you really wanted."

Eve snorted. "Yeah, well, my deadline is fast approaching and I'm no closer to the answer to that question than I am to finishing my project."

Without her sister's doubtful tone, Eve had already started to distrust the wisdom of her decision. She was over thirty and had experienced her fair share of lovers and relationships, not one of them seriously near engagement or marriage. Not that she needed the piece of paper or the ring—she just craved the soul mate. Someone who understood her gift, even embraced it. Someone whose presence alone could calm nerves rattled by work, or who would need her to ground his place in the world. Someone who would always surprise her with his intellect, his insights.

Someone who apparently didn't exist.

With all the dating she'd done and the friends she'd amassed, she figured she would have found someone by now. But she hadn't come close, making her suspect that she was, as the song said, looking for love in all the wrong places. She'd decided to take a year to figure out a new plan, clear her head and give her libido a much-needed rest.

Ha!

Luckily for Eve, Lacey knew when to argue with her older sister and when to let topics drop. After vowing to call Lacey back at a more decent hour, Eve hung up. She crossed the room and gently replaced the phone in the cradle.

The minute the device left her hand, a charged crackle surged through the air. For an instant, she enjoyed the play of the current, the sparks dancing over her skin as if a shower of static electricity rained all around her.

Then she realized she wasn't wearing any clothes.

She tensed, grabbed the discarded sheet from the floor, twirled it around her, then turned, only half-prepared for what she might see.

"Such a shame to cover such exquisite beauty."

Eve swallowed a gulp of air. Viktor Savitch stood before her. Despite that she could see partly through his thigh-high boots, long, lean legs, tapered waist, sculpted chest and defiant smile, there was no mistaking the image he projected.

*I am the king.*

Still, she had to be sure.

"Who are you?"

He arched a dark brow and even though his face was half-transparent, his intense blue eyes twinkled.

"You know who I am, Evonne Baptiste."

"How do you know me?"

He leaned back on her vanity and crossed his feet at the ankles. The delicate furniture remained steady under his non-existent weight. "I know you intimately, my sweet."

"That's not what I meant," she snapped. Ghost or not, she wasn't about to let him make her blush, despite the heat flushing her chest.

She drew the sheet tighter.

"There are things I know," he whispered, his voice rich with the brogue of a hundred different cultures. "The minute I came into your home, I learned all I could. What you eat. What you drink. What you dream. It's a habit I've formed."

"When did you come into my home? I didn't invite you."

"I'm not a vampire," he said with a chuckle, crossing his diaphanous arms. "I need no invitation. But, alas, you extended one when you brought my prison into your bedroom."

With concentrated effort, he reached down and flicked his foggy finger on the perfume bottle, knocking it a few inches aside. She gasped at his ability to move a solid object.

"Don't break it!" she commanded.

He eyed her though slits. "I will not return to this prison."

She swallowed, her heart slamming against her chest, not so much with fear for herself, but for him. As she suspected when she'd made the purchase, the glass bottle and Viktor Savitch were inextricably linked, though she'd never imagined how intimately! Had his ghost truly been trapped inside? If he destroyed the bottle, could he possibly inadvertently destroy the part of him that still wandered this Earth?

"You may have no choice," she said coolly. "If you destroy that bottle before we understand your connection to it, you could disappear forever. Is that what you want?"

He paused, clearly considering her warning. She'd always heard he was a clever man, raised in childhood by a legendary gypsy shaman—his grandfather—then later studying with a respected scholar and nineteenth-century chronicler of the Romani ways. She'd been driven to learn about this elusive man by forces she'd never truly understood. But never in her wildest dreams, not even after she purchased the perfume bottle, did she imagine she'd actually meet him—or at least, his essence.

She blinked a few times, then glanced at the window. Daylight was indeed dawning outside. Beneath the sheet, she pinched her arm. It hurt.

This was real. All of it. All of him.

In her entire life, she'd never seen a ghost. Heard them, yes. Thousands of them. But never, except in her dreams, had she ever made visual contact. She'd also never carried on a complete conversation. Snippets, only. Words. Phrases sprinkled between planes to exchange messages with the dead who had not yet left this Earth.

"You are amazing," she said, loosening her grip on the sheet as she walked forward, her arm outstretched. She stopped when her hand was mere centimeters from connecting with his filmy flesh. "Are you real? Are you really Viktor Savitch?"

He lifted his arm, palm up, his ghostly hand hovering just beneath hers. Warmth radiated from him as if he were solid, but an additional, metaphysical vibration sent a streaming reaction along her skin.

"You know I am."

She sucked in a breath. "Why are you here?"

He quirked his head, and a lock of long, dark, sinfully shiny hair dropped half over one of his sapphire eyes. "You beckoned me, Evonne Baptiste."

She shook her head. "How?"

He combed his hair aside with his other hand and glanced to the bed. "You called my name—don't you remember?"

With a start, she snatched her hand back, fisting her fingers against her chest. "No! I mean," she scrambled, remembering quite clearly now that she'd cried out his name with her orgasm, "yes, I called you, but that doesn't explain how you came here."

He dropped his hand. "Fate, perhaps. Luck, definitely."

She bit her lip, nodding, certain this could all make sense if she simply put the facts she knew into a logical progression. For years, she'd known the legendary bottle was tied to Viktor's past. She'd also known that the delicate knickknack had purported magical powers, having been crafted by a family of gypsy artisans skilled in the black arts. However, she'd had no clue, no indication whatsoever, that the soul that was once Viktor Savitch had been trapped inside the glass.

He reached out to her again, breaking her thoughts. Before she could stop herself, she extended her hand as well. The contact was brief, but charged. White heat shot through her body. Her knees quivered so badly, they buckled.

And when she looked up, he was gone.

## CHAPTER FOUR

"DR. BONNIE ANDERS, PLEASE."

Breathless, Eve had had just enough time to throw on a T-shirt, panties and shorts before she'd dug out the phone number of the bottle's previous owner and dialed the number. She couldn't wait. Not for coffee. Not even for a decent hour. It was just after six-thirty in the morning, Eastern Standard Time. For what she'd paid Anders for the bottle, the woman would just have to live with an early morning call.

The man on the other end of the line grumbled sleepily and sexily, something along the lines of, "Just a minute."

Eve swallowed and tried to steady her breathing. This was all too weird. She didn't exactly know what she would gain by this phone call, but before she decided what to do with her newly acquired ghost, she wanted a few facts.

"Hello?"

"Dr. Anders? This is Evonne Baptiste. I'm sorry for calling so early, but I must talk to you about the perfume bottle I purchased."

She heard an annoyed sigh on the other end of the line. "It didn't arrive damaged, did it? You need to contact the shipper. I had it insured, as you requested."

"No, no," Eve insisted. God, her brain was so scrambled, she was going about this all wrong. "I'm so sorry, Dr. Anders. Especially for disturbing you so early. The bottle arrived intact. But when we spoke prior to my wiring you the cash, you told me that you believed the bottle enhanced your own paranormal talent, as the legend said."

"Yes," she confirmed, her voice slightly breathy. In the background, she heard a sexy male mumble and if she wasn't mistaken, kissing noises.

*Aw, geez.* Had she interrupted the doctor during good-morning sex?

"Should I call back? This has to be a bad time."

Bonnie chuckled throatily. "No, please. The bottle spooked you, or you wouldn't have called so early. That's why I tried to explain beforehand, so you wouldn't be caught off guard the way I was."

*Too late.* "The bottle is exactly what you described. But what I need to know is, when you had the bottle, did you see him?"

A pause echoed over the line. "See whom?"

Eve shook her head. This wasn't right either. She tried a different tactic. She wasn't yet ready to admit to anyone, even someone who accepted the existence of paranormal powers, that she'd seen a ghost. A nearly solid, incredibly sensual ghost.

"Did you open the bottle? Dislodge the stopper?"

"No."

"And you never experienced an apparition of any kind while the bottle was with you?"

Eve heard a rustle of sheets, as if what she'd said had made Dr. Bonnie Anders sit up in bed. "No. Have you?"

"Yes."

She didn't hesitate with the truth, and maybe she should have. Eve knew Dr. Bonnie Anders was a psychiatrist. And right now, she was fairly certain the woman was assessing Eve's mental health. But then again, Dr. Anders also accepted the existence of paranormal activity, and Eve had read her articles on the rare existence of kinesthetic sensory perception. Even so, ghosts could be outside her expertise.

"Was the experience frightening?" Bonnie asked.

"No, just disconcerting," Eve answered, though the sweat beading at her temple and the rapid rate of her pulse would seem to make a liar out of her. "But I needed to know if my experience is unique."

"Sorry, no ghosts in my bottle. Apparently, it affects everyone differently. Since you told me you have the ability to speak with the dead, with the bottle in your possession, it's not unreasonable to assume you will see them as well. If this disturbs you, I'll take the bottle back. I had another potential buyer, one that wasn't too happy that I agreed to sell it to you before I gave him another chance to counteroffer."

Eve chuckled, not so certain she felt lucky. "Why'd you pick me?"

The rustle of sheets echoed over the phone line again. "I wanted to pass the object along to another woman, especially since you knew so much about its history. You'd appreciate it, and you were offering quite a bit of money, all of which went to a very good cause."

Eve nodded, remembering that Dr. Anders had sold the bottle to raise funds for a veteran's group. "Again, I'm sorry I woke you. But I think I'll hang on to it. I'll work this out."

"I'm sure you will. Good luck."

With the call disconnected, Eve marched over to the vanity table. The sun now streamed into her bedroom. The minute Viktor had vanished, she'd yanked open the blinds and turned on every light in the room, as well as the floods in the hallway for good measure. Not that sunlight would have any real effect on a ghost. Like Viktor had so charmingly pointed out, he wasn't a vampire. But she couldn't ignore the comfort of bright light, especially now, with the sunbeams glittering off the faceted surface of the bottle.

Though he'd said he wouldn't go back in his prison, she wondered if he'd had any choice. She picked up the base in one hand, the stopper in the other. After a deep breath, she replaced the top. She counted to ten, then removed the stopper. Her eyes darting around the room, she waited for him to materialize.

Nothing.

She couldn't deny that she wanted to see him again. She'd been enthralled with him and his legend for years. His sexual prowess had been legendary and totally counter to what she'd learned from her research on the Romani culture. Unlike modern hippies and bohemians who adopted some gypsy traditions, the Romani did not play fast and free with their sexuality.

But last night! Well, she couldn't deny the power of the experience. Her body still thrummed with the memories. At the first flash of sensual recollection, her nipples hardened, prickling through her shirt. She gave her thighs a little squeeze to squelch the intimate throbbing of her pulse. Her dream had likely been a point-to-point mirror of reality, yet while sleeping, she hadn't visualized Viktor physically present with her.

His voice, not his body, had seduced her. The water and the wind had whipped her into a frenzied storm, aided in the end by her own hands—at his bold suggestions.

And the experience had surpassed deliciousness—and despite her year of celibacy, Eve appreciated the power of sexual intimacy. Great sex had kept her in doomed relationships longer than anything else. She could only imagine how much more enthralling making love to Viktor could be, now that he had near-corporeal form.

She giggled uncharacteristically at the thought, but enjoyed the private joke all the same. Before heading back to the kitchen to brew her coffee, Eve put the bottle on her vanity, but left the top off. If Viktor wanted out again—if he indeed was back inside—she wouldn't deny him. For personal or professional reasons, this could all work out to her advantage.

The minute a past owner of the bottle, a New Orleans policewoman named Caitlyn Raine had contacted her, Eve's interest in possessing the magical heirloom had swelled. Rumors had persisted for years in the European Romani world that the bottle, created by the Romani family that had cursed Viktor

Savitch and perhaps even murdered him, still existed. Before that, the last she'd heard about the bottle was that it had been sold or traded in Glasgow. For years, she'd tried to track down information about the phial and its reputed magical powers, but she'd come up empty until the phone call from Caitlyn, who'd soon after sent the bottle to Dr. Bonnie Anders.

When Bonnie decided to sell the bottle to raise money for the psychiatric care of former soldiers, Eve had seized the opportunity, hoping to enhance her powers, hoping she'd have a clearer flow of communication with the gypsies whose spirits haunted her backyard. From what she could gather from neighborhood histories and the faded headstones, they'd lived in the same time as the gypsy king. She'd hoped that they'd known him. Or known of him.

She never dreamed she'd conjure the man himself.

She only hoped he *would* be back. She frowned. By releasing him this morning, she might have inadvertently helped him cross over. She combed her fingers through her tangle of hair and chided herself for being so selfish. What if that's exactly what he wanted? To cross into the Otherworld? To be free of this prison on Earth?

She stepped into the kitchen, not needing to turn

on any lights, thanks to the bank of glittering windows on the eastern wall of the house.

"He did not cross over."

The voice made her jump, but Eve wasn't entirely surprised to see the ghostly outline of an aged Romani woman sitting at her small oak kitchen table. As Dr. Bonnie had predicted, the bottle allowed Eve to see the spirit she'd previously only spoken to in brief, broken phrases.

"Jeta?" she gasped.

The woman smiled, nodding her head so that the beads woven into the kerchief tied saucily around her head tinkled. The sound seemed to echo, as did her voice. Just as it had once done only in Eve's head.

"This is powerful magic you've unleashed into your home. Powerful black magic."

Her frown was so pronounced, Eve could see the lines around Jeta's mouth clearly, though she could also see her refrigerator through the woman's partially transparent face.

"Is Viktor evil?"

Jeta shrugged and her hands rose gracefully like doves taking flight from her lawn in the morning. "Some say yes. Others would say his ways were wicked, even if his goals were true."

No longer startled or afraid, Eve slid into the chair

across from Jeta. This was what she'd wanted! This was why she'd cleared out her savings to purchase the bottle in the first place. To have a clear, uninterrupted conversation with this woman from the past.

"Did you know him?"

Jeta shook her head. "No, child. The Romani live all over the world. I was born in France, though I lived in just about every land of Europe before I came as an old woman to America with Nicholai and Alexis."

"They're related to you?"

So many questions swelled in Eve's brain, she knew she couldn't stay in a linear conversation if it killed her. She'd found so little information about the gypsies buried in her backyard. Most of her research came from apocryphal stories passed down by the Georgia families that had lived in and around Marietta since before the Civil War. Rumors of magic, prejudice and murder.

"Nicholai is my grandson. Alexis, well, she is his cousin. She had the gift of Sight, as did I. Nicholai was a great craftsman with wood. A carpenter."

"If you didn't know Viktor, how do you know his story?"

"Ah! The gypsies love a good tale, don't we? His life was short, but his story traveled far and wide. His demise at the hand of a black witch is the stuff of legend."

Eve nodded. The Romani people, with their strong oral tradition and growing written one, would embrace legends as bold and dark as the tale of Viktor Savitch. Such a story had the strength of drama to travel continents.

"You're sure he hasn't crossed over?" she asked, remembering Jeta's first statement.

Jeta's chest puffed and her eyes drifted closed, as if she was concentrating intently. "He is near. And crossing over is not what he wishes." She remained still, quiet for a few moments longer. Then again, she smiled. "Yes. I understand."

"What? What do you understand?" Eve's voice crackled with desperation.

When Jeta's eyes opened, Eve was startled by the brilliant gloss of her dark irises, like polished onyx. "He died violently. At another's hand and before his time. Like me. Like Alexis and Nicholai. Our spirits hope some day to rest, and we could, if we wished to leave. But those of us who remain on this Earth truly want something more."

A chill crept along the back of Eve's neck, so powerful she touched the spot behind her ear where the coldness originated.

"What? What do you want? What does Viktor want?"

Jeta reached out, much as Viktor had done less than an hour ago. Eve willed herself to keep her hand flat on the table. The aura of Jeta's hand emanated heat just as Viktor's had. The same tingle tickled over her skin, though this time, the soft, soothing effect calmed her, as if she'd been touched by an angel, rather than the devil himself.

"He wants to cheat death," Jeta answered. "His will is to reclaim the life he should have lived. And he needs you to help him."

# CHAPTER FIVE

VIKTOR LISTENED INTENTLY to the old woman. Yes, she understood completely. Maybe in the beginning, he'd merely wanted the freedom to cross into the Otherworld, to reconnect with his lost ancestors, to speak to his grandfather and beg forgiveness for adopting *gaujo* ways to control his wayward clan. But death had never suited him. He'd accepted the inevitable would occur, of course, but he'd had no desire to yield to murder. Besides, with her magic, his killer had made sure he couldn't cross.

She'd guaranteed that he'd spend an eternity imprisoned in glass and silver so lovely and intriguing, any woman who saw it would have to possess it. In that way, his tormentor ensured his continued torture. Beautiful, sensual, alluring women owned him. He could watch them, day and night, yet he couldn't have them. Couldn't touch them. Couldn't practice the many modes of seduction he'd utilized as king of his gypsy clan.

But now he could. He had. And yet, while the experience of making love, as it were, to Eve had made him visible, Viktor felt ever so slightly thinner. Less substantial, when the opposite should have been true. He had no doubt that his existence outside the bottle was only temporary. If he wanted to reclaim his solid form—which he craved beyond any other desire— he had to act now.

He slipped out from the stream of sunlight that had kept him hidden.

"Ah, I wondered when you would reveal yourself," the old woman said with a clever twinkle in her dark eyes. Instantly, she reminded him of his grandmother and he bowed in deference.

"How could I stay away from a creature as beautiful and responsive as our dear Evonne?"

Coyly, Eve glanced over her shoulder. Her eyes revealed nothing. The old woman laughed heartily and stood, though it was hard to tell since she was so tiny. Her shoulders were stooped, her body old and infirm as it had been when life was taken from her. But her gaze was sharp as a blade and Viktor knew to hold her in high esteem.

"You've studied my people," the old woman said

to Eve, slicing a cursory glance at him. "I don't have to warn you about the tongue of a gypsy man, do I?"

Eve turned away, blushing. "No, Jeta. I'll be cautious."

"Good. I won't be far."

And with that, she scooted across the room toward the door. The minute she passed through sunlight, she completely disappeared.

Eve inhaled, then released a long breath. "And our culture believes ghosts hide in the shadows."

Viktor chuckled, then moved so he could watch her face. She was beautiful beyond words, even with her eyes puffy and shadowed from lack of sleep. Her cheeks retained the sweet pink tinge of a woman who'd recently experienced skillful lovemaking. Even without the use of his hands, Viktor had made this woman call his name. The fact should have made him feel stronger, but instead, he was overcome by a wave that made his form flicker.

"Are you all right?" she asked, her hands braced on the edge of the table.

Viktor locked his gaze with hers. Her eyes were a golden, honey-brown, just a shade lighter than her hair, which fell in waves just beyond her shoulders. He must have lost some of the subtlety he used to master, because she looked away and attempted to run one hand through her hair while the other clamped the opening of her robe.

"I'm free, am I not?" he answered, choosing to ignore the fluttering sensation still waffling all around him. Being visible had an advantage, but outside the bottle, in the light, he felt like a vapor, a mist. He missed his body, his heartbeat, his power. He wanted them back. Today. And he'd do whatever it took to have his wish.

"How are you free?" she asked. "Or I suppose I should back up and ask how were you trapped in the first place? Jeta said you were murdered."

He crossed his arms over his chest. "Jeta is not of my clan. Nor of any other I've crossed paths with."

"She said your story was passed around, and she's right. I've found references to your demise, but mainly, just rumors that you disappeared. Some said you returned to live with the British professor, Richard Davenport-Dunn, who had taken you in as a child, but that wasn't true. His wife kept meticulous journals until the end of her life. She mentioned you in her early works. If you'd gone back, she would have mentioned you later as well."

He kept his grin inscrutable. "Ah, Lady Lynette. A vicious creature, too shrewd and clever to be trapped in a woman's body."

Eve did not seem to take offense, but instead, her gaze softened. "Sir Richard cared for her, and for you, very much. He never wanted you to leave, did you know that?"

He cleared the tightness in his throat with a cough. "Sir Richard wrote of me?"

Evonne popped up from her chair and disappeared through a doorway. He sensed he could transport himself into the adjoining room by simply concentrating on her aura and connecting with it, but she returned before he could try.

She tossed a dusty book on the table. The lettering was faded, but still glittered with flecks of gold. He'd learned to read English and the title caused him to frown.

*The Little Wanderers.*

"He wrote an entire book about the many children who passed through his home. But you were the first—"

"Sir Richard loved his work above all else," he commented, knowing his claim wasn't entirely true. He owed the educated Englishman for many a kindness, niceties the angry teenaged Viktor had never received with graciousness. Even now, when he realized the generosity of this stranger, Viktor couldn't completely discard the rage he'd harbored for having to live away from his family, his people.

For reasons Viktor still could not understand, he'd been sent away to honor a promise made between Sir Richard and his grandfather shortly before the *Chovihano*'s death. He doubted Jacques Savitch, his mentor and beloved *purodad,* knew what Viktor would learn in the Englishman's household, particularly from Lady Lynette, Sir Richard's ignored and insatiable wife.

"Sir Richard cared for you a great deal," Eve insisted. "He wrote of your departure when your uncle died."

"The leadership of the clan fell to me."

She flipped through the pages as if looking for something in particular. "He wrote that the clan was in great disarray, with much infighting. Several family members had broken away from the clan, only to be persecuted by the *gaujo.* He supposed if you hadn't gone, the clan might have dispersed or been destroyed."

"He was right."

Viktor forced his stare to remain on the book, but his mind wandered back to the discord and despair he'd found when he'd returned to his clan. During his ten-year absence, many clansmen had left. They barely had sufficient craftsmen and entertainers among them to earn enough to feed the children. With no *chovihano,* the sick had died or at least, never recovered. Only days after he'd taken the leadership of the clan, his cousin Marco had announced that he'd married a *gaujo* woman and intended to live with her in her village. In the interest of avoiding conflict, Viktor had let him go.

Only a year later, Marco's *gaujo* wife sought out the clan, half-starved and beaten. Marco had been hanged—wrongly accused of raping a village girl. Their only child had been stolen from them in restitution. Without his family, without the power of the clan, Marco had been alone. This lesson taught Viktor that survival meant keeping his family together. At all costs.

Eve's gaze met his and perhaps sensing his bitterness, she shut the book. "You succeeded in keeping your clan together, until you disappeared."

"Ten years later," he said. "The clan was intact. Powerful. We traveled to many lands together, collected enough wealth to keep our children fat and healthy. The *gaujo* we met looked forward to our return, depended on us to repair their wagons and adorn their homes and clothing. They healed our sick. I spoke their language, knew their customs. We created a trust."

She smirked. "An illusion of trust. Romani never truly trust the *gaujo*. Not really. We're like two different species—cats and dogs—rather than two different cultures in the human race. At least, that's what you would have been taught, true?"

He nodded. She did indeed understand how his people thought, how they'd thought for the thousands of years since they'd migrated out of India, escaping persecution after persecution by creating elaborate tales for the non-gypsies they met along the way. His ancestors told stories of a valiant pilgrimage out of mystical Egypt, full of pageantry and drama and magic and very little truth. They mimicked the Christian ways when necessary, adopted the rituals of other religions when it would keep them fed and out of prisons. The Romani adapted to the land and to the *gaujo* who could often make the difference whether they lived or died.

And to Viktor, they'd done more. From Richard Davenport-Dunn and his society, Viktor had learned the power of a woman's lust. Though the men strutted to their parliament and to their political meetings puffed up with self-importance, Viktor had spied a wondrous truth. A man besotted by a sensual woman would do anything for her. Sir Richard adored Lady Lynette so completely, he never realized that her encouragement for him to study the gypsies was a complex ploy to satisfy her carnal obsession with his people, particularly the handsome boys.

"That is the lesson I learned of the *gaujo* and the Romani," he admitted. "You know the truth."

"I've studied your culture," she explained. "I have a great deal of respect for it. My great-great-grandfather married a gypsy woman. He rescued her from a prison cell in Avignon, France, shortly before he immigrated to the United States through New Orleans, Louisiana."

Viktor grinned. He'd recently been in New Orleans, with a woman who seemed entirely unnerved by the presence of the bottle. As a result, she'd sent him away quickly. Not that he blamed her. His prison possessed magical properties that while harmless to the average owner, could wreak havoc with someone who had sorcery in their veins. From the moment Caitlyn Raine had removed the bottle from the charmed casket that cradled it, he'd sensed the presence of something mystical in her, but she hadn't had the power to release him. Neither had her friend, the doctor. Only Eve could set him free. Completely free.

"New Orleans brims with the magic of many cultures," Viktor concluded, knowing he had to bide his time before he broached the topic of his release with this alluring, but cautious woman. "I should like to return there."

"You remember New Orleans?"

"I've been aware of my travels since the beginning. I likely could not catalogue where I've been, but I could relay impressions, maybe describe a scent or a sound from every woman who's ever owned the bottle."

She licked her lips as he spoke, and Viktor thought he might go mad. Knowing she had gypsy blood, even a small dash of it, increased her power over him, like it or not. Yes, he'd manipulated many gypsy women in his regrettably short life, but inevitably, it was a gypsy woman who'd done him in.

"None of the women before me could release you?"

"No."

He watched her throat undulate as she swallowed. "And you never made love..."

"No," he answered, with a sly grin. He'd never dreamed he could have experienced something so enchanting as last night with Eve, especially not while still trapped in his prison. He could only imagine what they might accomplish now that he was, at least partially, free of the curse. "I wanted to, many times. The things I saw, trapped in women's bedrooms. The lovers they took. The secret fantasies they brought to life. I was like a child trapped outside a candy store."

She rolled her eyes, apparently unimpressed. *Gaujo* women today were entirely more apt to show and voice their displeasure than in his lifetime. Before, he'd associated such brazenness only with the women of his kind, women who understood the powerful magic they possessed that could make a man's life either paradise or perdition.

And yet, he thrilled at learning that Evonne Baptiste had Romani blood in her veins. The knowledge elevated her, made her an equal match. She was no simple *gaujo* woman to be finessed and beguiled to do his will. No, she had powers she couldn't begin to understand. Powers he could help her harness, control. Before he moved on, he would leave her stronger than before.

The challenge invigorated him.

Shyly, she drew her hand to her chest. "You're still quite the lover, even without a body. That was some maneuver, manipulating my dream, the water and the candle. I can't wait to see what other tricks you have up your, um, sleeve."

Her gaze locked with his, and the pink he'd noticed on her cheeks earlier bloomed bright and brazen. She blushed and she didn't care that he knew. She was bold, this one, but her audacity came more from her will than from deep within her soul.

Something stirred at this realization. Attraction? Lust? Most definitely. In huge quantities. But something more...as if someone whispered an important secret in his ear, but too softly for him to hear.

"You weren't afraid," he reminded her.

"Is that why you could—" she hesitated as she searched for the right word to describe what they'd shared "—contact me and not the others who've owned you?"

"Others who have owned the *bottle*, you mean. Perhaps," he mused, certain she understood that a man like Viktor Savitch could neither be owned nor contained. His release had only been a matter of time and patience. And, apparently, sexual desire.

"Have you spoken to the others?" he asked.

She shook her head. "Only to Bonnie."

"Did she help him?"

"Who?"

"The soldier?" Viktor answered, remembering the instant respect he'd felt for the man who'd ended up in Bonnie's bed. His wounds ran deep, and yet he faced the world with the humor and sense of adventure worthy of any Romani. "Her gift was one I'd never seen, except in a *chovihano* my grandfather once knew. A true healer."

"I don't know if she helped him," Eve answered,

clearly perplexed, and if he didn't mistake the slight tilt of her head, curious. "I can find out."

Viktor slid into the chair where the old woman had sat earlier. Her presence had been a great surprise to him. The Romani people had many rituals to ensure that their dead crossed to the Otherworld and as far as Viktor had been taught, gypsies were not apt to haunt the living, though they could be contacted by those with the gift. In all these years, he'd guessed he was the only Romani spirit trapped here. He longed to hear the story of the old woman and the others she'd mentioned, but that would wait. Now, he had more pressing interests.

He folded his hands in front of him casually, denying the urge that pushed him to attempt to touch Eve again. When he had this morning, he'd dispersed, shocked out of organized form, at least for a moment or two. The effect had been disorienting, and despite a century of captivity, he hadn't adapted to not being in control. He wasn't sure what had happened, but until he knew, he wasn't prepared to take another risk.

Still, the ache to touch her, to inch his fingers across the tabletop nearly made him forget the direction of their conversation.

"No need—I believe she achieved her goal. And after one hundred years of captivity, I'm more interested in my own future. There are so many possibilities now that you've broken the witch's hex." At her questioning look, he explained, "At the moment of my death, she cast a spell that trapped the essence of who I was, who I am, in that cursed bottle."

Eve's lips parted in a tiny gasp. Was it his imagination or did her slight intake of breath seem to sap the air around him?

She combed both hands through her hair, tugging hard enough on the roots for Viktor to realize the gesture was out of frustration more than from a quest to tame the wild strands.

"How? Such magic—"

"—is real. You know. You *can* speak to the dead."

She smirked again. "Wasn't much of a two-way conversation last night, Viktor."

With a strange sense of familiarity fueling her humor, Viktor matched her sardonic smile. And he so enjoyed the sound of his name on her lips. He'd liked it last night, and even more so now, spoken with such comfortable confidence. The woman inspired an admiration he'd never known before. She showed so little fear and faced unknowns with directness and humor. She was indeed the very woman who could beat the curse into submission, once he figured out how.

"Believe me, Evonne Baptiste, if I could have taken form, touched you, whispered so my breath curled around your ear, I would have."

Practically of their own accord, his fingers inched toward hers again. She sat back in her chair, but her hands remained flat against the tabletop. When they were nearly fingertip to fingertip, the urgent sound in her voice stopped his forward motion.

"How did you die?"

He flashed his gaze at her, then dropped his stare back to her fingers. Her nails were short, clean and polished with a rich gloss. Her fingers were long, lean and delicate. Her skin looked so warm, so inviting, he could practically feel his mouth watering in anticipation of her taste.

"How else does a man like me die?" he asked, his voice sounding far away and dreamy, as if spoken by someone else. He knew he shouldn't take the chance, but the connection forged between them last night was too powerful to resist.

He concentrated all of his force into his hands, then grabbed her. The magic held. She gasped, but unlike this morning, he didn't vanish. He remained at the table, her hands clutched in his.

"I died at the hand of a beautiful woman, a woman very much like you."

## CHAPTER SIX

EVE KNEW SHE SHOULD feel afraid, but no emotion stood a chance against the swarm of intense desire shooting through her every vein, her every nerve, her every sense. Need became a scent swirling around her nose, peppery and enticing, like a spicy exotic dish cooked over an open fire. Her eyelids drifted down against a smoky backdraft and instantly, flames formed in front of her. Night sounds rushed her ears. Crickets, music. A jovial accordion, perhaps a weeping violin. The instant she registered how her mouth had dried, the tingle of rich, sweet wine blossomed on her tongue.

Scenes from his life, perhaps? Maybe...the night of his death?

"What are you showing me?" she asked.

"What you wish to see."

"You can't read minds," she insisted, not entirely certain that her claim was true.

"You know who I was, Evonne Baptiste. The grandson of Jacques Savitch, the powerful *chovihano*. I can tap into the mysteries of the Otherworld, if I'm so inclined."

She swallowed. According to stories, Jacques Savitch had controlled his unruly tribe with magic for nearly forty years. A true shaman healer, he reportedly anchored his family to Romani traditions so tightly, he spread peace and tranquility to all who sought his counsel. But neither his son nor his daughter had shown talent for the arts of the ancients, and without someone to pass the gifts to, all could have been lost. Luckily, his grandson, Viktor, had shown great promise. But according to legend, Viktor never achieved *chovihano* status and even after he returned to his clan, never again attempted the shaman arts. So why now?

"Did Jacques teach you to use your gift for seduction?" she asked. She hadn't opened her eyes, but she felt his essence shift, as if her question unnerved him. Served him right. Though she hadn't moved from her spot at the kitchen table, she could feel cool grass and rich earth beneath her feet.

"I was young when he died," Viktor answered curtly. "He claimed to have sent me to the *gaujo* so that I understood their threat to our traditions." He shrugged. "I do not know. Yet by the time I returned to lead my clan, I was very different."

Her eyes flashed open. He watched her without blinking, his expression solid as stone. His chin was square and rugged and his skin, though gleaming with an ethereal light, retained his swarthy gypsy pigment. His nose gave his face just the right dash of angular sharpness, but his eyes truly set him apart. Deep-set and hypnotic, his irises flashed with blue flame. The regret in his voice, spoken through generous lips, clashed with the need in his gaze. He wanted her. Again.

Like last night, only this time, he'd give her more.

"You used your magic to seduce me. Powerful stuff. Why couldn't you use your magic to set yourself free?"

Again, her eyelids filled with lead and drifted down, blocking out his see-through image and replacing it with a very solid, breathtaking representation of the man he'd been on the night he died. He was dressed in sleek black pants, boots and a dark blue shirt that captured the rich color of his eyes. His vest, embroidered with a rainbow of threads, glittered in the firelight. He wore a frown that made his eyes stormy and his lips were drawn into a tight line. A man, dressed similarly, had just whispered something in his ear.

Eve swallowed thickly. "Where are we?"

"New Forest, just outside Southampton and Bournemouth. My clan had traveled there for a festival. We had craftsmen among our numbers, but the storytellers, seers and musicians were our stock and trade."

She nodded, certain he was showing her the night of his death. Legend placed Viktor's last appearance in New Forest in southern England.

"Is this a memory?" she asked, her voice a hoarse whisper.

"I'm showing you what happened that night."

In her mind, she watched him march through the encampment, joy and celebration all around him, and yet, she could hear the sounds echo as if the happiness was miles away. His scowl dominated the scene, which suddenly went black the minute he stepped into the leafy darkness on the forest's edge.

"Were you attacked?" she asked with a gasp, but after a moment, the scene refocused. He'd traveled some distance, to a single dark *vardo,* a traditional Romani wagon. A fire crackled outside, but no one sat near. Anticipation and fear, muted as if her ears were stuffed with cotton, made the scene painful to watch. Was he walking into an ambush? Did he know his attackers? Did he die slowly? By someone's hand or by magic?

Suddenly, she heard his footsteps crunching over the dried leaves and twigs beneath his boots. That was the only sound, until the wagon door swung open and a woman glided down.

She was dark-skinned, like Viktor, and her hair, black as the night, draped her shoulders like a shawl. The minute she spotted Viktor, she rushed him. Eve braced for the impact.

She felt only a slight shudder.

"Viktor! Why have you come?"

"I will not make the marriage, Iliana."

The woman's black eyes, lined with kohl, widened to rival the shape of the full moon. "You can't mean it, Viktor. You made the promise."

Iliana had whispered, but the power of the desperate fury behind the words echoed like a shout.

"I cannot honor my words. It was wrong of me to make that pledge. I will not condemn Yuri. I will not bring your *bengesko yak* into my family."

Eve knew the word. The evil eye. And this was not an accusation gypsies tossed around lightly. She remembered the crest on the wooden box where she'd found Viktor's bottle—the mark of the Dulas, a family reputed to have culled great skill in the dark magical arts. Was this Iliana one of them?

"We are powerful, Viktor, but with me, your

power will be infinite. Once I wed Yuri, you will have a mighty ally. Your wayward family will stay together. That's what you want, isn't it? What you crave?"

In the background, Eve heard Viktor's voice, muted and far away. It took her a moment to realize he was speaking to her from her world in the present time, not to Iliana in this strange half-memory, half-dream.

"Yuri was my cousin. The eldest of six boys, each more desperate to leave the clan than the other. Yuri was a widower, and the next in line to rule. He held sway over the part of the family I was having the most trouble controlling."

With a rapid succession of blinks, Eve returned to the present and watched Viktor's face harden with anger.

"Sounds very political," she said. "There was dissent among your clan. Since you had gone to live with the *gaujo*, you weren't entirely trusted by the men in your family. Not everyone agreed you should rule them. Many wanted to leave."

Viktor nodded. "The family was large, extended. Some had already left, others wanted to turn from the old life and embrace the *gaujo* way. They'd lost the magic of the ancients and it had been replaced by greed for possessions. I had to keep them together. I owed it to my grandfather."

Eve's eyes drifted closed and she watched Iliana fling her arms around Viktor and rub suggestively against his body. He tried to push her away, but she persisted, begged. Made lewd promises that jarred even Eve's sexually liberated ears.

"Had you seduced her first, before you betrothed her to Yuri?" she asked.

"Not in the sense you mean," he answered. "I charmed her. Led her to believe she was the most beautiful woman I'd ever met—that gifting her to my cousin in marriage was a great honor. I knew even Yuri could not resist her and that her power would help hold my family together. This, she knew. And yet, she misunderstood my personal attention."

Eve bit her lip, trying to fight the urge to watch as Iliana tore Viktor's vest from his chest and forced her hands into his shirt.

She distracted herself from the scene with more questions, knowing she had to fill in the blanks of the legend of Viktor Savitch. "She wasn't the only one, either, was she?"

"The others understood. The others took the passions I inflamed to their marriage beds. Satisfied husbands do not wish for more than they have. If I'd learned one useful thing during my exile, I learned that while women possessed no political power, they wielded great influence with their mates, particularly in the bedroom. The best way to ensure the cohesive continuation of my clan was to arrange strong gypsy marriages for the young men, the ones who burned most to break away from centuries of tradition."

In the dream, Viktor pushed Iliana away, this time with decisive force. Suddenly, a fog blocked out the action, though Eve could have sworn she saw movement behind them, as if a crowd had approached before Viktor's thoughts turned away from that scene.

"So you charmed young girls and then married them off to your clansmen?"

He chuckled, but the sound lacked humor. "Hardly young girls, Evonne. Widows, wives abandoned by their husbands with children to feed and protect. Women who knew the pleasures of the flesh. They didn't need me to show them, just to remind them of their beauty and innate feminine power."

"But Iliana—"

He interrupted her question with a flash of light that threw her back into the phantom scene. Viktor struggled against the arms and legs of four huge men, one gripping each of his arms and legs. A fifth wrangled a rope around his neck. A sixth man approached, just as burly and dark as the others, and placed the stump of a tree into the space between Viktor's legs.

"Don't be a fool, Iliana. You have the power to kill me, but nothing more," Viktor spat.

Iliana Dulas grinned at him, showing teeth that seemed a tad too sharp around the edges.

"You are correct, Viktor. I do not have the power to curse you as you deserve. So I will steal some magic from you."

A host of others swarmed around her. A young boy slammed a drum and a teenage girl shook a beribboned tambourine. Three old women, chanting, stood behind Iliana, who took a small pouch from one of the crones and tossed it into the fire. Sparks flashed and even over the distance of time, Eve nearly choked on the scent of burning sulfur.

The chanting grew louder as Iliana lent her voice to the song. She writhed in sensual undulations and the beating of the drum and quiver of the tambourine increased the cadence. With another flash, one of the old women stepped forward and placed a small wooden box on the tree stump in front of Viktor. She opened the casket and withdrew the intricately crafted bottle—the same one now sitting on Eve's vanity table.

Eve gasped, but the sound died quickly when the third old woman produced a thick-bladed knife. The blade captured the firelight and Eve's heart pounded as if she was there, afraid of what might happen— what she knew would happen.

She tried to close her eyes against the image, but realized her lids were squeezed tight. She didn't want to see more. She didn't want to see him die.

"Stop," she said.

Viktor didn't respond. Iliana sprang forward. Her eyes glowing with red-hot malice, she lifted the knife, chanting, swaying, chattering so that Eve thought she might lose her mind.

"Stop!"

The image popped out of her mind. Eve forced her eyes open and inhaled as if she never thought she'd breathe again.

Viktor leaned back into the chair, no longer touching her, his expression nearly inscrutable.

"Why so squeamish? You know what happened," he reasoned.

Eve shook her head. "I don't have to see your murder firsthand to understand the injustice. Was that your intention?"

He quirked a ghostly brow. "You are clever, Evonne."

She rolled her eyes. Yeah, real clever. She'd spent her savings to buy an object brimming with evil and black magic, an object made powerful with the blood of the murdered man sitting so calmly across from her, the same man who'd brought her incredible pleasure the night before. All to satisfy an intellectual and physical obsession?

Clever? Not exactly the word she'd choose.

# CHAPTER SEVEN

"So she stabbed you?"

Viktor shifted, his ghostly leg creaking, spiking with pain from the past. The shock and revulsion in her voice, the horror in her eyes, touched a part of him he'd long set aside—the part of him that hoped someone, somewhere, had mourned his death.

"She bled me, like a hog for slaughter. She used the blood to feed her hex. My body died slowly, allowing her time to trap my essence. She then charmed the bottle by enclosing it in the box, which was also protected by black magic. I would have been imprisoned for all time, I believe, if not for you."

Eve threaded her fingers into her hair, her palms pressing against her scalp, her head shaking back and forth involuntarily, as if she didn't want to believe—but did.

"Viktor, that's a horrible way to die. I'm very sorry."

He snorted derisively. "I don't want pity."

She glared at him, clearly insulted. "I'm offering you compassion. But if you don't want it..."

He glanced aside, suddenly needing to focus on anything but Eve. His eyes skimmed over the mismatched rugs she'd tossed all around her kitchen and the nicks in the polished wood floor. Viktor hadn't expected such emotional empathy from her. Their existences had been separated by centuries. He never imagined that anyone in his own time had truly grieved for his absence or his exit as leader. If they'd attempted to avenge him, the act would have sprung more from duty than outrage. He'd broken tradition, spit in the face of the spirits with his manipulations and schemes. And worse, he'd known all along exactly what he was doing.

He'd often wished he could blame his actions on misguided loyalty and desperation for his clan—but the truth remained that he'd hatched his plans of seduction out of bitter stubbornness. He'd been angry that his family had sent him away and for the price of their betrayal, he would not let them have what they wanted most—freedom to choose a new life. Had it taken one hundred years for him to learn the error of his ways?

He moved out of the chair, away from the table, away from Eve's soulful eyes. He drifted to the window, knowing the sunlight would mask his form as he looked out onto her expansive and verdant lawn.

"I apologize," he said after a long moment of yearning to feel the grass on his feet, the sun on his back. If he could go outside, would he feel anything? "Your compassion is more than I deserve."

She joined him, pressing her hands against the counter. "You didn't deserve to die."

Eve rubbed her face, and the circles beneath her eyes seemed darker than before. She'd done nothing to deserve this angst, but he needed her help. She'd free him. Could she do more? Or would he merely haunt her forever? Haunt this house, the scene of his release? Would he cross into the Otherworld? Or would he simply fade away?

None of those options was acceptable. He wanted to live again and Eve might be the key. He knew it. She could speak to the dead. When she'd called his name, he'd escaped. Perhaps if she did more than call his name, he could live again. This sort of magic was not unheard of in his culture. He'd been taught that women possessed powers men simply could not fully understand.

He turned to speak to her, but her gaze was lost in the bucolic scene outside, her brow scrunched in confusion. "I don't understand. Why did she kill you? Why didn't she just use her magic to control you?"

Again, his hands ached to reach out and touch the

woman beside him. Her allure was powerful, beyond physical lust, as much as he hated to admit that, even to himself. She fascinated him. So intelligent, sensual and sensitive. So open to accepting his pain as her own. So compliant to the realities of the magic that flowed through this world like the water of the oceans—timeless and beautiful, yet brimming with potential for disaster. Evonne Baptiste was precisely the kind of woman he might have finally chosen for himself a century ago—if he'd lived long enough.

Finally, she turned her weary eyes on him. "What did you mean when you told Iliana that she had the power to kill you, but nothing more?"

"I hadn't practiced shamanism for years," he explained, impressed that she'd picked up on the nuance. "But I was, thanks to the blood of my ancestors, too powerful for her spells and charms. Only in death, only with my own blood woven into the hex, could she truly punish me."

For a moment, Viktor thought he spied disbelief in Evonne's honey-gold eyes. She likely never thought anything so hellish was possible, she of her "civilized" *gaujo* ways. When her mouth curved into a frown, Viktor knew her doubts would not waylay her belief. After all, there was no reason not to believe him—a ghost standing beside her in her kitchen, showing her scenes from his past like flashbacks in a film, opening his heart and for the first time, telling a woman the entire truth that resided there.

"Punish you for what? Charming her? Treating her like a woman that men would desire? She didn't look so innocent and gullible to me, if you don't mind me saying so."

He chuckled. One flash of memory and Eve had understood Iliana completely.

"The Dulas clan was marked with evil. None of the other families would marry their women or take their men as husbands. They were dying out. I mistakenly believed the cohesiveness of the Dulas would help my family, but I was wrong."

"Would they have denounced the black arts?" she asked.

He shook his head. "It had been their way for too long."

"Why'd you even think of promising her to Yuri, then?"

Viktor suppressed a growl, an animalistic protest to his own outrageous pride. "I never should have accepted the offer of the Dulas to wed their daughter to my cousin. But I thought if any woman possessed the power to seal my hold over the clan, it was Iliana."

"But you changed your mind?"

Viktor nodded. Yes, he'd finally come to reconsider his dark plan, but too little, too late. "Yuri came to me the night before my murder with a young girl on his arm. He asked for my permission to wed her. He not only finally acknowledged my sovereignty over the clan, but he asked for my blessing."

Eve scratched her cheek absently. "Yuri appealed to your pride."

"He was a smart man."

"So you broke your word to the Dulas on his behalf. And Iliana was pissed."

He'd heard the phrase before, but the vulgarity didn't begin to describe the wrath of the Dulas witch. "Enough to kill."

"And now you want revenge?"

Viktor couldn't control the deep laughter that burst from his chest and mouth. "Revenge? For a crime over a hundred years old? No, I only want to reclaim what was stolen from me."

Eve licked her lips and her lids seemed even heavier than before. "Your life."

"Yes."

"And you think I can help you?"

"Yes."

"Why?"

"Because you freed me from the bottle. Because

by letting me into your bed, you strengthened me." He spun toward her and clutched her arms. He could feel her, but not feel her. The sensations wavered, as they should, between the realities of two distinct worlds— the world of the living and the world of the dead. "When we touch, a power surges through me. Sometimes, it weakens me. Sometimes, strengthens. The fact remains that magic is at work—because of you."

In response to his dramatic claim, she yawned. Long and wide and only as an afterthought did she lift her hand to her mouth. He nearly laughed again. Here he was, laying out the plan for his ultimate reentry into the world of the living and she was falling asleep.

"Sorry," she said, hardly sheepish.

He chuckled, genuinely. Warmth pooled where his belly should have been. He released her. "No apologies. Your lack of rest is entirely my doing."

She nodded. "You're right. I need a nap."

She pushed away from the counter and shuffled toward the door that led to her bedroom. Viktor moved to follow, but she stopped him with a flat palm and a stern look.

"Oh, no. I need *sleep*. I need to think. But mostly, I need to be alone. I don't think you're going anywhere you don't want to go, at least for a few hours."

Viktor grinned. He recognized her need for rest,

for space. Besides, he longed to explore his new boundaries, if there were any, of his transitional existence. Perhaps he could find the old woman or the companions she spoke of.

"I will not come to you until you call."

With that, he closed his eyes and with a forceful push, disappeared from her sight.

EVE STOOD IN THE KITCHEN, her entire body growing heavier by the minute. If she didn't retreat to her bedroom soon, she feared she'd collapse right there. Never before had she found communicating with the dead so exhausting, but the minute she flopped onto her bare mattress, she fell instantly asleep.

She didn't dream. When she woke, the sun was beginning its descent into sunset. Her head ached, but despite the discomfort, she turned toward the clock. Five o'clock. Her stomach growled. With care, she sat up, and after a few lungfuls of air, life and energy seeped back into her bones, veins and muscles. She showered and washed her hair. She fixed a peanut butter sandwich with chocolate milk, which she ate while staring out the window onto her garden. She thought she spied shadows flitting near the edge of her property, but in the twilight, she couldn't be sure.

She also couldn't believe that Viktor Savitch was

here and he needed her help. He claimed the touching strengthened him, but did that mean if they had sex all night, he'd be solid in the morning? She shook her head and snickered. As delicious as the prospect sounded to her and her starved libido, she doubted if even she could be so lucky.

*Still.* Would it kill her to try?

The possibility snaked through her like a forbidden whisper. Biting her lip, she washed her dish and glass and considered one downside. Both times that she'd tangled with Viktor, in her dream and then today in the kitchen, she'd left the experience weakened and exhausted. Communicating with the dead had always been somewhat draining, but never to this extent. If she strengthened him, did he do the opposite to her?

She didn't think so. Now that she'd rested, she fairly tingled with vibrancy, as if she'd just worked out at the gym. Her skin prickled with life and her heart beat steady and strong.

She had no proof that tangling with Viktor wouldn't hurt her, but she only had one way to truly find out. For years, his legend had piqued her interest. She'd listened to the lurid tales of his prowess and charm with unabashed interest. Now, she'd met him and had experienced his skill firsthand. She wanted more. She wanted whatever he could give.

She had nothing to lose, yet she could gain a chance at lovemaking that was truly magical.

In her bedroom, she pulled clean sheets and a fresh comforter from the closet. She made the bed, then dug into her lingerie drawer and found a silky gown. The gold color complemented her skin and eyes and the material draped over her body like a layer of sweet butterscotch. She dabbed a bit of makeup on her lips, cheeks and eyes, then dusted sparkling powder across her breasts and shoulders.

*Magical.*

By the time she had the fountain gurgling beside the bed and additional candles lit throughout the room, the sun had set. The sky outside glowed deep purple until the indigo streaks of night sucked the light from the cloudless heavens. After setting one last votive beside Viktor's perfume bottle, Eve closed her eyes and reached out with her mind.

*Viktor.*

Almost instantly, his presence filled the room.

## CHAPTER EIGHT

A WOODSY SCENT TEASED Eve's nostrils, enhanced by the subtle musk of a man inextricably tied to the outdoors. She gazed into the antique mirror hanging above her vanity and spied his glow behind her. He stepped nearer and his diaphanous form became more distinct. He wore the same blue shirt, colorful vest, tight pants and thigh boots as earlier, but in the darkness, his roguish appeal intensified. His glossy black hair and sapphire eyes captured the candlelight flashing off the prism of the perfume bottle and reflected such male perfection, Eve wondered if this was just another facet of an elaborate dream.

Without caring one way or another, she turned, an expectant smile teasing her lips.

"You follow orders very well. I'm surprised."

"You should be," he said. "I amused myself by exploring your land, meeting my kinsmen. They do not trust me."

"Should they?"

He quirked an eyebrow. "With you, yes. I would not put you at risk."

"Really? Why not?"

"You are the key to my release."

"Is that all?"

His face contorted with confusion, which he quickly banished beneath his charming grin. Many women had made demands of him, yet he'd never wanted to please one so much as he did Eve. And not just because she could free him, though he could not lose sight of her potential power.

"Being my savior is not enough for you?" he asked.

Tightness pressed against Eve's chest, forcing her breath more deeply. "I can agree to be your lover, Viktor, but your savior?" She attempted to swallow, but her tongue was thick and dry. "What if I fail?"

He smiled. "I have nothing to lose."

"What about your soul?"

He stepped closer to her. The atmosphere around them crackled and though she bet the effect was an optical illusion, the candles flickered and sparked. "I lost that years ago."

"You have a chance to get it back, now, don't you? If you live again, Viktor, you don't have to be the same man."

When he shook his head, his hair gleamed like streaks of ink, freshly drawn on glossy paper. "I can be only who I am, Eve. I am not evil, you know that. In fact, in some ways I can be very good. The needs you have—I can fulfill them as no other man can."

He toyed with the tips of her fingers, shooting tiny currents of heat into her bloodstream.

She smoothed her tongue across the sharp ridge of her teeth, trying to offset the powerful sensation of his palms brushing up her arms, skittering across her skin with spectral electricity, hardening her nipples beneath the silk of her gown. He noticed, because he dropped onto one knee and pulled her onto his lap. The thrum emanating from his ghostly flesh sizzled through her as his mouth hovered near the erect tip of her breast.

"You've searched a long time for a lover to attend you, fill you, challenge you. The men of your world have not satisfied you, physically or intellectually. Making love to you will be a path to your freedom— and mine. I'm sure of it," he claimed, his breath not warm, but hot and cold in quick succession.

He laved her breast and she thought she might melt in his mouth. He was greedy, possessive and rough—when he wasn't giving, free and gentle. His long hair brushed against her flesh above her plunging neckline, softer than gossamer. She lifted her hand to touch the glossy strands, but fisted her fingers before she could indulge.

"How do you know I can free you, Viktor?"

He lifted his gaze to hers. "Our connection grows more powerful with each touch, each taste. Can't you feel it?" He punctuated his claim by smoothing his hand around her backside, cupping her flesh possessively. His fingers dug into her so that she couldn't mistake the phantom sensation of sinew and bone. "We lose nothing by trying."

She nearly murmured, "Nothing," but he cut off her agreement with a hungry kiss. Mouth to mouth, Eve shivered, remembering when she used to test the energy level of batteries by swiping her tongue over the conductor tip. The shock had been mild, but revealed the power within. Now, the same buzzing energy sizzled through her, magnified a hundred times, throwing her mind into a shadow world of sensations and delight.

Viktor slipped his fingers beneath the straps of her gown and toyed with the thin strips, clutching and releasing, tugging and teasing so that she didn't know if he was going to let the gown fall gently off her shoulders or if he would rip the silk free. He distracted her with the skill of his lips and tongue, so that when he released her, leaving her clothing chastely in place, she barely had a chance to register her disappointment.

"What pleases you, Evonne Baptiste?"

With her eyes closed and her ears raging with the sound of her blood rushing through her veins, Eve had to work to understand what he'd asked. Sex pleased her. Men pleased her. Relationships, brief or not, tended to scare the shit out of her, but here she was about to make it with a ghost and fear was the last thing on her mind. Here was a man with real power, with influence over the elements and a line of communication with centuries-old magic, yet she wasn't spooked. Why?

If the explanation existed in her mind, it fled the moment he dropped his kisses to her throat. She arched her neck and turned her head so he could access that particular place below her ear that drove her insane.

He didn't disappoint, nipping and kissing and suckling until her balance wavered. She broke away, leading him with a crooked finger to the bed. She crawled across the mattress and waited for him to follow.

Standing back, he removed his vest and shirt, not by working the ties and buttons, but with a sweep of his hand. Eve caught a gasp in her throat at the beauty of him. His chest bulged with muscles defined by hard work and harder living. Dark hair offset the glossiness of his skin and for an instant, Eve realized she could no longer see completely through him.

He was solid enough for her to see the large circular shape of his male nipples and a ragged scar that crossed from his left shoulder to the top of his right hip. She reached out to follow the violent line with her hand, crawling onto her knees so she could reach him, touch him, learn him.

"Is this where…?" she asked.

"No."

He seemed enthralled by the way her finger traced the path, down, then up, then down again. Did he realize that touching him was addictive, irresistible, as if the pads of her fingers contained magnets drawn to the steel of his chest? The current zimming through her skin was strong and electric, yet at the same time, gauzy and hard to define. One moment she could feel him, the next she could not. But the tastes and samplings lured her, ensnared her. Bit by bit, the cravings for the low-voltage jolts of awareness overwhelmed her. Releasing him seemed impossible. Unthinkable.

He captured her wandering hand in his.

"The leftover of a barroom brawl. Nothing romantic or heroic. Does it repulse you?"

She stared up at him. "Never. Everything about you intrigues me. You've been in my life no longer than a moment, yet something tells me we could have been trapped together in that bottle and I still wouldn't know everything about you. You're a puzzle, a mystery. Unpredictable, even to yourself."

"I'm a simple man," he claimed, his voice insistent, as if he sought to convince himself more than her. He lured her hand to his lips, and though she closed her eyes to relish the moist feel of his mouth against her flesh, she couldn't help but contradict him.

"Liar."

He tugged her close, his hands cupping her cheeks, raising her higher on her knees so they were face-to-face. "Yes," he confirmed, his eyes hard. "I'm Romani. We tell the truth the *gaujo* want to hear. It makes no difference to the gypsy what the *gaujo* believes. We have our own truths. As long as we survive and flourish, what do a few lies mean?"

Eve tried to pull back, but Viktor held her fast. His lips teased hers as he spoke, his tone calm, his words hot with honesty.

"Will you lie to me?" she asked.

"Do I need to?"

She knew if she answered yes, he would accommodate her. He would create stories to placate her, to ease the echoes of apprehension she could only now admit she heard from the deepest part of her conscience. But if she said no, he'd likely tell her the truth, no matter how cold or calculating he would appear. Hadn't he learned that lying to someone with gypsy blood, even with only a few drops, could destroy him?

"No," she said. Emboldened, she grabbed the hem of her gown and tossed the material over her head. With as much grace as she could muster, she crawled across the mattress and settled into the pillows. "Make love to me, Viktor."

As he bent his knee to climb beside her, his pants and boots disappeared. His buttocks gleamed tight and contoured in the candlelight, his legs long and lean and muscled. He climbed over her, onto his knees, his hands on his hips, cocksure in the truest sense of the word.

"Are you pleased with what you see?" he asked without a hint of uncertainty.

She eyed him boldly, moisture pooling between her legs. An ordinary man with a physique like his would be impressive enough. In his supernatural state, he stole her breath.

"Are you?"

His grin rose a tad higher on the right side of his face. "I've never met a woman like you, Eve—so bold and unafraid. The temptresses of my time preferred coyness."

She stretched out her leg and teased his sacs with her toe. "Do you prefer coy?"

He groaned and she moved higher, stroking him with the slightly rough pad of her foot. He grew longer and harder as she aroused him. And yes, more solid. The tingling sensations of his ghostly existence lessened, but didn't disappear.

Viktor had been right. Making love to him might set him free. Sharing her sensual power with this specter from the past could give him back the one thing he wanted most—his life.

She knew the very moment he became aware of the change, slight as it was. His eyes widened, his chest expanded and his jaw dropped. Eve crawled forward and stroked him with her hands, dropping her head to trail a path of moist kisses along his shoulders, his breastbone, his nipples. The hard nubs were cool beneath her tongue, but his groan when she took a little nip put her nerve endings on fire. He threaded his fingers into her hair, absently massaging her scalp as her kisses dropped lower and lower, following the thin trail of his chest hair, diverting around to the smooth, sensitive skin on his sides and hips.

She cupped him, anxious to taste his cock, when he shifted and eased her onto her back. He captured her hands and secured them over her head, devouring her with his eyes and then his lips and tongue.

"I'll take the first taste, my sweet. I've longed to part your sweet lips with my tongue since the first moment I saw you." He slid a hand down her belly, burying his fingers in her moist cleft. "Oh, yes. The flavors will be plentiful."

On his way down, he teased and taunted her breasts. He laved the curved undersides and plucked her nipples until she thought she might orgasm right then and there. But just as the tide flowed toward the edge, he allowed her a sensual reprieve. He slid lower, caressing the insides of her thighs, one, then the other, as he slid her legs over his shoulders and settled in to feast his fill.

The minute his breath grazed through her tight curls, Eve knew the brink loomed. She braced herself, knowing the moment he tasted her, she'd come. She wasn't wrong. He dipped a taut tongue and instantly found her clit. Colors exploded all around her, glowing with hot light. She seized a breath in her lungs, her chest tight, her eyelids clamped, awaiting his next lick.

Only a second lick never came. In the midst of orgasmic overload, Eve blinked until her vision cleared.

Viktor was gone.

# CHAPTER NINE

GULPING GREAT GASPS OF AIR, Eve sat up. Her body protested, not yet done riding the wave of pleasure. She squeezed her thighs together, desperate to reclaim her ability to think, to speak.

"Viktor?"

She could feel his absence as if someone had dug into her chest and left a gaping, bloody hole. She grabbed her gown, pressing it against her as she ran throughout the house, hoping, but not expecting to find him in another room.

She stopped herself in the kitchen, forced calm into her mind, body and spirit. Then, with a strong push, she sent out a call into the realm of the ghostly spirits.

*Viktor!*

No reply. She called out for Jeta, but heard nothing. In fact, she'd never experienced such silence, as if—

*No.*

Had she sent him back? Had she sent them all back?

She tossed the gown over her head and wrangled with the straps until she was covered. She dashed out into the yard, yelping when bits of mulch and twigs bit into the soles of her feet. She crossed to the stone path that led to the gypsy graves and ran as fast as she could to the three lonely headstones.

She sat as close to them as she could, cross-legged, and chanted an old charm she'd learned from a gypsy in Yorkshire. This was how the woman had been taught to call the dead and, at the time, Eve suspected the Romani crone had made up the nonsensical string of words to entertain the *gaujo* college student who'd come to do research for her master's thesis. But she'd used the chant before when her conduit to the dead had been blocked, usually by extreme tension in her own life. Like when her mother had died and she'd been desperate to speak to her. For days, she'd chanted, fasted and rocked. For days, the dead had ignored her.

She'd never spoken to her mother, but she'd finally tapped into a spirit who'd claimed her mother had crossed over quickly. Would someone know if the same had happened to Viktor?

She had no idea how long she stayed outside, but the silence from the other side buzzed in her ears like static. Shockingly, Jeta, Nicholai and Alexis were nowhere to be found. She considered a trip to a nearby cemetery, but as she trod back to the house, another possibility assailed her. She ran to her room and found the bottle where she had left it—on the vanity.

Only this time, the top was firmly in place.

"Oh, God."

She cradled the glass in her hands and lifted the bottle near, snapping on the lamp. She peered into the facets, but saw nothing. She tugged at the top, but it wouldn't move. She knew Viktor was back inside. Trapped.

For how long?

And why?

"Viktor, I'm sorry. I don't know what happened. God, do you? Do you know?"

She pressed the bottle to the curve of her breast, so that she could feel her rapid heartbeat reverberate against the fragile glass. The silver worked like a conductor and a jolt of energy shot into her, sizzling through her veins and pulsing at the most intimate points in her body. She gasped. Her nipples hardened and a pearl of moisture slipped between her thighs.

He was there.

"I'll figure this out, Viktor. I have to."

The price she'd paid for the bottle became worth every penny the minute Viktor had materialized in her life. He was unlike any man she'd ever met, any man she'd ever meet in this lifetime. He knew things about the universe that no one else could ever fully understand. He'd done the unthinkable and, in return, had had the unthinkable done to him. And yet, he'd found a way to push aside his need for revenge and regret. He simply wanted to live. He simply wanted the life that had been due to him, though he accepted that he'd thrown it all away in a vain pursuit to keep his family together.

He enthralled her, intrigued her. She could spend a lifetime learning the minutiae of his life, his thoughts, his dreams. She could spend a lifetime with him.

Whether or not he wanted the same, she had no idea. She didn't even really care. Eve knew enough about men and women to know when a connection existed—a connection that might have existed for centuries and that transcended the boundaries of life and death. Was she being overly romantic? She didn't think so. It wasn't her nature. She didn't think she loved him yet—how could she when they'd known each other, really known each other, for less than two days?

But could she love him? Oh, yeah. For a lifetime, if given the chance.

But she'd never know now—unless she could free him again.

VIKTOR HOWLED IN FRUSTRATION, hoping, if even for an irrational instant, that the power of his voice would shatter the silver-enforced glass. He shouted and cursed in every language he'd ever heard until his energy was nearly spent.

He knew the keening was fruitless, but he hated the impotence of being trapped in his cage when life and love were just at his fingertips. Eve's fragrance, so sweet and musky, still clung to him, enveloped him. Her flavor lingered on his tongue. How had this happened? He'd been so close! For the split second before he'd dipped into Eve's sweet *yoni,* he'd felt a true and undeniable surge of blood through his veins. Every touch of her hand, every sweep of her lips across his skin had amplified the beat of his heart, the pull of his breath from deep inside his lungs. She'd led him closer and closer to living, then his freedom had been yanked away.

Had that been Iliana's plan? Had she cursed the bottle to retrap him if he ever came close to caring for a woman? If this had been her scheme, he couldn't think of a more potent punishment.

Evonne Baptiste, so unlike any woman he'd ever met and, yet, so familiar. Like a soul he'd encountered once before as a young boy in the woods, where the fairy spirits lived, back in the days when he still believed in the purity of Romani magic. Now, he couldn't even communicate with her. He'd been trying for what seemed like hours, though judging by the light outside, a day hadn't yet elapsed since he'd disappeared. Eve still wore the gold gown. Except for a few short absences, she hadn't left her bedroom. Hadn't slept.

Instead, she'd pored over books at her desk, had made a few calls on the telephone. She'd sat cross-legged on the floor, chanting words that he suspected he might have heard before many years ago, but if they were meant to break the wall of silence between them, they were useless. She brought food into the room and ate while she read. She'd drunk what he suspected to be an entire bottle of wine, then chanted again.

At first, she'd called to him. Only him. But when finally convinced he couldn't respond, she'd tried to reach the gypsies who haunted her land. Viktor found it odd that they had not responded. He'd spoken to them. He knew their deep affection for Eve. Why would they abandon her now? *Unless...* Perhaps they knew the secret to his release and wished to keep the knowledge buried. Keep him buried. Only he wasn't buried, damn it! He was caught like a lightning bug in a child's glass jar.

Helpless.

He gazed through a facet in the glass, watching Eve as she tilted back the last of her wine. God, she was beautiful, even when her soul was torn apart. How long had it been since anyone truly cared for him? Cared about not only his future, but about his spirit? His soul? Cared about his absence. Not since before he'd been sent to live with the *gaujo,* before the woman of the house had initiated him into the world of bedroom intrigue. He'd been young. Angry. So blinded by resentment and abandonment that he'd brought the *bengesko yak* into his family the minute he'd returned, ten long years before he'd met Iliana Dulas or her wicked family. No matter his aim to keep his family together, he'd used the *gaujo* tools of seduction and intrigue to achieve his goal. If he had simply shown his family loyalty and respected the old ways, he wouldn't have been murdered and cursed, perhaps for all eternity.

But he also would never have met Evonne Baptiste. He would have died decades ago, a continent away. His legend would never have intrigued her, inspired her. He accepted that even if he never broke free of the curse, knowing that she cared about him, if only for a moment, brought him the only solace he'd experienced in a hundred years.

For the first time since his idyllic childhood, he'd

found someone to care for, someone he'd actually trust with his heart, if given the chance. Watching Eve weep from the other side of the bottle, unable to comfort her, unable to beg her forgiveness for drawing her into his cursed existence, weakened him more than any black magic ever could.

After one hundred years trapped in the bottle, time meant nothing to him. If he could have lived and breathed and walked the Earth as a man again, he would have devoted whatever years he had left to capturing Eve's heart. He didn't realize until this moment how his anger had dissipated, how his own heart yearned.

For life. For love.

For Eve.

Only he could not have her, unless she found a way to set him free.

THE BOX.

The voice popped into Eve's brain, waking her with a start.

"Viktor?"

He wasn't there. She grabbed the clock and yawned. An hour before dawn. She'd slept on the floor for four hours, and her body ached with exhaustion. Her heart bled with sorrow. She'd known him for only a few days, but he'd been ripped from her at a moment of intense intimacy. She wanted him back, dammit!

*The box.*

"Jeta?"

Eve scrambled to her feet, but she knew before she dashed into the hallway that she was still alone in the house.

Box? What box?

Eve trudged back into her room, scanning the dresser and vanity table, her mind muddy with ragged emotion. Her eyes lit on the perfume bottle and suddenly she knew what Jeta meant.

The box! The casket. The scarlet-lined wooden crate the perfume bottle had come in. Where had she put it? Viktor said that Iliana had used the box to seal the curse. Was it the key to freeing him again, perhaps permanently?

She slid onto the floor, fairly certain that the last time she'd seen the box, it had been on her bed. Before Viktor had seduced her and she'd stripped the sheets. She pushed her hands blindly beneath the dust ruffle, yelping when her nails cracked on something hard.

Excitement shot through her, but she paused and took a deep breath, hoping she possessed the power to use whatever magic or clue she found. She couldn't bear to think that all of what she'd experienced over the past few days was for nothing. She'd finally opened her mind to the possibilities of love, to the off chance that she'd finally found a man who could hold her interest and share a passion for the culture she studied, respected and loved. Maybe she hadn't found love before because she'd been meant to love a gypsy.

Better yet, a gypsy king.

She settled onto her bed and picked up the box. The crest carved into the inside bore no secret clue. She felt around for secret compartments, turning the box this way and that, pressing her fingers over every inch, prodding and jiggling every hinge. Desperate, she grabbed a razor-knife from her desk drawer and carefully cut out the lining. Beneath the stuffing—made from human hair, if Eve guessed correctly—she found another carving.

She translated the word, but it wasn't in Romani. It was in French. The Romani likely had no translation for such a word.

*Surrender.*

Was this the key? But she'd surrendered to Viktor! Body, mind and soul. She'd allowed him intimate access. She'd agreed to share whatever sensual exploration he thought would help him free his soul.

Unless...she wasn't the one who had to surrender?

Eve climbed onto her bed, the box cradled in her lap, her brow frozen high over her eyes and her jaw lax with shock. She closed her mouth with a pop. She'd give Iliana Dulas one bit of credit—when she designed revenge, she went for maximum irony.

Eve didn't have to surrender to Viktor in order to release him.

He had to surrender to her.

## CHAPTER TEN

"YOU HAVE NO CHOICE," Eve whispered, her lips pressed intimately against the bottle. "Surrender to me. Do you hear me? You have to relinquish all of your power, all of your control."

Viktor couldn't believe the depth of her request. Surrender? Him? The most powerful gypsy king in the history of his clan reduced to a slave? Again? Hadn't he donned that role as a young man with Lynette? And what had that humiliation gained him other than the disdain and mistrust of his own clan?

"Trust me, Viktor."

*The most powerful gypsy king in the history of his clan...and now, the most impotent.* Viktor was proud, but he also wasn't a fool—not any longer. Now, he had nothing to lose and a world to gain—a world with Eve, if she'd have him. Fifty years ago, maybe even as recently as ten or five or even three days ago, his pride would have kept him entrapped. His pride and his arrogance. No matter how much he'd wanted to live, he'd wanted to preserve his legacy more.

Now he realized his legacy had already found a place in history. No matter what he did today, the past could not be changed. Surrendering to Eve, fighting every instinct bred into his soul, meant a chance to build a new life.

Concentrating, he formed a picture of himself in his mind. Outside the bottle. On his knees, subjugated before the woman who already held him in thrall. Deep in the center of his chest, a place once empty filled with devotion and deference.

*I am your slave. Do with me what you will.*

His essence expanded, grew heavy and hot. Tendrils of smoke seemed to stretch out from where his chest began, forming into arms, legs, fingers, feet and hair. When he opened his eyes, he was right where he imagined. Right where he belonged. He looked through his transparent hands into Eve's red-rimmed eyes.

"Don't speak," she commanded, her voice wavering, but strong.

He swallowed, but obeyed, a tiny smile teasing the corners of his mouth. He had a thousand questions for her, and he knew she would have an answer for each and every one. She wasn't just stunningly beautiful, she was damned clever and incredibly resourceful. So why did she look unsteady, unsure?

Still clutching the perfume bottle, her fingers were white-knuckled. He feared she'd crack the glass and cut herself if he didn't warn her, but he hadn't forgotten her directive of silence. He wanted Eve. Completely. He would make no mistakes this time.

Even so, he had to fight to bow his head.

"Good," she said, a sigh of relief rushing out with the word. "That's what you need, Viktor Savitch. A touch of humility. Perhaps a dose of personal risk. When you made love to me before, you focused on my pleasure, my body." Confidence strengthened her voice. "Not that I'm complaining, but to turn all your charms on me, you gave only what was physical. To break the curse, you'll need to give more. I'll need your obedience. Your trust. Your love. Do you understand?"

Viktor swallowed, his tongue thick in his mouth. Thick and dry, but feeling more and more solid by the moment. The concept was unthinkable—a gypsy man obedient to a woman in the bedroom? He'd been an obedient lover once in his life, as a boy. Could he bear the experience again, this time with Eve, a woman he craved so much he could barely control his desire to take her?

He swallowed his objections, knowing the situation would not be the same because the women were so unalike. With Eve, his dedication sprang from his heart and from his admiration for this woman who wielded great magic and power over him. And she always would.

"I understand completely, my sweet," he answered.

Her breasts rose with her huge inhalation, and a glorious smile. "Good. Undress."

He moved to wave his hand over his body, but she let go of the bottle and grabbed his wrist. A sizzle shot through him. If he regained solid human form, would he miss the burning electric current that sparked between this world and the next?

Not as long as he had Eve he wouldn't. They would generate an energy all their own.

"No," she said, her grip tight, insistent. "Use no magic. Take your clothes off as a man of this world would."

She released him and stepped back, still cradling the perfume bottle between her breasts, inspiring a jealousy he never thought he'd feel toward his prison of glass and silver. When the back of her thighs collided with the edge of the mattress, she sat, her eyes reflecting a myriad of emotions ranging from desperate anxiety to keen expectation.

Viktor shrugged out of his vest. He stretched his

fingers, then, looking down, yanked the ties on his shirt. He grabbed the ends to tear the material apart, but she stopped him.

"Slower," she said, her voice husky and deep. She placed the bottle on the center of her pillow, then leaned back casually on her elbows, striking a pose he knew he'd practiced on many occasions just like this one—only he'd been the one on the bed. "This may be the last time I see you in such luminous form. I want to remember."

"May I speak?" he said, tugging his shirt from his pants.

"Of course. Freely...unless I say otherwise."

Her amber eyes twinkled impishly. She was enjoying his servitude. Surprisingly, so was he. He removed his shirt with the patience of a man he didn't know, enjoying how her gaze swept over him, how she tugged her lower lip between her teeth, how her breath seemed to quicken with each inch of flesh he revealed.

He released the button on his pants. "Has a man undressed for you before?"

"Not for free," she noted wryly.

He stopped. "You've had to pay a—"

"No! But I've been to bachelorette parties. Do you know what that is?"

He nodded, kicking his heel against the floor to loosen his boot. "A wild, frivolous party where women celebrate the impending marriage of a friend by getting drunk and sometimes naked with hired dancers."

Eve's laughter brought tears to her eyes. "You do pay attention, don't you?"

"I was once owned by an American woman in Amsterdam. She brought the tradition with her. Besides, women fascinate me. Always have. That perhaps was the best part of my entrapment, being exposed to so many beautiful and interesting women all over Europe and the United States."

The mirth in her expression was tempered by a pouty frown. "So many women in life, so many even in death. You won't stay, will you?"

He paused, knowing her question was a test—one he knew he could pass, once he had the time to show her. But for now, he put off answering her query until he'd obeyed her command. There was no sensuous way to remove his boots while standing. He gestured toward the bed. "May I?"

She nodded.

He sat and tugged both boots off before he answered. "Must I settle down to be released?"

With a shrug and a shake of her head, she silently

answered his question. Was disappointment holding her tongue? Or relief?

"I'm a different man now, Eve. A different man living in a different era. The Romani ways of today are not that of my ancestors. The wandering, the borrowing rather than owning, already had lost its luster for them during my lifetime. Too much of the world is owned. A gypsy who cannot wander free is just as trapped as a ghost in a bottle."

She inched closer to him. "There are clans still in existence, Viktor, who move and wander. If you wish to find them, I can help you."

He turned, fighting with all his might not to grab her hand or shoulder. The need to touch her threatened to overcome him, but he hadn't forgotten the curse or the magic still zinging through the room.

"Will you go with me?" he asked.

"What?"

He shrugged and removed his other boot. "A slave can go nowhere without his mistress."

She scooted an inch or so away. Her gaze darted to the perfume bottle, her expression brimming with regret.

"After tonight, you won't be my slave anymore."

*How seductively naive.* Her claim was true, but only in the most basic sense. The moment he'd revealed himself to her, he'd known the course of his existence had changed. With no more willpower left, he reached out a tentative hand and caressed her cheek. Her skin was so warm, so pliant, so soft. The pad of his thumb felt rough in comparison. He wanted nothing more than to pleasure her, please her, show her the depths of the passion they shared. He wanted to seduce her, but knew he could not. Not unless she commanded him.

"I'll always be your slave, Eve. How could a man be anything less with you?"

She pulled back. "You'd be surprised."

He shot to his feet, stepped two paces away and then dropped his pants to the floor. He kicked them aside and stood, arms akimbo, naked as the day he'd been born and just as vital with the true spark of life imminent within him.

"As will you be, by my obedience." He bowed low, pleased to see how long and hard his cock was, all for her. Never in his life or long punishment of death did he think he could ever want a woman so badly as to want to give her everything he could offer. But with Eve, he'd give her that and more. "You need not command me for you to have my heart. I freely would give you whatever you wish, whatever you truly desire."

Eve pressed her lips together, unsure, still suspecting that Viktor was simply playing a role to win his freedom. He was after all, a gypsy. Better, a gypsy king. Playing to the crowd was second nature—only he hadn't had an audience to entertain for a very long time. Could he be sincere? Did he really wish to stay with her? Forever?

The look in his sapphire eyes surpassed sincerity, with a dash of uncertainty that tugged at her heart. The power to release him from his curse was inextricably bound to her need to know if he spoke the truth. To put him to the test, she'd have to drop her own inhibitions.

"I don't believe you. You'll need to prove to me that you truly wish to stay."

"I will."

She stood and dropped her gown to the floor. She stepped out of the satin and stalked around him, smoothing a palm across his pecs. Once behind him, she spread her hands over his buttocks. Hard and warm, his skin tingled in her grasp.

"Move toward the bed," she ordered.

He complied with two steps forward.

"Bend over."

He did as she asked, his hands braced on the mattress, the muscles in his arms taut and glistening.

She licked her lips, then touched every inch of him, exploring his expanse of bared flesh. She kissed his hip, the small of his back. She dipped her tongue in the sweet crease of his buttocks, tickling, teasing and taunting his sensitive flesh with light fingers.

When he groaned, she stepped away.

"What do you want?" she asked.

"To touch you."

"No," she said. "Stand up. Step back."

She spun around him and resumed her position on the bed. She spread her legs slightly. Cool air swirled around her and the pulse of wanting him hard between her thighs intensified.

*Soon,* she told herself. *Very soon.*

"First, you must touch yourself."

His eyes widened. She caught his quick glance toward the perfume bottle. Perhaps even Viktor had his limits.

She dropped her hands to her knees, then drew a single finger up her inner thigh, to the soft curls there. "You watched me pleasure myself. Don't I deserve the same?"

He complied, widening his stance to compensate for the loss in balance. He cradled his cock in his palm and began a slow, stroking motion that enthralled her. She watched his chest heave, his eyes drift closed.

She nearly bit her tongue with the need to taste him. "Come closer," she ordered.

He closed the distance, leaving just enough room so he could continue to massage his sex until she knew he couldn't get any longer or harder. A sparkle of moisture on his tip caught her eye and she couldn't help but swipe the bead with her tongue. She ordered him to stop, then took him in her mouth and suckled him until he begged for mercy.

"Please, Eve," he moaned.

With a grin, Eve ended the sweet torture. He dropped to his knees in apparent exhaustion, but when she spread her thighs wide, he didn't hesitate. He tasted her just as intimately, his breath ragged against her mons when he requested free rein with his hands.

She granted his wish. In seconds, he had one hand on her breast, tantalizing her nipple, the other dipping deep within her as his tongue worked magic over her clit. But she'd orgasmed twice without him inside her. She wouldn't do so again.

"Stop, Viktor."

He complied, his lips moist and glossy as he pulled back.

She cleared her throat, certain she could speak with no authority while her senses reeled with intimate delight.

"Lie down, on your back."

When he did, she climbed atop him. The combination of hard and wet brought them together instantly and completely, so that Eve cried out in ecstasy at the perfect contact. Vibrations beyond the physical world strummed through her and she had to breathe hard to contain her release.

She braced her hands on his chest, moving to the music only her body could hear. He toyed with her breasts and whispered a litany of words that ranged in language from English to Romani to nonsense born of pure sexual want and desire. Before she could stop herself, foreign words spilled from her own mouth, increasing the motion and rhythm of their lovemaking. The volume and echo of the chant deafened her, but she couldn't stop, wouldn't stop, not until—

With one definitive thrust, Viktor broke the boundary between the physical and spiritual worlds. As orgasms racked their bodies, the air around them swirled. Photographs flew from the walls. The bed linens flailed as if they lay in the eye of a tornado. Viktor's eyes widened, and he grabbed Eve and tugged her down tight against his chest, wrapping his arms like bands around her. She gasped when, through his transparent skin, she could plainly see blue and red veins, the orange of cartilage and the pink of muscle. He screamed in what she knew to be agony and all she could do was close her eyes, hold him tight and pray the powers of fate wouldn't fail them now.

# *EPILOGUE*

STILL HALF-UNCONSCIOUS, the sudden sensation of a blanket warmed Eve's bone-cold skin. She stirred and snuggled beneath the heat, a heart beating beneath the supple skin cradling her cheek. Her eyes fluttered open and she pushed up, her muscles sore and protesting. Viktor lay beneath her, solid and breathing and beautiful. The curse had been broken!

But he was still asleep. Who had put the blanket over her?

Eve grasped the crocheted wool to her naked breasts. Jeta stood brazenly at the edge of the bed, laughter in her aged blue eyes. In the doorway, Alexis, a raven-haired beauty, glanced aside shyly. Nicholai, handsome and slender, watched the scene with brazen interest.

And all three were as solid as the former gypsy king.

"Jeta? What happened?" Eve gasped.

At the sound of her question, Viktor woke. With

a grunt, he pulled up onto his elbows and surveyed the suddenly crowded room. Eve palmed his cheek, turning his face to hers, loving the heat of his solid flesh against hers, steady and strong. "Viktor? Are you all right?"

His grin could have rivaled the sun and all the stars put together. He thrust his hands into her hair and yanked her into a long, lingering kiss. He didn't seem to care that they had visitors and after allowing him to plunder her mouth, she didn't much either.

Nicholai, however, cleared his throat. Twice.

Viktor pulled back, but his eyes captured hers with their life and vigor. "I'm alive, Eve. Thanks to you, I'm alive!"

He pulled her close and for an instant, Eve wondered if he'd ever let her go. She didn't care if he never did. The magic had released him. Now she had a real chance to tame this magnificent gypsy king.

Although tame wasn't quite the right word, was it? She wouldn't want him tamed in any way, shape or form. She had a feeling she was going to fall hard for him just the way he was.

Her laughter spilled onto his and broke the kiss. Even Alexis grinned from ear to ear, although she had trouble keeping her eyes in their direction. She appeared nearly ready to faint when Viktor flung the blanket aside to retrieve his pants. He bowed deferentially to Jeta, then continued to dress. Once finished, he turned to the old gypsy, who stood as solid as he did in the middle of her bedroom.

"What magic did you conjure, woman?"

Jeta shook her head calmly, the beads on her scarf tinkling. "No magic from me," she said whimsically. "The expression of your passion and need for life, true life, expanded beyond this room. It opened a doorway between the plane of the restless dead and the living. When the time was right, we simply walked through."

With a nod, Viktor accepted Jeta's explanation. Eve, however, didn't quite understand.

"What are you talking about?"

Jeta cleared her throat, but Eve heard the distinct sound of a giggle beneath the cough. "The magic you stirred with your lovemaking reversed the curse, opening the gateway between worlds. After speaking with Viktor, I suspected this might occur, so Alexis, Nicholai and I were ready. We live and breathe now, Eve. Thanks to you."

Jeta shuffled to the bed, took Eve's hand and gave it a gentle kiss. Then she waved her arms toward her grandson and his cousin, shooing them out. "Now, I don't know about you, but I'm in the mood to cook.

Nicholai, build a fire in the yard. Alexis, see what Eve has in her kitchen that can be turned into a decent meal."

And with that, they were alone, separated from Eve's new houseguests by a closed bedroom door. Viktor immediately dived back into the bed. When his weight hit the mattress, the perfume bottle Eve had left on the pillow bounced into the air. Eve screamed, but with deft hands, Viktor caught the phial before it hit the ground.

He held it up for her to see, then snuggled back into the bed. He was staying. She could feel it in her bones. For now, at least, he was staying.

"So, what do you suggest we do with this?" he asked of the glass container.

She shrugged her shoulders. He turned the bottle over and around, examining it as if he'd never seen it before. She supposed he hadn't—not from the outside, anyway.

"You can destroy it, if you wish," she suggested.

He tugged at the stopper, which didn't seem to want to come loose. Eve grinned, but remained quiet. He was locked out, hopefully forever. No more curses! She had no idea if the bottle still possessed magical powers to enhance psychic phenomena, and at the moment, she simply didn't care.

"No," he answered, stretching across the bed to

put the bottle well out of reach on the bedside table. He turned and enveloped Eve in his arms, settling onto the bed with her against him as if he was content to remain there for the rest of his life. "The bottle is magic. It brought us together."

"And you still want to stay?" she asked, hating herself for being so uncertain.

"Didn't I say I wanted to stay with you, Eve?"

She quirked her brow. "Pardon me for doubting, but you are a gypsy. Not exactly known for telling us *gaujo* the truth, remember?"

A sudden seriousness knocked the contented smile off his face. He turned toward Eve and brushed his hand gently across her cheek, then ran his thumb softly across her lips. "I am a gypsy, Eve. I will always have Romani blood surging through my veins. But I'm also a man. A man who's never met anyone as fascinating and beautiful and kind as you are. I surrender my heart to you, Evonne Baptiste, for as long as you want it."

Eve's heart swelled with so many emotions, she couldn't name a single one. Except, maybe, desire. The minute Viktor leaned forward and captured her mouth in a kiss, an undeniable need broke from the swirl of sentiment. She kissed him back with all her passion, all her love and suddenly understood why the magic they'd conjured had expanded beyond the two of them.

Viktor hadn't been the only one to surrender. Eve had, too, and even the combined connection between reality and the Otherworld hadn't been able to contain the power of their love.

And, perhaps, it never would.

\* \* \* \* \*

*Viktor's search for true love may be over, but Nicholai's is just about to begin...
Look for Blaze #146, UNDENIABLE,
available next month*

## Coming in July 2004
## from Silhouette Books

Sly McEwen's final assignment for top-secret government
agency Onyxx had gone awry, leaving only questions behind.
But Sly had a feeling Eva Creon had answers. Locked inside
Eva's suppressed memory was the key to finding the killer
on the loose. But her secrets may have the power to destroy
the one thing that could mean more than the truth...
their growing love for each other....

*Available at your favorite retail outlet.*

*A determined woman searches for her past.*
*Will true love stand in her way...*
*or fulfill her deepest desire?*

**Don't miss the emotional second installment of
this new continuity series from Silhouette Books**

# LOGAN'S LEGACY

Because birthright has its privileges and family ties run deep.

# SECRETS & SEDUCTIONS

**by *USA TODAY*
bestselling author**

# PAMELA TOTH

Determined to uncover the truth about her
mysterious heritage, Emma Wright went to
the Children's Connection—and straight to the adoption
agency's handsome director Morgan Davis. She expected his
help...but she didn't count on falling in love with him....

***Coming in July 2004.***

## Silhouette®

*Where love comes alive™*

Visit Silhouette Books at www.eHarlequin.com

LLS&S

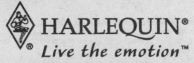